ELIO^2

Divided Loyalties

Larry W. Miller Jr.

Larry W. Miller Jr.

This is a work of fiction. All of the characters, names, incidents, organizations, and dialogue in this novel either are the products of the author's imagination or are used fictitiously.

ELIO[2]

Other books by Larry W. Miller Jr.

Fantasy Titles:
Trials of an Arch Mage – Book I Discovery
Trials of an Arch Mage – Pern and the Giant Forest
Trials of an Archmage – Pern and the Mystic Library
Trials of an Archmage – Book IV ascension/Circle of Darkness
Long Live the Queen
Balance lost / A Strange Friendship
A Kingdom of Unity
Revenge of the Brotherhood
Caitlin's Secret
In the Hands of Rogues
Thomas the Dragon's Coming of Age

Science Fiction Titles:
Droptroopers: Gauntlet of Fear
A Watery Crash
The Last Wizard of Earth
Conquest of New Eden / Sins of the Father
Alvarez Shipping Company: The saga of Myrlita Alvarez
Space Station Blues
To Choose Eternity
The April Summers Story
First Citizen
A Public Divided: the forgotten mission
EL10
Flight of the Nostos: Eternals among us
Flight of the Nostos: The new Eternals
Flight of the Nostos: Mirrored Realities

Urban Drama Titles:
Fade to Gray
Emergence of a Titan
In Earth's Defense
Dissention of the Gods

Religious Science Fiction Title:
Sarah's Miracle

Fictional Biography Title:
The Adventures of Shooter

All of these titles are available from Amazon.com. If you are looking for books in print form, creatspace.com has been acquired by Amazon.com so both versions of my books reside in one convenient location! You can see and preview all of my books from my author's page at the following URL...

http://www.amazon.com/-/e/B00DGIFLZC

Coming soon...

Flight of the Nostos Book 4!

Dedication

Here we have Elio, the little robot with a big heart. His story wedged between two *Flight of the Nostos* novels. He just wouldn't wait until that series ended. (There are six books in it so far.) Stories like this come from life and the people around us are a big part of our lives. So let me take a moment and elaborate on who was involved, directly, or indirectly in the creation of this story...

First of all, I'd like to point out some on-line friends that have shared in the experience that we call life. Esa, Coheed, Tuna Bandit, Best Sell By, Goblin (name shortened), Wuss, Sausizzle and finally, Smash. All of you and probably more that I didn't mention by name have had an impact and are valued by me.

Secondly, I want to mention people at work who also share in the daily experience and thus the formative part of my brain. Plus, I write these stories at work during breaks and lunches. So, thank you to Waldo, Hugo, Jesse, Eddie, Belayneh, Greg, Verdin, Sergei, Davis, Kim, Ruben and all of the receivers and shippers at Level10.

Finally, the people that have always been there. Family. You already know who you are but I must mention you here. My sister Julie, whose Birthday is it today as I write this. Aunts, uncles, cousins, the lot. Nancy, David & Linda, and let's not forget Danny. Ed and Mom. After all, without Mom, none of this would ever have happened. I love you all and thank you for being there for me.

A New Mystery…

The planet loomed before them. A big brown and green ball full of mystery. Ripe for the taking. The stories and writings all lead here. The planet itself was covered in thick clouds, obscuring the surface. The maddening twists and churning in those clouds suggested pretty severe weather conditions. The given name of this rock in space is Ladius232. But the name fell short trying to describe the world that hung in the sky before the archeological crew.

Emma looked at her boards with piqued curiosity. What was actually down there on that hostile world? The atmospheric disturbances made her scans useless. The land was beneath a thick layer of electronic noise. They would have to go down there personally to find out the answers. But could their scout ship be able to penetrate that much disturbance as well? It was a question for an engineer, not an archeologist.

Captain Sean Harris sat in his chair, looking at the view in front of him. The world looked nasty and hostile to him. He had not been in charge for as long as he had without learning at least a little bit about keeping his people alive.

"Tell me again, how important it is to get down into that soup." He said to his navigator.

"Sir, we have followed an ancient trail of breadcrumbs to this very planet. It will either be the next clue, or the actual prize." The young woman replied. Her name was Sharon Osling. Sharon's family had always been spacefaring and she had signed on to this ship early in her career. If she had been closer to headquarters, she would been promoted much faster. Her dedication to duty and her focus on the job were unquestioned. She simply preferred life out here, on the fringe of societal space.

The captain was not convinced about proceeding to the planet. "Elio, what do you think?" He asked. The crew was used to him asking the little robot for advice. Elio was much older than any of them and had a vast repository of information that any historian would give their right arm for.

"Sir, we must go down or abandon our quest." He replied simply.

"But we could lose the drop ship in that." The captain complained, pointing at the viewscreen and the turbulent planet below.

"Yes, we could. But if we do not try, we will have wasted three months to get here and a lot of fuel that we cannot recoup. Which is the lesser evil?" Elio asked. The captain was used to the little robot winning every argument. In fact, he played this game more to reaffirm his own feelings than to find out what the robot is thinking.

"You're right about fuel and feed costs. Nothing is free in outer space." He replied soberly. Then he turned back to his navigator. "Prep the drop ship and send a team down. Make sure they have an engineer with them in case that storm breaks something. They'd be stuck down there without the ability to come home." The captain warned.

"Yes sir." Sharon replied curtly. Then she pressed the appropriate buttons to carry out his orders. It was very professional compliance.

Captain Harris looked at Elio. "Don't even think of volunteering for that engineering slot." He warned. "You are too valuable to lose on a mission with such a high risk." He explained.

Elio rotated his metal body side to side like a human shaking his head. "I would go, but I knew you would say that." He replied. "Permission to inspect the vehicle?" He asked.

"Granted, make sure that they can come home." The captain replied.

Elio extended his legs and walked off the bridge. Emma was not far behind.

The navigator turned in his chair. "Sir, you know he's going to try to sneak on board."

Sean smiled. "Of course, he is. But now I am officially on record telling him not to go. That allows me to discipline him when he gets back." The captain replied.

"But you just told him he was too valuable to risk on this mission." Brandt complained.

"Yes, I did. But he doesn't consider his worth the way we do. If I told him just how valuable he is, he would tell me that I am not treating him like every other crewmember, and he would be right. This way, he will get to go, and the company will see that I was against it in the event that something bad does happen."

"But you are clearly allowing Elio to go down to the planet where he might not make it back." Brandt protested.

"Yes, it is a risk we all take every time we step on board a spacecraft. We all know the risks involved. Elio more than most." Captain Harris explained.

Brandt was satisfied in that response and something in the captain's tone had made that acceptance mandatory. "Yes sir." He said in conclusion.

The captain nodded and smiled. "Besides, if he goes, the drop ship has a better chance of coming back. A much higher chance than if it goes without him. I have never seen anybody with the acute ability to think on the go and to come up with solutions on the fly like Elio. They will be in good hands. Er- you know what I mean." He said faltering at the end.

* * *

Elio made his way down to the drop ship bay. It was not a very large section of the ship since the actual drop ship was not much larger than a school bus, but it still had to maintain the little ship it was attached to without endangering the research vessel it was in. That meant that lines were run in "safe zones". Pipes and conduits were all routed according to code. The walkways were all clear of obstructions. The lights were turned down to only thirty percent. It made the entire bay look dark when compared to the rest of the ship. But the pilot of the drop vessel would be plunging into total darkness. With a darker bay, it made that transition much less dangerous.

"Okay, we've got orders for this tub, let's get it together people." Foreman Pippa Duncan ordered. The bay crew was a tight knit group, able to handle things as a team. She knew that her people knew what to do. She had drilled them often enough and they had worked together long enough to know what each other was doing without looking or asking. The checklist was being filled out and the systems were all being checked and double checked. People were moving about the craft everywhere you looked.

Emma was in her pressure suit. It was what one wore underneath a space suit, and it was also what one wore when dealing with a potentially hostile environment. The amount of equipment she had with her made more than one eyebrow rise at the sight. It was like a tourist that overpacked for everything. Despite that, nobody said a word to her about the excessiveness. The gear was taken, weighed, and stowed as per protocol. The ship's balance had to be maintained. Emma herself was led to a waiting room where coffee and snacks were offered.

Other members of the team were notified as well, and they began to make their way down to the bay. The procedure was the same for each member of the group. They all ended up in that waiting room, enjoying the food and beverages before beginning their journey.

Elio, however, was not content with others doing the checklist and making all the inspections. He pulled up the inspection log and began making his own checks. The crew were actually used to seeing him now and they did their best to step aside as he moved about the exterior of the ship. He was checking antennas, rigs, wiring diagrams, everything. His arms moved so fast that to appearances they were a blur. His legs moved just enough to allow access to the next item on his list, and the next. Due to Elio's help, the actual time for this pre-flight had been reduced by thirty percent.

Once it was all done, he stepped down to view the ship from the side. He was considering stowing away on it. The captain had warned him not to go. He had told Elio that he was too valuable to risk on this flight. But Emma was going. Emma was his best friend. Elio could not bear to see her leave him into the unknown. It was then that he made his final choice and vaulted onto the ship to tuck in neatly next to the engine cell. He anchored himself properly and even shut down so that his power signature did not alert the others of his presence. Once underway, he could make the crew aware of their unexpected guest.

Pippa looked at the logs and nodded her satisfaction at the jobs her crew had done. In fact, they had done really well. She browsed the names and saw Elio among the crew. This made her suspicious.

"I want a head count on that ship." She ordered and two members of her maintenance crew headed back to the ship to begin a search. They started with the inside of the vessel but there was nobody inside. The cargo was strapped in, and the instruments all read clear and green.

The crew did not know what they were looking for, so they did not immediately suspect the top of the ship. They instead reported back that the ship was clear.

Pippa was not fooled by this. She stepped up to the ship herself and began to look around. She inspected the exhaust tubes, the underbelly of the craft and even under the front canopy. Nothing out of the ordinary was there. She climbed the ladder to the top and it didn't take long to spot the round robot nestled into the workings.

"Elio!" She shouted.

Elio's lights came on. He rotated his body to point his sensors at the voice where he saw Pippa. "Are we there yet?" He asked.

Despite her anger at catching a possible stowaway, Pippa laughed. "No, we are not there yet." She said, still chuckling. "We do not treat stowaways all that kindly." She retorted.

"I was going to protect Emma." Elio stated flatly, trying his best to sound innocent.

Pippa made a come here gesture and Elio began to detach from the top of the ship. He moved over to her, still, every ounce of him seemed like an innocent child. He even stayed low and looked up at Pippa when he reported.

"You need to answer for this." Pippa stated and then started back down the side of the ship. Elio lowered himself down and then waited for Pippa on the bay floor. She seemed to take his speed as a sign of insolence. She was angrier when she got to the floor herself. "I think we need to talk to the captain." She added.

Elio made a gesture that was supposed to be a shrug. It didn't sit well with Pippa. She marched towards the bay entrance and stopped just as the doors were about to activate in front of her. Elio was following at a respectful distance. When she stopped, Pippa turned around to glare at the little robot.

"You are not allowed to stow away on board one of my ships." She said clearly and distinctly. "Therefore, you have to register as crew." She said, surprising Elio completely. Her snide grin showed that she understood what she had just done.

"Now get on board and strap yourself in correctly." Pippa ordered and Elio complied gleefully. The foreman simply sighed and watched the happy little robot go.

Some of her crew had watched the entire exchange since leaving the ship. She eyed them and shrugged. "It's not like I could have prevented him anyway." She said in defense. Then she moved to the break room where the mission crew was waiting.

ELIO[2]
"You may board now. Your friend is already on board." She said and then she closed the door again, not explaining herself or anything for them.

The crewmates eyed one another and then they all got up to check out the ship together. Their gear had been stowed and the pre-flight was complete. All they were waiting on now was themselves.

Emma moved with the rest of the small crew. They moved into the ship, and she saw Elio right away.

"Elio! How did you get the captain to let you come along?" She asked.

"I was a stowaway." Elio replied. "Then I became a crewmember." He added to ease the sudden tension that was thick in this small compartment. "The captain did specify an engineer, did he not?" Elio asked in protest to the thoughts of his new crewmates.

"Well, yes he did." Emma replied for him. She had been on the bridge when the order was given.

"No matter who is here now, we have a mission to do." It was their pilot, Jamal Frost, who had spoken. He was in business mode which meant no-nonsense. "Everyone, strap yourselves in and get ready to drop." He ordered. On a mission like this, the pilot was usually the one in charge. He obviously expected to be judging by his attitude.

Emma did her best to strap in and remain quiet. The others did the same and soon the light status on board went fully green.

"About time." Jamal muttered and he hit the release switch.

The bay doors opened beneath the small craft, and it literally dropped out of the mother ship. The initial surge of energy came from the artificial gravity and once clear of the gravity envelope the drop ship continued to glide down and away from the primary vessel. The planet loomed before them, taking up all of the front window as they were nose down. The engines fired up and soon they were nearly level.

The stars were bright above them, and the ship that was their home looked smaller and smaller. The planet, on the other hand, continued to grow. The atmosphere was rough at the onset. It buffeted the little craft around terribly, but Jamal handled the controls like the veteran he was. The heat was making the hull outside glow. The internal temperature was usually heated to allow people to remain comfortable inside, now it was cooling them to keep them from cooking. The turbulence suddenly stopped, and the craft hit a pocket of gloriously lit sky. The clouds below them were churning and dark. But the sky above them looked angelic. The golden amber hue of the sky brought a sense of awe at the power and splendor of nature.

"Don't get too comfortable." Jamal warned. "We're about to drop into what amounts to a hurricane. The visibility is going to be nil so I will need all my concentration on the instruments to keep us on course. No screaming or sudden outbursts please." He warned.

Elio unhooked and made his way to the front where he reattached to the bulkheads. "I will assist you." He said. Jamal looked at the little robot as if he had just offended his family.

"How are you going to help me?" He asked, sounding quite skeptical.

Elio cocked his body forward and pointed his projector at the wind screen. "My sensors can penetrate this noise for a short distance. I will project onto the window what is ahead of us." He replied.

Jamal was startled. He wasn't sure whether or not to believe the little guy. "Show me."

Elio shot his sensors forward and scanned the immediate area and then projected that onto the windshield in real time. He used his extending legs to lock himself in place to stabilize the image.

Jamal felt like he could see everything now. The haze was still in front of them, but the landscape had been laid out as a grid on the windshield. "Fine, keep that up." Jamal said. His tone was substantially happier though his words did not indicate that.

The ship plunged into the swirling winds. The immediate sensation was of falling in several directions one after another. The ship was being tossed about like a toy in bath water. Jamal fought for control even as the ship began to stabilize. Elio held solid as a rock and displayed the ground plane and any obstruction well before they could actually hit anything.

"We're going to have this rough chop all the way to the ground." Jamal informed them. "This is going to get sketchy." He warned.

"It's sketchy already." Emma protested. "If not for Elio and his enhanced sensors." She pointed out. Nobody argued with her either. The ship continued fighting the winds and Jamal managed to turn the craft into them. Their forward progress was slowed greatly, but the ship was cutting through the gale forces now instead of being buffeted about. It became a much smoother ride.

The flat area of land they sought to land on suddenly appeared in the grid and Jamal angled them just a bit to head there. The ship was still coming in slowly. The headwind had practically stalled them in place. All of the passengers and crew looked white knuckled except for Jamal and Elio. Jamal was the image of calm focus and concentration. Elio was locked in place doing his job and letting Jamal have the key information he needed, as best as his sensors could show.

They continued in at an agonizingly slow pace, barely making headway. Suddenly the window showed them debris flying past. Tree tops were being broken off and whipping around in the air.

Jamal said. "If one of those hits us…" The sentence was not finished. Nobody was prepared to contemplate that reality fully. It was just too frightening. The ship was still descending and still moving forward but you could walk at the pace it was making. More debris sped past and smaller pieces were bouncing off the hull.

Elio made a sound, and everyone looked at him. "The landmass if close. But trees cover this area. It is not as flat as it seems." He said. He updated the display to show massive trees dotting the landscape.

Jamal was flabbergasted. "How accurate are these positions?" He asked.

"Fairly accurate, five percent error possible." Elio replied.

Jamal shook his head. "This just gets better and better." He said and he dove the ship down through the trees, trusting in Elio's imagery to guide him. They glanced off of a particularly large branch but missed the trunk. The sound of rending metal could be heard though.

"That's going to need fixing." Elio commented.

"Do you wanna' drive?" Jamal asked, losing his temper.

"No, I am only supplying the data for you to do so." Elio replied. He put no emotion into his response. The ship bounced again and this time everyone looked at Jamal.

"Hey! It's not my fault." He cried.

"Veer twenty-seven degrees left and level out." Elio commented and Jamal almost didn't react in time. He pulled hard on the yoke to comply with the instructions and the nose of the ship came very close to the trunk of a mighty tree. The tree was as big around as the ship was long. It would have been certain death if they had struck it with any force. Jamal was shaking. His nerves were shot.

"On second thought, I will drive." Elio suggested. The ship hovered around the tree and then set down beside it. The tree was mighty enough to allow a reprieve from the wind. Visibility was no better, but Elio could see well enough. The howling could still be heard from inside the craft.

Jamal unstrapped and backed away from the pilot chair. "You, you saved us." He managed to say.

Elio turned briefly to face him. "It is what crew does for one another." He replied. "I will begin repairs on the damage if you will suit up and begin the survey. If there is something of value here, we need to find it sooner rather than later. The night temperatures will be cold, very cold. Make sure you are back in the ship before the sun goes down." Elio commanded.

"With the storm out there, how will we know?" Emma asked.

ELIO[2]
"The winds will die down a small amount and the temperature will drop dramatically. If you notice a five-degree, drop in temperature, get back in a hurry." Elio commented.

"Maybe you'd better accompany us then. In these suits, we may not notice a five degree drop in temperature." Jamal commented.

"As you wish." Elio replied. He seemed happy, almost giddy to be on mission once again.

The others all began to put on their outer suits. This environment looked to be a challenge one and none of them wanted to take anything for granted. Once outside, Elio began scanning the ship for damage. His body was practically immune to most of the things that could kill humans here, but the odd stone travelling at hurricane velocity still held lethal capacity. He continued to scan upwind as far as his sensors could reach even as he worked on various parts of the ship while the rest of the crew suited up.

The mission had truly begun.

***

Back on board the main ship, several sets of eyes watched the telemetry feed as the drop ship continued on its treacherous journey to a hostile planet. The screen view had been enhanced to show the little ship as it dove for a massive storm. Ionization from hitting the atmosphere began to light up the little craft, but soon enough it dropped out of view. The telemetry feed stopped almost immediately, as predicted. The surface of that world was incredibly hostile to ship-board sensors.

"Well, that's that until they ascend once again." Captain Harris commented. He stood up from his chair and rubbed his hands together. Well, we have some time while we wait, I think I'll get some coffee. This could be a long night." He stated and he left the bridge. The duty officer took the mantle even as the doors closed.

"Enter into the ship's log, I have the command." She said as was required by protocol. She was slightly perturbed at the captain's lack of decorum by just leaving without giving her the command chair. She had to take it for herself. She put it down to the worry he must be experiencing over the drop ship crew. Then her attention was pulled back to duty and she checked all the read-outs on the chair for proper function. The captain's slight had already been forgotten.

****

ELIO[2]

Captain Harris made his way to the galley and ordered his coffee. It arrived hot and steamy, with the perfect mix of sugar and cream just as he had specified in his profile. He eyed the cup but somehow, he didn't feel like having this particular coffee. He set the cup back down and considered other options. For the size of his crew, the menu of food items available was quite vast. He felt overwhelmed every time he looked at the full menu. He stared at the menu for some time, but nothing jumped out at him. He sighed and picked the coffee back up. A couple of warm sips later and he was happy once more. Inside, though, he was all torn up.

Captain Harris felt worried for the drop mission crew and what they might find down there. Part of him felt concern over what the masked planet held in store for his people. There were no scans of the surface and thus no details to be gleaned from them. Finally, he was insanely jealous of the drop crew for they were living the adventure he had always dreamt of. He wanted to be an adventurer. He had gone into archeology to realize that dream. But he had been promoted too quickly and found himself locked on board the main ship when someone else went down and experienced the danger and possible rewards of an expedition. Even that robot had done so much more than he had. The little machine, the smallest crewmember on board, had lived many lifetimes worth and had done amazing things. The captain was so jealous of him that he could hardly bear it. He moved back towards the window and peered out. There was the planet, all swirly and ominous splayed out before him. He wanted to grab it by the hand and force it to give up its riches to him. He wanted to at least set foot upon this new world and see for himself how it felt under the real gravity and the real winds blowing in his face. But alas that would not happen. His duty was clear, and it was locked to the command chair on his bridge. He was a slave to duty and the impossible planet would get to sting his eyes with regret even as he rejoiced in his crewmates.

The coffee was about halfway down when he turned away from that window and the planet that seemed to mock him. He wanted to get away from here so that it lost its power over him. He also knew that would be useless. Another planet or another base would come up and he would revisit all of these feelings again. In truth, he had experienced them to some degree each time he sent some people to a site. It was just the life he had chosen. He sat back down and leaned back in the chair.

His fingers rapped on the table as he considered his next move. He had an indeterminate amount of time to wait. He could go over his duty logs and clean up any discrepancies. He rejected that idea so fast it hardly touched the surface of his brain. He could research the next link on this chain, assuming that the crew found nothing down below. He didn't want to jinx the mission by assuming it was going to fail. Then he remembered Elio's database. They had lost the first one to the corporate dogs who had taken it as soon as they were aware of it. They had thought that it was Elio himself they were taking. But the Captain had saved the little robot from those sharks in the water. Elio had constructed another backup device. It had his knowledge in it, well, at least at the time of transferring. Maybe this planet was mentioned in there.

Captain Harris felt a surge of hope and he got up again. He put the coffee cup back on the tray and headed down to the lab. He finally had something to do. Even if the planet wasn't mentioned, maybe there was another clue as to where they should go next.

He had a lighter step as he made his way through the ship. Personnel simply got out of his way. His sense of purpose was engaged once more, and nobody wanted to get in the way of that.

The backup unit sat in the lab in the corner, powered down to conserve energy. The button on the left of the access panel was the on/off button. Sean pushed the button and pulled up a chair to interface with the device. The tiny keyboard would be inconvenient, but then nobody could overhear his request either. He wasn't sure if that level of paranoia was needed here, but one had to remain cautious when dealing with this database.

Query:
What is the ancient name of the planet Ladius232?

Data Result:
Ladius232 is not listed in this database. The location coordinates referenced refer to planet Acheron.

Query:
Who lived on Acheron?

Data Result:
Acheron is the ancestral home of the Treshnik Tribe. The Tribe consisted of an empire of over two hundred worlds that all died out in the same era. Estimates on the fall of their empire are one hundred and twenty-five thousand years ago.

Query:
How do you know about something so ancient as that?

Data Result:
Acheron data was recovered by an archeological team on star date... unknown. The team was forced to evacuate when planetary defenses activated, creating violent storms and electrical discharges disabling any and all approaching aircraft.

Query:
So, sending a ship down into that storm is a mistake?

Data Result:
Planetary defenses were activated so no craft could land. The visual and electronic sensors would be useless. The countryside was planted with a variety of large obstacles to prevent landing. Success rate calculated at extremely low.

Query:

Can the planetary defenses be deactivated?

Data Result:
Unknown.   Insufficient data on the Treshnik technology base to formulate a probability. Theoretical projection doubtful, but not impossible.

Query:
Can I get a message to the drop ship that has already penetrated the defensive storm?

Data Result:
The defensive electrical storm is designed to disrupt sensors and communications.   Communication is impossible within its influence.

Query:
Is there an old device in this database that can help the team succeed?

Data Result:
There is no device on file that could assist the current team.

Captain Harris leaned back, unhappy. He reached up and turned the backup unit off. He now felt that he had been missing critical mission information when he sent those people down. Why hadn't they asked Elio about this before? He had the same data as this backup unit. Of course, they hadn't specifically asked about this planet and its origins, but he did have useful information about it. He made a note to change his protocols when approaching a new place. Consulting the database, or Elio himself, would become one of the first things he did from now on.

The good captain left the lab in destroyed spirits. His crew was down on a hostile planet that had been rigged to stop them from finding anything. Yet he had sent them there to do exactly that. Elio was with them though. He had seen the crew manifest include the little robot at the last minute. With his knowledge, there might just be a chance. He hoped they would ask him some key questions to get to the information he had just found. He wanted to set them in the right direction. How could he tell them where to look? An idea struck him, and Captain Harris moved quickly once more. He entered the bridge at a trot.

"I want a probe sent down to the planet, close to where the ship went in." He announced to the surprised bridge crew.

"A probe sir?" The duty officer asked as she stood up to relinquish the chair to him.

"Electronic messages will not get through that static down there; I want to send a regular handwritten message to them." The captain remarked.

"Sir, the likelihood of them finding the probe in all of that static are astronomical against." She pointed out.

"Nevertheless, I want this done." The captain replied.

"Yes sir, what message do you want to send?"

The captain thought about this for a moment. "Ask Elio about the Treshnik defense system." He replied.

"Yes sir." The duty officer replied, having jotted down the message as requested. "Will this make sense to them?" She asked before turning to carry the message down to the probe. The captain just watched her go.

"I hope so." He said under his breath. The rest of the bridge crew could not hear it.

***

The Survey Begins…

The planet itself wasn't all that bad. The soil was rich with nutrients and wildlife seemed to be thriving, if not all that large. The storm itself did not move. The event seemed to be fully localized. That meant that it was probably not natural. Of course, that hardly mattered when it was slamming you in the face. Despite the protective gear, they all felt the rush of the wind as it pushed them and slammed them repeatedly.

Elio's legs would not hold him in that wind, so he remained a ball. The wind pushed him like the others, but his body shape allowed most of the force to redirect around him. He made his way to a place in the ground where his sensors detected a possible cave. He wanted to establish a base of operations there, out of the storm. It was the most logical pursuit, so the crew had agreed right away. Jamal had led the way in the beginning, but he seemed just as lost on the ground as he had found himself in the air. So, he relented and allowed Elio to lead. The little robot was a good choice because he was small enough to avoid most of the power of the storm. He also had superior sensors to find what they sought. The only problem was he couldn't step over a vine in his ball form. As soon as he extended his legs, the wind blew him over. He couldn't jump over a rock. He had to be helped from time to time. But the progress was rapid enough that they did indeed reach a cave entrance and were then out of the storm.

The cave appeared natural. The echoes said that it was deep. The floor angled down and away from the entrance and broadened as if something large had used it for a ramp. It was not, however, smooth. Sharp stalagmites jutted up in various places and the footing was treacherous pretty much everywhere. The accompanying stalactites seemed to hang over each stalagmite as if it formed its brother by dripping there. Perhaps it did. The minerals provided a bit of sparkle when hit with the suit lights. It wasn't enough to see by, but it was enough to highlight the dangerous protuberance. The sounds of dripping water could be heard farther down the cave.

"This is a good start." Jamal commented.

Emma was already setting up a portable sensor station. "We've got to find out what is in this cave before we are forced to sleep here." She said.

Elio looked down the cave. In here he could use his legs. He lifted himself up and scanned as far as he could see. "I detect nothing moving for about eight hundred meters." He declared.

"Well, at least nothing is going to jump us now." Jamal replied, a bit sarcastically.

"You know that we know so little about this planet. How could you be so non-compliant about simple security measures?" Another crewmember asked. It was Janet Hoskins. Janet's specialty was geology. She was a rock and mineral specialist and she had already taken a sample of the glittering stalagmite.

"Hey look, I am no optimist." Jamal replied with his hands in the air. "I saw that storm out there and no matter what we find in here, we still can't get back to our ship in space through that." He said.

Emma stood up again. "Elio landed us in this soup, not you. I'd take his word on whether or not we can get home long before I took yours." She rebuked.

Jamal made a dismissive gesture. "So, the little robot is in charge now, great." He said, in a self-deprecating tone.

Emma put her fists on her hips. "He has been on many more missions than we have. It would be foolish not to take advantage of his experience and expertise." She countered. "But if we're going to make it down here, we need everyone working together. So, stow your attitude and do something useful." She commanded, her tone hardening as the sentence trailed out.

"All right, all right, I'll scout out a bit and see if there is anything edible in here." Jamal said.

"We brought provisions, but fine, do that." Emma replied.

ELIO[2]

Janet moved closer to Emma. "It looks like you're in charge, not Elio." She said and she smiled as she said it.

"He needed to be put in his place. I hated to do it. But we need to stay focused here." Emma explained.

"Oh, I know." Janet countered. "It was just good to see him dropped down a notch and someone finally had the nerve to give him some truth. Well, done." She said and then she went back to check on her gear. For her part, Emma returned to Elio.

"Okay, so we're down here in one piece. What's next on the agenda?" She asked.

Elio had been going over some things and was startled by her query. "Sorry, I was thinking." He replied at first. "I do not have an agenda. However, the mission requires us to find any ruins or writings that have been left behind here." He reminded her.

Emma rolled her eyes. "Of course, it does. We're archeologists." She replied. "I mean specifically now, what do we do next?" She asked.

Elio took the new question and suddenly felt a bit of embarrassment at his previous reply. "My apologies, I am only a robot you know." He said in explanation. "The next part of the mission should be to follow this cave to an underground settlement." He said. Emma's eyes went big.

"Do you know that for a fact?" She asked.

"No, but what we are looking for is a ruined settlement for a species that lived here a very long time ago. I suspect that due to the storm activity, their main settlement had to be underground. So, I brought us to the closest place I could find." Elio replied.

Emma gazed away at the massive cave structure. "We could spend days down here and find nothing." She replied. Then a thought struck her. "What makes you think we are looking for an ancient race here?"

Elio moved closer to the cave wall and popped up his projector. "This planet was not always called Ladius232." Elio began. "It was not always covered in storms. The storms are a planetary defense system triggered by the last people to come here." He said. The projector blinked on and showed a wall of writing. Not just writing, but of a warning.

> *Travel beyond this point is forbidden. Automated systems are designed to trigger for any unauthorized trespass. Consider this warning final.*

"You see, this is not the first time I have been here." Elio admitted.

Emma stared at the little robot in surprise. "Why didn't you say something earlier?" She asked.

"The mission requirements needed me to remain silent on this. I was not about to interfere with the mission." He replied.

"But our lives were in danger!" Emma protested.

"Not at any time. I came along to make sure of that. I have calculated the coordinates of the old installation and theorize that we should be able to reach it through this cave system. It will be much easier than moving on the surface." He declared.

"No argument there. But this means that you already know where it is we need to go. We are not searching for something; we're simply going to pick it up." Emma complained.

"To some degree, your statement is accurate. But I remind you that my database is large, but not exhaustive. There could easily be threats that I am unaware of. The artifacts you seek could have been removed by others seeking them." Elio challenged.

"I think we'll find whatever it is down here pretty secure." Emma replied hotly. "Who would be crazy enough to fly down here to get it?"

"Unknown. I don't know everything." Elio replied. He had missed her sarcasm completely.

ELIO[2]

Emma stood up again. "So, which way to the artifacts?" She asked. Elio lifted his body up and rotated to the correct angle. He extended his mining tool to indicate where he was facing.

"That way, about three kilometers away." He replied.

Emma looked that way as if she could see through stone or even the darkness before her. Then she looked back at Elio. "Where were the people when they triggered the planetary defense system?" She asked.

Elio was surprised by the question, but he swung his arm around to the correct angle. "It is that way, much farther. It is at least thirty-five kilometers away." He replied.

"What were the other people after? Emma pressed.

"They wanted answers from a people called the Treshnik. The Treshnik inherited their technology from an even more ancient race, as I mentioned before, they died out long before humans evolved. The Treshnik died out more recently, but still a long time ago by your standards. But their systems and thus their artifacts are very powerful. There might be something useful, if not terribly valuable down here." He concluded.

"Useful for whom?" Emma asked.

Elio made his equivalent of a shrug. "We are on an exploration mission. Maybe we'll get lucky and find some real answers." He offered.

"If he knows the way, why aren't we heading out now?" Janet asked.

"We're establishing our base here first. We don't need to carry everything down there, do we?" Emma asked.

Jamal was wandering around. "I don't see why not, you carried it all this far." He replied. "What's another three kilometers?" He asked.

Emma looked around at the camp they had. If they found what they were looking for, it could be a lot more comfortable. At least it would be farther away from those storms. "Okay, have it your way. I was just following standard protocols. But obviously standard protocols didn't account for having Elio with us. They don't account for actually knowing where you are going and not just exploring until you stumble across something. We'll set up camp at the dig site." She announced.

The crew began to pick up their gear once more. Jamal was his usual self. "Just pick a good spot."

The group managed the walk in less time than would have been believed. It helped greatly that most of it was downhill. They had descended deep into the rock, or mountain, or whatever this was. They reached a point where the natural stone turned into carved smooth stone. The stone had been polished so that it shined brightly when lit. There was an entrance, but it was solidly closed. The group decided that this would be their new camp site. It was a nice cool temperature down here. The walls and floors were dry. The ceiling looked to be polished just as much as the walls were. Whoever did that work had a lot of patience.

"Elio, do you know how to get in this door?" Emma asked. She had taken to asking him first before trying to figure out anything. It seemed his database covered practically everything.

"I'm afraid not. I do recall this door, but it was already open when I went this way before." Elio replied.

"It is so strange having someone who has actually been here with us on this mission." Janet mentioned. She moved over to Elio and patted the top of his dome. "They told me that you were valuable, but I didn't understand just how much. It is not about credits, but about history. You know things that people have forgotten. You have the keys to things that we don't even know exist anymore. You are special." She said.

Elio would have blushed if he had been able to. "Thank you." He managed to say instead.

Janet sat down beside Elio. "So, you don't know how to get past that door?" She asked directly.

"Not now, but I will look into it. I hope to have an answer soon." Elio replied.

Elio was scanning through his visual records of the last time that he was on Acheron. The images were mostly of boring stuff. There was scant little about archeology since he was not programmed for that mission. He was a security surveillance robot. He was looking for misconduct. He managed to find a scene that contained this door and he played it. A human walked up to the door and placed their hand to the left of it at hip level. An access plate formed beneath the hand and lit up. The door slid obediently open. Elio lifted himself up onto his legs and walked over to the door. Interested, Janet followed him. Elio's sensors could not detect the access plate. He knew that it was there and still could not see it. He turned to Janet.

"Place the palm of your hand on the wall here." He said, indicating once more with a drilling tool. It had become his favorite pointing instrument.

Janet shrugged and placed her hand on the wall. She expected to feel cold stone, but her hand came into contact with something that looked like polished stone but felt more like glass. The access panel appeared beneath her hand and the scan checked her hand.

Elio did not know what they were looking for, but they obviously found it in Janet. The door slipped open and stayed that way.

"You did it!" Janet cried excitedly. The rest looked over to see the door open and they were up like a shot.

"What did you do?" Emma asked as she approached.

Janet was the one who responded. "Elio told me to put my hand on a particular spot and a plate appeared and let me in." She explained.

Emma glanced around. "Let's get our stuff and get in there then." She pressed. She was not ready to let this gift go to waste. But she did have a cautious side to her. "Place a rock in the doorway after we are through. I don't want this thing closing us in." She said, voicing her concerns.

So, they moved through with their gear and Jamal was forcing the largest rock he could shift into the open doorway. "That ought to hold it." He said with a sigh. He brushed his hands off and then picked up his gear as they moved farther into the facility. As the group got about ten meters down the corridor inside, the door closed, splitting the rock in two. The half of the rock inside looked crumbled where it was struck.

"So much for that idea." Emma stated and then she turned back down the corridor. "I guess there's no turning back now, we'd better find something down here." She stated.

"It won't be long now; we are inside the complex itself." Elio informed the group.

"Oh, do you need to lead the way?" Janet asked.

"Oh no, that is not necessary. The path is clear and brightly lit. You'll have no problems finding your way down here." Elio said reassuringly. "Do watch for traps though." He added as an afterthought.

"Traps? You never mentioned that before." Janet complained.

Elio lifted himself up to peer at Janet. "Actually, I did. I told you that the storms outside are part of an elaborate security system. This was all set off by a trap." He told her in response.

"So, we are in a maze of pitfalls and traps?" She asked for final clarification.

Elio made his shrug movement. "Maybe they don't work anymore." He offered.

"The storms are still brewing outside." Emma pointed out.

Elio shifted from face to face and back again. "Point taken. Just be careful." He added at the end. They really had no choice but to go forward anyway.

Emma grabbed Elio and pointed him at her. It was not a customary move for her. "Tell me, can you sense these traps before we hit them?" She asked.

Elio considered what he knew of the layout of this place and how many years had come and gone since that time. "Some traps are more easily detected by humans than robots." He replied. "If I sense one, I'll let you know immediately." He promised.

"Good enough." Emma said and let him go.

Janet moved closer to Emma and whispered. "What was that all about? Do you control him like some kind of pet?" She asked.

Elio? No, nobody can control him. He is sentient. He chooses his own path. I just wanted him to understand the danger we are all in and to alert us if it becomes necessary." She explained.

"You talk to him like he's a child." Janet whispered.

"Sometimes you have to. He is old, but he has only been sentient a brief portion of his extended lifespan. In essence, he is a child. Just a very special one." Emma explained.

"Yes, and a valuable one everyone keeps telling me." Janet replied under her breath.

"Most people think he is just a robot, but he is a life-form now. Despite the fact that he can rebuild himself when he needs to. He has learned how to think and act like a living being. He has emotions and reactions to things just as we do. Do not underestimate him." Emma warned.

"Underestimate? Are you expecting trouble from the little robot?" Janet asked, beginning to sound alarmed.

"No, not as such; but he did know what planet this is and he had been here before without mentioning it to anybody, especially Captain Harris. He has become a bit too human. An omission such as that may have been criminal." She said.

"Criminal? Can a robot be a criminal?" Janet asked. This was obviously something she had never discussed or even thought about before.

Elio was a machine, so he could not be prone to disaster. He could not be persuaded into doing something he didn't want to do. He was strong willed and had machine tolerance built right in. This made him a valuable asset. But, if his perceptions required him to do the wrong thing but for the right reasons, he could do so. In fact, he probably would do so. Had he done so already by withholding the information? Most likely he had.

The entire idea bugged Emma terribly. Janet was beginning to feel the same way, but she was still quite enamored with the little robot. "If he does something wrong, we can call him out on it, right?" Janet suggested. "Just like any other crewmember." She added to seal the deal.

Emma nodded. "Indeed, we could and should. What if someone comes to harm because we were not informed of a threat?" She asked.

"Elio wouldn't do that." Janet replied quickly. She had raised her voice just a bit and both women looked around quickly.

"We were just discussing what he could, or even would do. Do not make any assumptions now. Approach this with scientific curiosity. We must watch him for our own safety as well as for the mission." She concluded.

"So, I have violated your trust." Elio broke into their conversation. "The risk was there to be calculated, but the decision was the correct one." He said and both women stared at him incredibly.

"Explain your logic in this." Emma demanded.

"It is quite simple." Elio began. "The last time I was here, I was sworn to secrecy regarding this place due to the nature of the traps and the people that were lost here." He said.

"Who swore you to secrecy?" Janet asked.

"The Treshnik." Elio replied simply.

"You were in contact with an ancient alien species?" Emma asked in shock.

Elio made a nodding gesture. "Not the people directly, of course, but their computer here." Elio replied.

"Are you violating this oath by telling us this now?" Emma asked.

Elio seemed to consider this carefully. "My responses are being carefully filtered to prevent that, but we are on the border of doing so now." Elio responded. "Please know that I trust all of you implicitly, but I understand if you do not trust me. I do have your interests in mind when I make my decisions. You are my crewmates. It is a bond we share that cannot be broken." Elio declared.

"But your vow to a lost people, or to the computer here more precisely, is just as solid in your mind, right?" Janet pressed.

"Actually, yes. But I will not allow any of you to come to harm if I can prevent it." Elio stated.

"If you can prevent it? That doesn't sound all that reassuring. If your ancient vow prevents you from preventing it, then we are still screwed." Emma protested.

Elio seemed lost between the two women arguing with him. "I am here to do a mission and that mission I will do." He said, voicing his protest at their argument. "Part of my mission objectives is to ensure that all of you return to the ship with me. Do not mistake my caution for a lack of caring or a lack of sincerity. I will do my job." Elio stated and it felt as if he had put his proverbial foot down.

Emma crossed her arms. "Fine, we'll see just how dedicated you are when the time comes." She said and it sounded more like a challenge.

"Good, then let's get back to work. We have wasted enough time here bickering." Elio said. He was on the move before either woman could raise a new fuss over the slight.

Janet eyed Emma. He sure acts like a living being, doesn't he?" She asked and Emma nodded but moved along at a brisk pace for

ELIO[2]
Elio was leaving them behind. Janet had no choice but to follow
or be left behind and most likely become lost in this place.

***

37

The Treshnik encounter...

Captain Harris was studying once more. He had dedicated a two-hour segment of each day to learning what Elio already knew. He had made query after query when he suddenly realized that he was seeing things out of context. He changed to viewing the data sequentially. This meant that an event might be made up of a dozen log entries and now he would watch them in order. It would take longer than jumping around would, but the thought of missing something important was too much for him just to do things quicker.

He pressed the play button on the top of the backup device and the projector obediently began to display the relevant file.

Several people in regular space suits of older design were loading into a shuttle. They were going to head down to the planet presumably. Captain Harris could see this but could hear nothing. He reached out and tapped the audio button for more volume. The sounds between spacesuits were transmitted to each other, but Elio did not have radio communications. So the image was still silent.

"Why do they have helmets on before they launch?" the good captain asked, but there was no answer.

The shuttle lifted off the deck less than twenty centimeters and began to taxi out of the main ship. Apparently, the drop mechanism had not yet been implemented. The shuttle proceeded to a physical door that slid aside to allow them to leave. The shuttle then moved forward until it was clear and then it angled towards the planet.

The first thing Sean noticed upon viewing the planet was the lack of storms all over the surface. The planet looked lush and green. It had sparkling oceans as well. It looked like a perfect habitat. The shuttle made its way towards the planet using some kind of rocket thruster. Reentry began and the image on the windshield was hidden as a heat shield slid into place. The pilot was flying on instruments alone. A small display showed part of what was ahead of them. The shuttle buffeted about quite a bit, but nobody was panicking. In moments, the heat shield slid back out of the way and wispy clouds could be seen. The sky was open and blue. The pilot moved slightly to the left and Elio moved up as if called for. His sensors pointed at the window for the most part but now they were noting the switch panel. Without audio, it was impossible to tell what they were trying to capture here, but soon enough Elio slid back to his stowed location and the image resumed normally.

The shuttle sailed down easily and made a soft landing on a control pad near a large building built right into the rock. The crew unstrapped and made their way to the rear of the shuttle where the back opened up to allow them egress. The people were talking amongst themselves and making hand gestures. They moved as a group towards a large door in the front of a massive building. There were several people outside it, presumably guards. They did not look human! Each was about the size of a human, but that is where the similarity ended. They had multiple eyes scattered around their heads and webbed hands and feet. The skin tone was more like a frog or a lizard than a human, but it did not look wet. They seemed to be comfortable in the air and sunshine.

The crew of the shuttle moved with purpose towards them and stopped when one of the guards held up their webbed hand in a gesture of halt.

The alien speech was the first thing that Captain Harris heard on this recording. It sounded like garbled gibberish, guttural and harsh...

"gnish gnocket dacoorum snart." The first creature said Each sound was accompanied by gestures and movements. The humans responded with some kind of sign language. Sean could not understand a syllable of the alien speech, yet these people seemed to respond as if they understood it all. The signs ended and the lead human bowed. The guards stepped aside and allowed entry. Elio skittered right past them. They didn't even seem to notice his passing. He moved just behind the crew and when they all got inside the door closed behind them. The sound of air movement was loud, and Elio recorded it fully. The humans were able to remove their helmets after that.

"Can't believe that you are so good at that." One of them was saying as the helmet seal broke.

"You know what it takes to learn this." The response sounded like it had been said many times in the past.

"Yeah, I know. But I don't have a knack for languages, and you do. Is it a problem that I recognize that?"

"You know it isn't only that. But thanks." The man who was speaking looked around as if surveying the room that they were in. "This is better than the holding tank we were in before." He mused.

"You know that they have to take extra care when dealing with us. The toxic spores in the air can kill us after a few hours' exposure." The lady said.

Captain Harris gulped. "Toxic spores? Is my team in danger?" He asked, but the backup device simply continued playing the file.

"Yes, I understand that, but we have been in negotiations for weeks now. You would think that better accommodations could be arranged. Maybe they could come to our ship." He offered.

"You know that they fear being taken Lucas. They would never set foot in our ship." The woman replied. Just then she turned to face Elio. For a brief second, her nametag was visible. It said "S.Taylor". Now Captain Harris had at least partial names to apply to these mysterious people in the past, Lucas and S. Taylor.

"I still say they've been dragging those webbed feet of theirs in all of this. The mineral rights we seek would not affect them at all. They're stalling for something." Lucas replied.

"Shhh! Keep your voice down. Do you want to offend them just before we make the deal?" Taylor asked.

"C'mon Selene, you know they can't understand our spoken language." Luca replied.

"Do you want to bet your life on that?" Selene replied.

Lucas did not answer right away, he was suddenly distracted.

"Lucas Salinas, are you listening to me?" Selene asked.

ELIO[2]

Lucas looked up once more and smiled. "I always listen to you. I just don't always respond." He explained.

"You can be infuriating sometimes." She informed the smug gentleman.

Elio watched the entire exchange and did not speak up at all. He simply recorded the event and made notes as to motivations and study. Then his sensors detected movement close by.

"Our guests are arriving." He announced and both humans stood up straight and watched the door. True to Elio's word, the door opened and the Treshnik negotiators entered the room. They were wearing ceremonial clothing woven from what appeared to be the finest silk. The vibrant colors had been somehow gleaned from nature. It was a dazzling display.

Elio brought his focus to the newcomers and settled in to continue recording this event.

"Gnashish gnruk sirvenko delinsh." The ambassador of the ancient race said with his hands out to the side in a grand gesture of welcoming.

Lucas lowered his eyes to the floor and made a similar, but smaller gesture. "We thank you for the honor of your time." He said formally. His hands moved in small circles as he spoke, and his eyes remained hidden from view.

"Garforth trrnok detruntial forscht." The ambassador replied. His arms fell back to his side, but his right foot canted out ever so slightly. The quick movements of the neck muscles were the only clue that the creature was hesitant. Abalom nostrium gershank decorum. He said and he stood up straight and tall.

"Pause playback." Captain Harris commanded, and the scene froze in place. He addressed the backup unit. "Is there a translation for these events?" He asked.

The little unit seemed to consider his request by executing a search of its own. After a little more than a minute, the machine responded.

"There is a partial translation package available for the Treshnik dialect, but the accuracy is calculated at only sixty-three-point-oh-seven percent." The machine responded.

"Fine, please engage the translation matrix and replay this file." Captain Harris ordered.

The paused screen vanished as the file was reset. When it came back on, there were subtitles of the translation for both sides across the bottom of the image.

The improved playback…

"Welcome to our humble house." The first creature said. The humans responded with some kind of sign language. The signs ended and the lead human bowed. The guards stepped aside and allowed entry. Elio skittered right past them. They didn't even seem to notice his passing. He moved just behind the crew and when they all got inside the door closed behind them. The sound of air movement was loud, and Elio recorded it fully. The humans were able to remove their helmets after that.

"Can't believe that you are so good at that." One of them was saying as the helmet seal broke.

"You know what it takes to learn this." The response sounded like it had been said many times in the past.

"Yeah, I know. But I don't have a knack for languages, and you do. Is it a problem that I recognize that?"

"You know it isn't only that. But thanks." The man who was speaking looked around as if surveying the room that they were in. "This is better than the holding tank we were in before." He mused.

"You know that they have to take extra care when dealing with us. The toxic spores in the air can kill us after a few hours exposure." The lady said.

"Yes, I understand that, but we have been in negotiations for weeks now. You would think that better accommodations could be arranged. Maybe they could come to our ship." He offered.

"You know that they fear being taken Lucas. They would never set foot in our ship." The woman replied. Just then she turned to face Elio.

"I still say they've been dragging those webbed feet of theirs in all of this. The mineral rights we seek would not affect them at all. They're stalling for something." Lucas replied.

"Shhh! Keep your voice down. Do you want to offend them just before we make the deal?" Taylor asked.

"C'mon Selene, you know they can't understand our spoken language." Luca replied.

"Do you want to bet your life on that?" Selene replied.

Lucas did not answer right away, he was suddenly distracted.

"Lucas Salinas, are you listening to me?" Selene asked.

Lucas looked up once more and smiled. "I always listen to you. I just don't always respond." He explained.

"You can be infuriating sometimes." She informed the smug gentleman.

Elio watched the entire exchange and did not speak up at all. He simply recorded the event and made notes as to motivations and study. Then his sensors detected movement close by.

"Our guests are arriving." He announced and both humans stood up straight and watched the door. True to Elio's word, the door opened and the Treshnik negotiators entered the room. They were wearing ceremonial clothing woven from what appeared to be the finest silk. The vibrant colors had been somehow gleaned from nature. It was a dazzling display.

Elio brought his focus to the newcomers and settled in to continue recording this event.

"It is good that you have returned." The ambassador of the ancient race said with his hands out to the side in a grand gesture of welcoming.

Lucas lowered his eyes to the floor and made a similar, but smaller gesture. "We thank you for the honor of your time." He said formally. His hands moved in small circles as he spoke, and his eyes remained hidden from view.

"We understand you want rocks." The ambassador replied. His arms fell back to his side, but his right foot canted out ever so slightly. The quick movements of the neck muscles were the only clue that the creature was hesitant. "How do we know that you will leave some rocks for us?" He asked and he stood up straight and tall.

Lucas held his posture. "Do you use the rocks? We understood that your affinity for your world lay directly with its wildlife, people and energy." He said with a series of hand gestures that took several seconds to get through.

The ambassador bowed ever so slightly. "Your words are true... to a point. We value the universal energy. The energy of life and the soul of our world. What you suggest would steal some of that soul from us and the world would be diminished." The alien went through a series of movements just as complex as Lucas had just performed.

Lucas glanced at Selene. Then he turned back to the ambassador. "My apologies, I was unaware that your connection included the rocks. Let me explain what we need." He said through a pantomime that everyone patiently waited for him to complete. "We seek not the rocks, but the veins of mineral within them. We use that to power our ships in the sky. There are a great many uses for this mineral. It can be used to heal. It can be used to clean. It is very versatile." He explained.

The ambassador was getting agitated the longer Lucas communicated. "Does this not tell you that what you seek is powerful? It is the soul of the rocks you wish to steal." He said through very agitated gestures. "We would be fallen from the favor of our planet's grace if we allowed you to steal the very lifeblood of our world." He said. His meaning was strong, and the movements were precise and almost violent.

Lucas felt that this situation as getting out of hand. He knew how important that these mineral rights were. He understood what they meant to the fleet. He also knew that these people were very religious. The fact that they had tied the very minerals he sought to their god was terribly bad news. There was a chance that they would not part with a single gram of the valuable stuff. This was made even worse by the simple fact that you could search a thousand worlds and never find another with such a rich deposit. This was an all or none sort of situation.

"I apologize for our misunderstanding. Of course, we do not wish to harm your beloved world. That was never our cause or intention." He said. His nervousness was making his gestures a bit sloppy. Things were going from bad to worse. Mistakes could change a word and kill the meaning of his sentence. He drove on, tying to make his case.

"The minerals we seek only exist on a few worlds. They cannot be the souls of the world because all of them would then have it." He explained. The ambassador and his fellows were getting very agitated.

"Do not preach to us about what our world is and is not." The ambassador commanded. His movements were so sharp they may have been militarily taught. "It is we who decide what is right and what is wrong for our world. You are no longer welcome here." He said. His gestures finished with an undeniable ending and Lucas lowered his head in defeat.

Lucas began to retreat with Selene behind him. Elio was still watching the Ambassador for some reason. It was then that the ambassador flinched. He made a religious gesture, "Heretics!" and he drove a long spike from his wrist into Selene's back and out into Lucas. Both humans were run completely through and fell right there in the doorway. The looks of shock and surprise on their faces would haunt Captain Harris for a long time. Elio lifted himself up to address the Treshnik.

"I realize that the humans have committed sins against your world. I do not share in their views on this. May I be permitted to exit and return to the ship to explain that they are not welcome down here?" Elio asked.   The Treshnik were quite surprised to see the little robot communicating with them using his version of their gestures.

"It is granted. You are to tell them not to come here evermore." The ambassador said. His grim and determined gestures were perfect, of course.

Elio turned and left the aliens in their place. The door closed behind him and would not open again. Elio made his way back through the lush green place to the shuttlecraft. There, he initiated the autopilot to take him back up into orbit and to the awaiting ship.

ELIO[2]

"Elio to home base, I report the mission is a failure. The negotiators have been slain and we have been ordered not to come to this world." Elio transmitted to the main ship. "Full report to be filed as soon as I am back on board." He declared for the protocols that were required.

The recording ended.

****

Down on the planet there was a cold stillness in the air. Most of the crew had already settled into a darker spot in the old building. The day had been quite eventful and now they were settled in for rest. Elio took watch since he required no sleep. His sensors could see farther than human eyes in the dark anyway. He perched himself on the wall overlooking the corridor that led to the camp and the crew itself. He had laid out sensor modules about the place and any sound would alert him right away of anybody was approaching.

The building was just as he remembered it. The floor was dustier, but then nobody was cleaning it. The walls were laid out the same as he remembered them too. He could navigate this place fully if the assumption was made that nothing had changed at all. But that was an assumption he was not ready to make.

Elio did his best to keep the others in line, but he knew that sooner or later, one of them would touch something that they shouldn't. The automated defense systems were likely still active. After all, the storms were. He had deactivated several traps during their search of the grounds. Basically, Elio was on full alert on this planet. He dared not think if they had come down here without him. The crew would probably already be lost. The crash landing on the planet would have stranded them here and if they had managed to find the cave, they would not have located the door mechanism. If they had managed to open the door, the traps therein would have finished the job. Yes, the calculations of the crew's survival rate without him were abysmal. Yet none of that mattered. He was here with them. He had done his part to ensure that they moved forward while still feeling in charge. He had done well. But he also knew that bigger challenges awaited them deeper in. But this time the humans were not looking to take away any of the planet's vital energy. No, this was just to study the Treshnik base and to determine what kind of people they were.

Elio felt a tingle in his circuitry. Was something coming? He checked his readings, but nothing was active. He checked the crew and Emma was stirring. He looked closer and she looked to be in REM sleep. She was dreaming. That was something he wished that he could do. But he had a job to do watching the group, so he set that idea aside and continued monitoring.

***

49

Emma's dream…

Emma stirred and awoke. She looked around but the room was quiet. Her crewmembers were scattered around her all sleeping. She checked for Elio, and he was watching the hallway just as agreed. Everything seemed to be right. Why had she woken up then? She pushed herself up and stood, brushing the dust off her hands. Nobody else seemed to move at all. Elio didn't even react to her getting up.

"That's strange." She said softly and even the sound didn't make him turn her way as it usually did. Was the little robot broken? Was it asleep? Elio said he didn't sleep.

"Your friends are fine." A voice said, startling Emma. She looked and saw an apparition of a tall person with webbed hands and feet. Its skin was almost lizard-like, rough looking, but he or she was see-through!

"Who are you?" Emma asked.

The being, or apparition, or ghost moved without stepping. "I was once the guardian of this place. But that was a long time ago. My name is Aeolia. I had a rank once but that matters not once you are dead." She said.

Emma felt curious instead of fear. "I am sorry for your loss." She said automatically. "Can you tell me more about your people?" Emma asked.

"So, you are not here for the soul of our world?" Aeolia asked.

Emma shook her head.   "No, we are here as archeologists, not surveyors." She replied.

"It is good. Our world has seen so much death. The storms have taken so many." Aeolia said.

"I know that they are a problem. We came down in them just barely." Emma replied.

ELIO[2]

"Yes, the little one was involved." Aeolia replied moving towards Elio. "We know this one. He is breaking a promise in bringing you here." She said.

"I know very little about his encounter with you ages ago. I do not understand the limitations he is working under. But it is not his fault that we are here. We followed a trail of archeological breadcrumbs to this planet to find the remnants of your people for study. I admit that I never expected to speak with one of your kind." Emma commented. "How is it you speak English?" Emma asked, suddenly realizing that they were speaking to each other fluently.

"I do not speak your language, but I do speak to your thoughts. Your mind translates your thoughts into your own language for proper understanding. But it does not work when you are awake." Aeolia explained.

Emma looked around. "But I am awake." She replied.

"No, you are still sleeping. Please forgive this intrusion, but we needed to know what your intentions are." The webbed one explained.

"We are only here to learn, and maybe, to find some valuable artifacts for our historians. If you guide me to the things we need, I can assure you we will touch nothing else." She offered.

"You are a curious people." Aeolia responded. "You will search everywhere, touch everything." She made a gesture similar to a shrug. "You understand that we no longer care about this base. But we do care about this world. Take nothing that comes from the ground. You can have any of our constructs, but nothing naturally occurring."

Emma paid close attention. "I understand and comply. I will tell the others."

"There is no hurry, you can do that when you wake up." Aeolia replied. "I am certain that as an explorer, you have questions for me." She sat down and a ghostly chair seemed to form under her. She motioned her hand to another chair that looked and felt very real. "Have a seat and we will talk." She offered.

Emma smiled. "This is the opportunity of a lifetime." She said with some excitedness in her voice.

"As I presumed." Aeolia replied.

The two spoke for quite some time about the culture that existed when Aeolia's people roamed these halls. Emma found their beliefs to be much the same as hers. They believed in balance in all things. They believed in natural beauty. They believed in honestly and truth. They also believed in protecting what cannot protect itself. Emma spoke at great length about Elio and his contributions over time. Aeolia spoke of Elio and the time he was here and was allowed to leave. They had a lot of common ground.

"We are out of time." Aeolia proclaimed. Emma wanted to shake her head, but something told her the alien was right. She bowed and accepted it.

"Thank you for this discussion. I value your input more than you will know." Emma told her.

"I am in your head. I can see just how valuable this is to you. You cannot lie to me just as you cannot lie to yourself." Aeolia replied. "But your friends are worried, it is time to go." Aeolia vanished and Emma's eyes popped open. To see her crew's faces looking down at her.

"Ah, so you're back with the living." Jamal stated tartly.

Janet looked concerned. "We were going to wake you, but Elio insisted that we not touch you. He said you were communicating."

Emma got up slowly. Her head hurt a bit. "I was. I had a long talk with Aeolia of the Treshnik people." She declared and the mouths of her crewmates fell open in unison. Emma looked past them to Elio. "She had good things to say about you." She declared and Elio lifted himself up a little bit.

"I missed talking to her. My circuitry apparently was not compatible." Elio stated.

ELIO[2]

Emma turned to the rest of her crew. "We have been given permission to take any artifact that is Treshnik made. We are forbidden to take anything that is naturally occurring." She told them.

"Natural stuff can't be all that valuable." Jamal commented. "Did she tell you where to look?" He asked to press this mission on.

"Actually, no." Emma admitted. "But Elio knows, don't you?" She said.

"Affirmative." Elio replied quickly.

"Wait! You knew which way to go the entire time?" Jamal asked.

Elio made a little move that was akin to a partial shrug. "I had the data, but the Treshnik had not allowed me to use it. I was under oath." He told them.

Emma moved closer to Elio. "Yes, Aeolia told me that you did violate your oath by bringing us to this world." She said.

"I didn't bring you here, I only protected you since coming here. It was a very close interpretation that I was using to remain legitimate." He replied.

"You can be a little sneak, can't you?" Janet commented.

Elio made his shrug move again, but more pronounced this time. "The mission required me to be a bit sneaky, if that's how you want to phrase it." Elio countered. "The alternative was to warn you not to come down and risk your total loss if you didn't believe me. I chose the more assured method of accompanying you with a sideways permission from the captain." Elio informed them.

"I saw the captain tell you not to go." Emma replied.

"Yes, on the surface, for the logs. I read between those lines as he knew that I would." Elio replied in protest. "He knows that I am a crewmember now. He has to walk a fine line between allowing me to do my job and saving me from doing my job. He still views me as a valuable piece of history. But he promised to let me be my own robot." Elio continued. "He is in a bad predicament over this."

"You eased that somewhat by building your backup unit." Emma pointed out.

"I did. In fact, if I hadn't done that, he would never have allowed me to escape onto this mission. You can bet every credit you have that he is up there consulting with that backup of my database even now." Elio said.

"Then he may know more than we do. You haven't old us everything, have you?" Emma pressed.

"No." Elio's short answer surprised them all. "You know that I have restrictions on my data. This world contains even more than most. I am bound by galactic law not to reveal items concerning weaponry and defense systems in space. You know that already. On this world, I am not supposed to allow anybody to take anything naturally occurring from this world." Elio conceded.

Emma's eyes lit up. "That is exactly what Aeolia told me." She confirmed.

Elio lowered his electronic eye just as a human would look down at the floor. "I wish I could have seen her." He said sadly. "She spoke in gestures and movements." He added.

"Not to me. She spoke mind to mind. I understood every word in pure English." Emma reported.

Elio looked up again. "Really? Then there is a probe here somewhere." He concluded excitedly. The crew began to look around nervously.

"Why do you say that?" Emma asked.

"The Treshnik people were water breathers. Their vocal skills were disquieting to the ears. They could not produce sound like you do at all. They developed their communication of body language much in the same way cats do." Elio explained.

Emma looked confused. "Cats? They have vocal cords. In fact, they have two sets." She pointed out.

ELIO[2]
"Elio made a dismissive gesture. "Yes, they do. But they do not communicate with each other vocally. A series of movements and gestures is all they use, and they can convey all of the important things they need to without speech. They only 'speak' to people who speak to them." Elio countered. "But that is neither here nor there." He added to stop this tangent conversation.   "If you received thought transmissions and your brain turned them into English, then you were in proximity to a transmitter, thus a probe." Elio concluded.

"So, we have been monitored in here?" Janet asked.

"Undoubtedly." Elio replied.

"The Treshnik are still here then, somewhere?"

Elio shook his round body like shaking one's head. "No, they died out some time ago. What is left behind are automated systems. The probe is a surprise to me but a happy one. If I can interface with it, I might be able to contact them and explain us to them." He said.

"I just did that." Emma injected.

Elio turned to her. "You did?" he asked.

"Yes, we had quite the conversation. She told me about the world and the balance they believe in. She told me about their beliefs, and I told her ours. Her concern was mostly about the world itself. I told her that we were interested in her people, and not this world." She finished.

Elio made a sound, kind of like a tsk-tsk. "You do know why I was here before, yes?" Elio asked.

Emma looked at the others of the crew and nobody knew why he had been here before. "No, I'm afraid not." Emma replied.

"This world is rich in minerals. Specifically, the ones that we use in almost all of our systems. Propulsion, medical, and many others. It is why we were here and the Treshnik considered this a threat. They killed the crew I was with. They only allowed me to leave to warn others not to come here." Elio admitted.

"But you let us come down here. How could you do that if you knew it was a death sentence?" Emma asked.

Elio canted a bit during his reply. "I came along to protect you. You didn't know it was a threat to you and I could head off any traps that could do the job. I expected fully well to contact them and explain our nobler cause. But if they are now extinct, and it appears that they are, we could profit heavily from those mineral rights." Elio put forth.

"But that is exactly the type of thoughts that gets people killed down here." Emma protested. "Consider our mission of an archeological find profit enough. If we can shut everything down, then maybe we branch out. But for the time being, we have to remain pure of thought to avoid detection." She informed them. "These probes can see into our minds." She insisted. "Not sure about yours though." She added for Elio.

"If I manage to interface, then the same will hold true for me. I am aware of the risks, but I am on two missions now. Yours, and the one I was originally sent here to accomplish." He declared.

"The people that sent you on your old mission are long since gone. That mission has expired with them. Focus on keeping us alive and completing the current mission. That is an order." Emma commanded, putting her foot down.

"An order?" Elio replied. "You mean, like a real crewperson?" He asked.

Emma did not relent. "Yes, like a real crewperson. You have to abide by our rules just like we do. I will not have someone running around as a potentially hostile base with an agenda of their own. Focus on your job and I won't have to send you back to the ship." She said. Her words hit Elio like rocks.

"You would send me back to the ship?" He asked.

Emma crossed her arms. "Indeed, I would. There are repairs to be done out there if we are take-off from this rock again. You know that already." She told him.

ELIO[2]

"But the traps, how would you avoid them without me?" Elio asked, he sounded desperate.

"We would manage, it would just be slower." Emma assured him.

"Do I have your word that you will only work this one mission?" She asked him directly.

Elio considered his directives. Above all of them was not to alienate Emma. He could sense that she was serious about this. He checked the others quickly. It was a very human thing to do. They looked just as adamant as Emma was. Elio considered his position and finally relented.

"I promise that this mission is my only focus." He said solemnly.

Emma switched moods like a lightbulb. "Great! Let's go find those artifacts then." She said excitedly. The abruptness of her emotional change caught Elio off guard.

"Really? Just like that?" Elio asked.

Emma looked back to him. "Of course. I trust you as much as I trust anyone. If you promise me, I'll believe you." Emma replied.

Something in Elio suddenly felt warm. It was not physical heat, but an emotional heat. He felt good. It was somehow soothing. This was something he had never felt before. He felt trusted, like he belonged. This was better than any feeling he had tried so far. He wondered how he had missed this one before. Then Emma cleared her throat and he looked up at her. She was looking down at him expectantly.

"So, where do we go next?" She asked when he failed to take the hint.

Elio lifted his body up to be even with Emma's eyes. "I think we need to go to the main control room." He replied. Then he turned toward the closest wall. His projector shined the floorplan around them with a green dot on the room he had chosen.

"You can do that?" Janet asked in surprise. "You have the floorplans to this whole facility?" She asked.

"Most of it. You recall that it has been a long time since I was here, but most of the walls remain right where they were." Elio explained. "If we find a discrepancy, I will adjust this floorplan for accuracy." Elio offered.

Jamal distracted them all. He had picked up his gear and was ready to get moving once more. "Good enough for me." He said and he headed off in the direction the map had indicated.

"Wait up. What about the possible traps?" Janet called after.

"We've been sitting around too long. Let's get this done so we can get back to the drop ship and fix it up." Jamal replied even as he continued walking down the corridor.

Emma grabbed her bag as well. "Alright people, it's time to go." She said and the rest of the crew shuffled to catch up to Jamal.

* * *

ELIO[2]

Captain Harris sat in his bunk. He had been too tired to sleep lately. Worry creased his brow as he considered his crew both in the sky and down on the planet below. The financials were bleak. They were low on supplies, and they were low on credits. Yes, they were corporate sponsored, but they had yet to see any credits come from that source since they had started this trek. The path that led to this planet had consisted of five jumps and that cost a great deal of time and fuel. They needed to score here. The path back was still available, but only just and they would not be able to pay the berth fees if they used all of their food and water up. That didn't even include paying the crew itself. The man was miserable.

He had a small reading light on to allow him to review the figures, but in all reality, he hadn't even needed to look. He knew how many credits were in the accounts. He knew the fuel levels and he knew the consumable supplies level as well. They were running thin to be sure.

"I need a break." He muttered softly to himself.

"What sort of break?" A voice answered him, and he looked up. A Treshnik woman was there, but only in a ghostly, see-through form.

"Who are you?" He asked, still freaked out that an alien hologram was standing next to his bed.

"I am the guardian of the world below. My name was Aeolia. I understand that you sent those humans down to my world despite the warnings that have been posted against such action." She accused.

"Warnings? What warnings?" Captain Harris questioned.

"The storms cover the planet. Surely you noticed that much at least." The alien woman pointed out.

"Well yes, we did see the storms. But we are on an archeological trip and the evidence we found pointed to this world. Is this world still inhabited?" He asked.

Aeolia looked sad. "Alas, it is no longer inhabited, but it is still protected. You need to pull your people back. Do not let them violate our base and grounds." She said.

"With the storms in place, I cannot contact them to recall my team." The captain replied.

"Hmmm, then we are both suffering from troubled circumstances." The woman replied with a shrug.

"You came here to tell me to remove them. Can you tell them to evacuate down there?" the captain asked.

"I have spoken with Emma. She tells me that you are interested in only the artifacts of my people and not the planet. But I sense discussion about something called minerals. We have heard that word in the past when humans wanted to steal the life force of this world." Aeolia explained.

"The mission is purely archeological in nature, I assure you." He replied.

"I understand that you are in financial straits and that the life of my world could help you." She told the captain. "I do not understand how this is so, only that it is." She admitted.

"I don't know what the lifeblood of your world is, so I have no idea either." Captain Harris admitted as well.

"Your robot knows. It was here before. It knows about our world and the riches hidden within it. I do not understand its thinking, but it told me that it wants only the artifacts. Then it tells the rest of the crew that there is more wealth here than that. We are concerned about the robot's motivations." Aeolia explained beseechingly.

"I honestly do not know enough about your world to speak intelligently about what Elio knows. I will reserve any statement until I learn more." The captain said.

"Admitting that one doesn't know is better than jumping forth blindly. We accept your reply and will also wait until more information is available." She said. She began to vanish, but Captain Harris stopped her.

"If there are valuable minerals on your world, is it possible to have just a little of it to cover our costs?" He asked.

ELIO[2]

"We shall discuss this when we meet again." She replied. "I am trusting you to be a man of your word." She warned and then she vanished.

"Well, that was interesting." Captain Harris said rubbing his head with both hands. Sleep would be even more difficult this day.

***

Elio made good time through the maze that is the underground complex of the Treshnik. The crew, being merely human, were scrambling to keep up with him. It was like he knew every twist and turn. They reached the double doors of the control room before the morning was gone. For a complex of this size, which was an accomplishment all in itself.

Emma bent over, trying to catch her breath. "Give us a few minutes before we try to open the door." She said, panting and gasping during that sentence. Elio moved away from the door and sat in the corner. Whatever he did to amuse himself, that is what he was doing now. His body looked completely inert. Something was going on in that electronic brain though. The others ignored him while they caught their collective breaths and rubbed aching feet. The packs were all on the floor now. The crew were sitting on them.

"This place is huge." Jamal complained.

"Yes, and we have only crossed a portion of it to get here." Emma replied.

Jamal looked up at her. "How do you know that?"

"When Elio projected the map, the control room was in the middle of it. That means there is at least as far as we went to go if wanted to cross the whole thing." She concluded.

"I don't want to do that." Jamal replied. "At least not without a good rest and some food." He said.

The mention of food reminded them that they had not eaten in a while. Stomachs gurgled with the realization, and they set up lunch right there in front of the double doors.

Field rations were always rough. The tubes and bars they could carry were nutritionally balanced, but not the best tasting things you ever had. It made them all miss the food machines on the ship. The tablets that fulfilled the rest of their dietary needs were even less satisfying.

"I wish someone would make this stuff more palatable." Someone complained.

ELIO[2]

Elio went back online at the sound. He checked around the room and saw the crew eating their lunch. "They cannot make the portable food taste better or people would eat it all the time. It is like a hospital bed not being comfortable. If you feel well enough to complain about the bed, then you are better. If you eat the field rations, then the regular food will gain a greater appreciation in your mind." Elio explained.

"That makes sense, but it still sucks." Jamal complained.

"I'm afraid I can do nothing for the rations. I am not equipped as a chef. I am, however, fortunate to not need the nutritional sustenance to survive. However, if I am too long without a charge, my circuits may go inactive. My power plant does require shut down from time to time. Most of that is due to cooling my systems. But the problem exists and resembles hungry or tired in humans." Elio offered.

"Fine, so none of us are the perfect person." Janet spoke up.

Elio had a reply to that as well. "Actually, as unique individuals, we are all perfectly suited to our destiny. It may take a while to determine what that should be, but sooner or later everybody meets their destiny." Elio posed.

Emma wiped her mouth, having finished her meager fare. "Really, have you met your destiny?" She queried.

"I have, several times. I am fortunate to have lived for a very long time and I have run across destiny more than once. The hard part is recognizing it when it happens. Most people only view their destiny through reflection upon their past events and actions. I have many videos about this subject, but we are on a mission right now." Elio explained before the requests could come in.

"You are correct about that." Emma replied. "I am happy to see your focus has returned." She told him.

"Then you are ready for the doors to open then?" Elio asked, sounding a bit excited himself.

"You can open them?" Emma asked.

"Of course. Not all doors are sealed with traps. Most of the time when I cannot open a door, it is because of the danger it poses to the crew. I will not endanger you needlessly. If I manage not to endanger you at all, only then have I succeeded." He announced to the group.

"Well, it is a little relief to know that your mission parameters require you to keep us alive and well." Janet put forth. "But we really need to find something to take with us quickly. We still have ship repairs to perform, and our good captain is waiting up there, probably in a nervous fit. He can't contact us to see if we even survived the crash he couldn't detect." She added.

"Yes, you are right about that. Perhaps we can get a beacon up above the storm layer and get a little piece of mind for our leader." Elio suggested.

"A beacon? Do they have that sort of thing here?" Emma asked.

"They most certainly should. I honestly do not know if they actually do, but if not, there is enough raw materials and salvageable components here to make one ourselves." He offered. The small task offered something the crew had been short on, hope.

"Well, we'll see about this beacon project. It would be even nicer if we managed to turn off those storms. It would make returning the ship to working order much easier. Not to mention the return flight to get back into orbit." She followed.

"Yes, that would be good. But the controls were so far away according to Elio." Jamal pointed out. "Didn't he say kilometers?"

"He did." Janet confirmed. "But we still have artifacts to find before we can even consider going home. I'm not willing to give up and go back empty-handed." She concluded.

"That's not my first choice either." Emma confirmed. "We will find stuff here. Be very careful what you touch. We don't know how any of this technology works. Blowing ourselves up now would be a tremendous waste." She warned.

ELIO[2]

"It would be career ending." Jamal agreed. "I think we can all be just a bit more careful from here on in." He suggested.

"Well, it could make you famous. But the proceeds would go to your next of kin instead of you. So, if you would like to enjoy the fruits of your labor, I recommend caution." Janet echoed.

"I think we all need to stay focused." Elio said. "But I can help somewhat with the artifacts." He offered. The whole group took notice.

"Just how can you do that?" Emma asked, being the first to voice the question.

"The control room has a special section that I think you will find interesting. Here, let me open the door and I will lead you to it." He said.

Emma waved an arm at the door in a "By all means" gesture.

Elio moved to the door and lifted his body up. His tool arm extended to the top of the doorway and touched a sensor. The door slid into the wall as if it had never been there at all.

"So, you do know your way around this place." Janet added appreciatively.

Elio moved in and the group shuffled in behind him. The control room looked huge. Compared to the corridors and holding rooms they had witnessed so far it was a massive construct. The whole of it was at least ninety meters wide. It was also carved from the stone as if by some kind of machine. The walls of stone were perfectly smooth. The length of the room was the impressive part. It curved back and away from them and disappeared. What you could see was more than one hundred and twenty meters.

Elio seemed to take the dimensions of the room in stride. He was still ambling along to whatever it was that he wanted to show them. The room was filled with wonders. Consoles and controls all seemed to be made from either stone or wood. The actuators looked like crystals, or gems. How could any of this work? There was no metal to speak of.

Elio seemed not to notice any of it, so good was his focus. He stopped in front of a compartment and his mechanical arm touched a gem at the top of it. The compartment opened. Inside it were various pieces of handheld equipment. They were obviously meant to be held by webbed hands, but they would be usable by humans if the humans understood the functions.

"These are amazing, but what do they do?" Emma said. She reached out to pick one up and Elio stopped her hand gently.

"Careful what you touch. We have all been warned." He said. "This one," he continued indicating a smallish device near the left edge of the compartment. "...measures seismic activity when set on the ground. It can sense tremors many kilometers away and report them all to the central console display." He explained.

Emma looked at the little robot. "Do you know the function of all of these devices?" She asked.

Elio did a negative gesture and added. "No, only a few that I have witnessed being used." He replied. "But this equipment compartment would pay for our trip easily." He added for emphasis. "Given enough time to experiment with them, I am certain that we could ascertain the function of each device without much difficulty." He said helpfully.

Emma looked around. "Are we allowed to take them though?" She asked.

"A good question." A new voice said. It was a projection of Aeolia in the control room. Her image was standing in the middle of the room. Her arms were out to the side and her eyes seemed to bore into Emma.

Jamal hid behind a console. Janet moved closer, but not too close. Emma got up and walked purposefully over to the apparition.

"I meant what I said before, we do not wish to harm this world. We are interested in you, as a people. How you think, what you knew, the kind of industry you deployed and the gadgets you created. These are all indicators of the level of a civilization or society." She explained.

ELIO[2]

Aeolia bowed slightly. "I agree. In that it shows me how far you have advanced as a species or civilization. You do not fear me?" She asked. It sounded like a strange question to Emma.

"No, should I fear you?" Emma replied.

"Not necessarily, but your people seem to." She said indicating the two others hiding in the control room.

Emma glanced around and then returned her gaze to Aeolia. "Most people fear what they do not understand. To some extent, I understand you." Emma replied.

"You speak wisely for such a young people." Aeolia replied.

"Thank you, but the question I asked remains unanswered. Were you planning to tell us what we can and cannot take?" Emma asked.

Aeolia smiled. "We are no longer here. I cannot physically stop you from taking anything, even the planet's heart. I only beseech you to avoid damaging anything permanently. The world does not belong to us, nor does it belong to you. It is a part of nature. Just as we were, and you are. We must all live with nature, or we all will die from its absence." She said.

Emma bowed deeply. "I fully understand you now. Know that I will never hurt the world in which you lived. I only wish to learn from it and from you to understand the truths you learned while you existed here." She said and it sounded solemn.

"Then you have the wisdom you need already. What more could I possibly teach you?" Aeolia asked.

"First things first, can you tell us what these devices do so that nobody gets hurt trying to find out?" Emma asked.

"A reasonable request. But one I am anxious in granting. Those devices seem small and insignificant, but actually possess great power." She replied.

Emma nodded. "I suspected that, and it is why I asked for guidance to avoid an abuse or misuse of that power." She replied.

"You are quite gifted in public speaking. That is a skill that most people do not possess. I wonder if you realize just how rare it is to always say the right thing.

"I do not say the right thing all the time. It is something I have been working at for some time. But I try to do the right thing always. That usually leads me down the right path. Once there, it is easier to be the person I need to be and say the things I need to say." She explained.

"Very well, I will point you to the instructions for these devices. It is stored in the system's memory. You will find a great many things there. I am sure that you will find pretty much everything you need in there and thus are then able to leave this world in peace." Aeolia offered.

"I have only two more questions for you if you would indulge me." Emma spoke up.

"Do you have stored a history of your people and their journey?" She asked.

"It is also in the archives you seek." The figure replied with open arms.

"Finally, can we shut off the storms outside so that we can leave your world without incident?" Emma asked.

Aeolia's smiled vanished. "You have asked us to open this world for anyone to land. That is something we are not prepared to do." She said.

Emma held up her hands defensively. "No, just to leave this world. If you restart them after we have gone, that would be satisfactory for us and still protect your world for you." She suggested.

Aeolia seemed to ponder on this. That was strange for it was considered that she was a recording, and a recording would not need the processing time. But the apparition stood in a thinking pose for longer than expected.

ELIO[2]
"Your plan is agreeable. I have consulted with the last of our people and they agree that this is an acceptable compromise to our statutes." She replied. It sounded very formal this time. Her smile returned at the end of her delivery.

"My final message is for your robot friend." Aeolia told them all.

Elio stepped forward and settled in before the apparition. "You have violated the trust we put in you. But after reviewing the people that you brought here, it is understandable. You serve people with good moral character, and they have only the brightest and purest of intentions towards this world. Therefore, we absolve you of your transgression and free you of the burden of secrecy. You may share with them whatever you wish. Just follow the same guidelines concerning this world and its health." She said and it sounded like a mixture of admonishment and absolution.

"I am happy to be relieved of this burden of secrets. My friends and crewmates deserve to be warned when the danger is present, and I was not allowed to come clean about my involvement here. It is something my logic circuits have been struggling with." Elio stated in response.

"We trusted you and now that we understand more of your decision-making process, we trust you even more. You walked the fine line between the wording of the rules and the intention of the rule. That takes more consideration and logical thought that we gave you credit for. Please forgive our oversight in this regard. After all, to us you were merely a machine." Aeolia said.

"Elio is more than a machine." Emma protested.

"Indeed, he is. It is our oversight that we didn't see that before." Aeolia admitted. "In fact, we are pleased that our misdeed and poor judgement got the opportunity to be rectified. You will all find that this little robot, Elio, has all of the information stored in our computers. You may access it at any time through him. But I must ask that you leave this planet in peace. You may take the gadgets, of course, but please be very careful with those. The information in Elio's brain will guide you about their use."

Elio looked up at the apparition and his manner seemed sad. "Is this the end for our conversation?" he asked.

"It must be. We have to sleep now. Your people need to return to your ship, and you are now loaded with our history. You are our caretaker. Be careful who you show our secrets to." Aeolia urged. "We have earned our rest. It is good that we passed the torch to you. The little robot that held our future and our past in his mechanical hands. It seems ironic now. But so very fitting." She said and then the apparition was gone.

Emma moved first. She started putting the devices carefully in her satchel. Elio lowered himself back to the ground. Janet and Jamal just stood there, watching this happen as if the apparition had not spoken. They were most probably in shock.

Emma stood up, slinging her satchel over her shoulder. "I'm ready when you are." She said to Elio. Then she glanced at the others. "Get your stuff together, we're getting out of here." She told them.

"What about the storms?" Jamal asked.

Emma looked down at Elio. "Well?" She asked.

Elio froze in place for a second. "Accessing... storms are controlled by... accessing... the storms are off for two hours." He reported back.

Emma looked back at the rest of the crew. "Then we'd better get moving then." She ordered.

The group headed back the way they had come. The traps were all disabled, and the doors were open only on the path they needed. They had an easy route to follow, and they made the most of it. They reached the cave and had to stop for a moment to catch their breath.

"I need to rest." Jamal said. His pack looked to be sliding off the side of his back. Janet looked no better but made no verbal complaint.

Elio lifted his body up a bit. "We have to be in orbit in one hour and twelve minutes." He informed them. "Unless you want to fly through those storms once more." He added for emphasis.

ELIO[2]

Jamal was the first one back up. "Uh no, I don't want to think about that anymore." He admitted and then he pressed the others up the cave and out into the open. With the storms gone the landscape looked stripped. The continuous winds had pulled leaves from trees, smaller brambles had managed to survive the torment, but they were brutally misshapen and looked quite dangerous.

The ship was not far now and without the storms to slow them down, it was in sight rather quickly.

"Begin those repairs." Emma ordered Elio even as the others went inside and began stowing the gear and Jamal began the pre-flight.

"If there is anything out there that could survive all those years of storms, we do not want it coming for us." Janet said and Jamal seemed shaken by the notion. His hands were moving like a man possessed, going through the checklist.

For his part, Elio was busily repairing bits of the ship that were required for flight. They had taken a few hits in the stabilizers, and he was welding them back together. His speed was that of a machine, but the timer was still ticking, and time was running short.

"How much longer Elio?" Emma asked through the radio on board.

"Not much longer, had a little trouble with some circuitry on panel A. But it is progressing now." Elio explained.

"We don't have a lot of time." Emma reminded him.

"I agree… there. Coming in now." Elio replied.

The little robot rolled in, and his robotic arm tapped the controls to close the hatch. He moved with speed to the front of the small craft. "Engage the engines now." He said. Jamal hit the switch and the engines came to life. The status board went green, and Jamal smiled.

"You are a handy little thing." He commented.

He is a member of the crew." Emma reminded him. "Get us off the ground." She ordered. Then she turned around. "Strap yourselves in, we don't know how this is going to go." She ordered.

Everyone was strapped before the ship cleared the massive trees. Once they were clear and into open space, Jamal pointed the craft at the planet. "Time's up." He said to the rest, and they all watched out the front windshield as the storms spun back up from tremendous generators around the planet. In minutes the entire atmosphere was storms once more.

Emma gawked. "However it is that they do that, it is most impressive." She commented. Then she put her hand on Jamal's shoulder. "Take us home." She ordered.

"Yes ma'am." Jamal replied and he turned the ship around. "Shuttle to mother ship, do you read?" he asked in the radio.

"You made it out?" The words lacked confidence and sounded striking to their ears.

"Affirmative, we are enroute to you now." Jamal replied.

"Did you find something?" The captain asked.

"You'll have to hear about that when we get there." Emma replied. "For security reasons." She added before he could protest.

"Understood." Then after a pause. "Will I be happy?" He asked.

Emma smiled. "I think you'll be ecstatic." She replied. "See you when we arrive."

The shuttle made its way back to the main ship without incident. The crew were subject to quarantine and decontamination as per protocols. After all, they had been down on an alien planet. Who knows what they might have contracted down there?

***

Debriefing…

Elio's decontamination was the easiest, so he was out of the quarantine quite a bit before his human crewmates. The shuttle itself was undergoing maintenance and further repairs. He was required to report to the captain as soon as he had been deemed fit for duty. The little robot actually maintained his own level of repair, so he was cleared as soon as it said his diagnostic was clear.

"Sir, Elio reporting as ordered." The small robot said as he entered the captain's quarters.

Captain Harris looked at the little robot. There were some signs of wear on his metallic body. Scratches that needed buffing out. But the overall effect was not unwelcomed. He had been through a lot reportedly.

"Before you begin your report, I must ask you about Aeolia." The captain told him. Elio seemed surprised.

"How do you know that name?" Elio asked, still finding his bearings.

"She visited me here while you were down on the planet. She was concerned over your earlier mission." Captain Harris pointed out.

Elio made a gesture that would have meant something to Aeolia but meant nothing to the good captain. He changed tactics and resorted to speaking once more. "She was there when I was on this planet before. She is someone of some importance as I recall." Elio began. "She was also downloaded into the computer as the base's guardian." Elio explained.

"But she was in this very room." Captain Harris complained.

Elio updated his information on holographic transmissions. "I was unaware she had that ability. However, that does not affect the mission parameters and will not impact my report." Elio stated, trying to get this report back on track.

The mission as stated was to try to recover artifacts of value from the Treshnik people. This has been accomplished. But we have acquired so much more." He said. The captain's eyebrow rose as if to ask what.

"We have recovered their entire database." Elio stated. The captain's other eyebrow rose to match the first one. His eyes were wide.

"Does that mean what I think it means?" Captain Harris asked.

"Yes, we have the sum total of their accumulated knowledge, to include the descriptions and functions of the artifacts that we have recovered. We have their math, their science, even their social greetings and languages. Those are all gesture based by the way." Elio continued.

"What can you show me?" Captain Harris asked.

Elio seemed to pause. "I have yet to go through the data to remove anything that violates our laws." He replied. "After all, weapons and defensive systems are forbidden. The storms down on the planet were artificially generated. That constitutes a defensive system." Elio explained.

"Okay, how long will it take you to go through and remove the illegal data?" Captain Harris asked.

Elio considered the amount of data and his own interest in the subject work. "I would estimate about two weeks. The variables involved make it only an estimate. But there is a substantial amount of data in here." Elio said.

"In here?" the captain asked.

"Yes, they transferred all of their information into me." Elio replied.

"So, your database has new entries in it from them?" He asked to verify.

"Yes, I am nearly full now. As the data is cleared, I shall transfer it in blocks to the backup device as soon as possible." Elio added.

"How much did they know?" The captain asked.

ELIO[2]

"I honestly do not yet know. But they did have an advanced society and were attuned to nature. It is this last part that has caused them to protect this world beyond their own lives." Elio explained. "Like I mentioned before, we got a lot for our historians to digest. We should do well financially for this run." He concluded.

Captain Harris stood up. "Very well, begin working on that data. I want to see something as soon as it is available. In fact, if you find any good stories, let us set up a time to review them as a group in your lab." He suggested.

"I am sure that something will present itself. These people were remarkable." Elio replied. Then he did a sort of bow and left the captain to his thoughts.

***

For the human part of the drop crew, things weren't going as easily. Cleaning and decontamination were only the first parts of their process. Then came the quarantine. They were locked away, together, in a cell with only the basest of comforts. Nothing soft could be arranged since a possible virus could reside in it. So hard surfaces were all they had.

"How long are they going to keep us here?" Jamal asked for the umpteenth time.

"You know very well how long we are going to be together, so stop bringing it up and answer the questions." Emma replied. They all had questionnaires on their mission to be filled out on wall displays. The process was not all that difficult, but in this tiny cell, privacy was non-existent. The group would simply have to continue despite the rest of their team being able to view their responses. If nothing else, it would keep the complaints about each other down. Now if they do that, the offender will see it and be able to react right away. They could not escape each other in this tiny cell, so the argument would not end until it reached full completion.

Fortunately, the complaints that could have been given were then withheld. There would be no blotch on anybody's record. There would be no arguments for them to work through. What they did have was a shared experience that they wanted to talk about.

"Do you think that Elio will tell them everything and that they won't even need our reports?" Janet asked.

"It is quite likely that he will tell them everything. However, they will still want our reports to corroborate his statements." Emma replied.

"We did really good down there. We got the goods they wanted, and that little guy got the database. We should all get bonuses for this run." Jamal said, pleading his case.

"If the money is good enough, we just might get bonuses at that." Emma replied, trying not to break his hopes. But there was nothing in their contracts about bonuses in this situation. For excessive danger, yes, but not for completing the mission as required. If there was, nobody would want to leave a site until they had earned that bonus.

ELIO[2]

That might jeopardize what they were after in the first place needlessly. She kept that in mind but did not say it.

"If anything, that database could teach us so much about how they lived and what they knew." Janet offered.

Emma nodded. "You are right about that. I cannot wait until I get a hold of Elio and ask him what he knows." She said. Her determination came through in her speech and the other two backed off on the subject.

Jamal moved to the central table. "So, anybody want to play cards?" he asked.

Neither of the women took him up on the offer. Jamal sighed and went to lay down. "Fine, let me know if you find out anything exciting." He said.

"You'll be the first." Emma said, it sounded sarcastic.

Janet moved closer. "What is with that guy?" She asked.

Emma shushed her with a look. "There's no use discussing such a thing while we are still in quarantine." She said softly, very softly.

Janet took the hint properly and backed off. She did, however, make a personal note to ask the same question later, when they weren't locked in with the person they were going to discuss.

Despite all of the possible tension, the quarantine ended after the allotted time, and the trio were released.

"I've got to get a real shower and then head to the lab." Emma stated. "I'm sure that Elio has already jumped ahead of us processing that data he received." She added as an afterthought.

Janet moved closer once more. "If you don't mind, I'd like to see some of that data for myself. We all risked our lives down there and I would be interested in knowing what we found." She said.

Emma agreed. "I'll see you at the lab then." She offered. She looked over at Jamal.

"I don't want to hang around in your stuffy old lab. Just let me know if there is any profit in what he found." He told them and then he left with both women shaking their heads at him.

***

Reuniting the crew…

Elio was busily working on his database. He had already done two dumps to the backup device. As he continued, the realization of just how much data they had accrued was becoming obvious. He had school lesson plans and curriculums for things that humans had not even discovered. The information was fascinating to Elio. He was perusing it even as it transferred. Much to his dismay, the Treshnik people had developed weapons as well, terrible weapons. In fact, it was this fascination with weaponry that had eventually led to their downfall. It was a path that humanity had followed for quite some time before the laws were enacted that saved them from a similar fate. Elio was crunching numbers and letters and enjoying the entire time. The door to the lab slid open and Emma entered.

"Ah, you are out of quarantine!" Elio nearly shouted. His excitement was genuine and sounded odd from a robot.

Emma stepped forward quickly and placed her hand on Elio's top. "Just what have you been doing while we were trapped in that little room?" She asked. While it might not have been scathing, it was a bit accusatory.

"I have been filtering the data for illegal information just like we did with my original data." Elio replied.

"I see." Emma said. "Just how much data did we get?" She asked.

"Tons." Elio replied. "I could tell you a figure once this pass has completed. I am deleting illegal data, so the amount is changing." He informed his partner.

"You are doing this is sections, right?" Emma asked with interest.

"Of course. Two downloads have already been processed into the backup device." Elio declared.

Emma glanced over at the device. "So, I can look at it there and not slow down your process?" She asked.

"Yes, it is why I started working in blocks. I understand your urgency to get something valuable out of our mission. I started with the artifact descriptions and instructions. This should allow a team to begin studying right away." Elio said with a bit of pride.

Emma blinked. "Yes, it shall indeed." She replied. She moved over to the backup unit.

"Please show me the newest data entries." She ordered.

The machine began to comply. Emma expected a video display but what she got surprised her. The projector did indeed come on, but it did not display a moving picture. What was displayed was a full terminal display screen. A directory of choices appeared before Emma. She pointed at one and a red dot appeared in the display, tracking her finger. She highlighted the one she wanted and said "Play"

The option she had chosen was also not a video, but it was educational...

One of the artifacts they had brought back with them was displayed on the wall. The various parts of it were labeled and then the image exploded into its components. An explanation of each part was given and then the unit came back together on the wall. The item spun around slowly showing all sides. Then it was gone and in its place were a list of uses.

"Pause." Emma said and the display stopped right where it was.

"Elio, have you seen these?" She asked.

"Yes, quite nicely done are they not?" Elio replied.

"I've never seen documentation this complete. It is complete enough that if we understood the materials involved, we could produce these items ourselves." She commented.

"Indeed, we could." Elio agreed.

"How much more is in there?" Emma asked.

ELIO[2]

"A lot. At the current rate I am going through this, it will take about three more days to complete the filter process." Elio replied. "More if my processes are interrupted for questions though." He warned.

"My apologies." Emma said. "Please continue with the process."

Elio went silent once more, obviously working internally.

Emma returned to the display. "Please move on to the next item in the list." She commanded and the backup unit obediently moved to the next file and restarted its display on the wall.

Emma continued looking at all of these items until she was satisfied that she had viewed them all at least once. Then she returned to some of the more interesting ones. These gadgets had immediate value to her and the crew. The real problem was that they might have to give them all to the company. At least they would if they were not dangerous. After all, weapons were still not allowed.

Emma rubbed her eyes. "That's good stuff." She commented. Just then Janet entered the lab.

"Good stuff?" She said as she had only caught that last line when the door opened.

"The information on the artifacts we recovered." Emma began in explanation. "The complete instructions on what they are and how to use them are in the database." She concluded.

Janet smiled. "That is really helpful." She replied. "That means that nobody has to keep trying things until we find out what they do. That could be dangerous after all." She said.

"I agree." Emma stated. Janet looked over at Elio. The little robot had not spoken to her when she entered and that seemed odd.

"What's up with him?" She asked pointing a thumb at Elio.

"He is processing the data to remove any illegal information." Emma replied. "There is just so much stuff in the database that it is going to take a while. A few more days I'm afraid." She finished.

Janet frowned. "That long, eh? He is a computer on legs. If it takes him that long, how long will it take us to understand what we found?" Janet asked.

Emma laughed. Probably months, maybe years without Elio's help. We are so lucky to have him." She replied.

Janet moved over to Elio. "Hello my little friend." She said.

Elio startled her by rotating to her. "Oh, hello Janet. I am glad that you have visited us. If you can forgive my bad manners, I am busy collating and filtering data for storage and study." He explained.

"By all means, go right on ahead." Janet replied.

"Thank you for your understanding." Elio replied and went silent again.

She turned back to Emma. "You know, sometimes I think he is more human than we are."

"I think you're right. He is very considerate for a person, let alone a machine crewmember." Emma agreed. Emma pointed at the backup unit. "He has already put a bunch of data in here so we can view it while we wait for him to finish getting the data ready for us." She offered.

Janet pulled up a chair. Her face was equal measures of excitement and curiosity. "Okay, you've got my undivided attention." she replied.

Emma addressed the backup unit once more. "Please show us the next file." She said.

The backup unit's projector lit up and the wall before them displayed a diagram. It was the diagram of the base they had just visited.

"Wow, that display would have been helpful if we had it beforehand." Janet commented. There was a note of sarcasm in it.

"Yes, but we did have Elio. Most of this information was already inside of him when we went in." Emma explained.

"Then why did we have to fumble through this?" Janet asked.

ELIO[2]

"Elio was under a binding contract with the Treshnik to withhold their secrets. He only helped us when it wouldn't violate that directive. Once the hologram freed him of that restriction, he became much more forthcoming." Emma elaborated.

"So, we need to know if he has any prior concerns when going on a mission with him." Janet concluded.

Emma glanced over at Elio. "I don't think he would have let us come to harm. But yes, we need to make sure everything is on the up and up when going on a mission." Emma confirmed.

Janet made a sound like a sigh. "So, that's the downside of the little guy. He is so old that he might have agreements with ancient cultures." She stated. It sounded so fantastic, but that is exactly what had just happened.

Emma took the cue and moved closer to Elio. "Elio." She said. The little robot lifted up to address her appropriately. "How many other cultures do you have secrecy agreements with?" She asked directly.

Elio considered the question carefully. He lowered his body back to the floor and stopped his filtering process in order to being this search. It took a few moments for him to scan his database for the answer. When he replied, it startled both women in the room. "Seventeen." Elio replied.

"What? You mean that you have directives from seventeen ancient cultures?" Janet asked for she had regained her composure first.

"Not ancient cultures, but cultures." Elio replied cryptically. "For instance, your culture forbids knowledge of weapons. That is one of the seventeen cultures." He replied.

Emma picked up on the gist here. "So, how many of your directives relate to cultures that have gone extinct?" She asked.

Elio checked his short list and tried to verify the validity of the data. "As far as I can calculate, seven of the cultures have gone extinct, or been reported to have. Five others have had no contact for a long time but have not been verified to no longer exist." He replied.

Emma did the math quickly. "That means that you have active directives from four other cultures to our own." She said, trying to nail this down.

Elio considered his list and the response, and it all checked out. "You are correct."

Emma was close now, really close. "You are a member of this crew. The mission of this ship and this crew are your top priorities." She stated resolutely.

"I was monitoring our progress during the mission and following the protocols of both agreements." Elio replied.

Emma shook her head. "That's not good enough. I need to know that you are going to do the right thing and not follow some outdated rule from a people that do not exist. We are your people now. We are the ones that you belong to as a crewmember and friend. We are the ones that demand your loyalty." Emma said, laying out her stance clearly.

"I understand." Elio replied. "You understand that your words do not free me of my prior commitments?" Elio asked.

"What I am telling you is that commitments to a people that no longer exist are already null and void. There is nobody left to be loyal to." Emma replied, getting exasperated.

"You also understand that I am a robot. I follow orders and directives without question. I have followed the line thinly for you already. But follow the line I did. I cannot break one of the instructions given." Elio stated.

Emma flipped her hands up in exasperation. "Then how can I trust you?" She asked.

Elio seemed to get confused. "The simple fact that I follow all of my directives qualifies me as trustworthy. Is that not enough for you?" He asked.

ELIO[2]

Emma sat down and stared at the little robot. "I need to know that you have our backs when we are on mission, regardless of your prior commitments." She argued.

Elio didn't pause this time at all. "I will always protect my crewmates. I will always stay on mission. Even if there are prior commitments, I will do my best to get things done as required of me." Elio promised.

"But…" Emma pressed.

"But I cannot ignore my prior commitments. You know that just as much as you know that I will protect you. I made sure that you didn't blunder into traps. I made sure the craft landed without hitting the trees. I made sure that everybody we had with us made it back. Is that not enough?" Elio asked.

Emma considered his points. The mission had gone extremely well, despite the storms and the hologram. Elio had delivered the database and not shown it to anybody else so that his commitment to the no weapons law remained consistent. He really had done everything he could to make sure all criteria were met. It made her wonder… had she?

"It is enough." Emma relented.

Elio went back to his processing, satisfied that he had made his point. His work would still take days. He was gifted in that sleep was not necessary. If he had been human, the task would have taken markedly longer.

Emma had a new awareness of Elio. He had worked very hard to follow all of his directives and she had been selfish to think that only hers mattered. She had placed the little robot in a situation that made it even harder for him to achieve his goals, and he had managed to do it. She began going over her interactions with him in her memories. She had always considered him as a commodity, an archeological find. Something that belonged to them. She noted his intelligence and had even fought for it, but in the end, she considered him as a useful tool they all owned. He had asked to be treated equally, as a crewmember, as a person, as a friend. She realized now that she hadn't done that.

She felt ashamed of this and made a vow to herself to amend that. From now on, Elio is a person.

She wondered what she could do to make it up to the little guy, but nothing came to mind. He didn't seem to need anything. It was not like she could get him a bottle of wine to say that she was sorry. A robot couldn't eat or drink anything. She would consider this later and make it up to him somehow. In the meantime, she would get back to perusing that new data. After all, this was exciting.

"Please continue with the current file." She instructed and the backup unit un-paused the display.

***

Involving Corporate…

Captain Harris was looking over his report. The mission had been a success, but it had been too good of a success. The corporation was already watching for him and his next find. Elio had started a frenzy of profit seeking and the backup unit they had taken had provided a lot of information for them. Now the good captain and his crew had discovered another cache of information and technology. It was like a second lightning strike to the same tree. He wondered if he should downplay what they found to keep the dogs from sniffing at him any closer.

The problem with that was that the data was extremely valuable. The gadgets recovered alone could change life as they all knew it. Humanity was on the brink of a new age based upon this discovery. Could he downplay that? He also had the added problem that Elio had brought back the data inside his own memories. He couldn't report that, or the corporation would come back for the little robot. They thought they already had him. They did not consider him as a person. The poor little robot was just a thing to be exploited for the greatest profit possible.

So, he had to tread very carefully in this report. Captain Harris didn't have any hard facts to give in it yet. That would change fairly soon though. Elio was already working on extracting the new data and filtering it for legal purposes. He understood the dangers of unfiltered data. The ship had been boarded once before for this very problem. It only underscored the importance of discretion.

He read his report so far...

> *Preliminary report for planet Ladius232:*
>
> *We have discovered the ruins of the lost civilization of the Treshnik. We have recovered artifacts that are still functioning and by a stroke of luck, have the instructions to said artifacts. We have managed to gather some intelligence too in the form of an old database, but that information is still pending*

actual retrieval. Updated reports will keep you apprised of our findings as they occur.

Captain Sean Harris, commanding.

This was a short report as reports go. The fight to tell them how much what they found was worth and the fear that they will come and grab it once again waged within him. His next report would see so much scrutiny that it was frightening. But all he could do now was to wait until his team figured out what they actually had, exactly.

He hit send and sat back in his chair. If it was the right move or not was now irrelevant. He had committed himself and his ship to it now. At least they had some time. The message would take three weeks to reach corporate home. Hopefully, they had enough time so that they could send a second message before hearing back on the first one.

* * *

The automated communication machines on various repeater nodes sent that message, along with a lot of other traffic, through the subspace network. The speed of the system was the limiting factor due to the vast distances. Profits and losses were determined by who made the decisions faster, more reliably. That meant that the more reliable the system they used to communicate, the better the decisions and the more profitable a company could be. Oskar Golden sat at his desk where he monitored the communications traffic, searching for gems of information that could directly affect the bottom line. He had developed a series of search filters and had been perusing the hits when the little message from Captain Harris appeared before him. The little ship out in the outer reaches had gained prominence recently by finding a robot with an intact database in it. The robot had been claimed and even now was in a lab where several scientists and accountants were going through its data with a fine-toothed comb. This message, however, made his eyebrow rise not because of the information in it, but the obvious omission of information in it. The captain was up to something.

Oskar pulled up Sean Harris' file and read about his competency and his track record. He was nothing really special from a profit standpoint, but he was reliable and trustworthy. Oskar scratched that risen eyebrow. Something here didn't add up.

The idea of a ship captain being lucky enough to retrieve two ancient databases was ludicrous. The odds were so stacked against such an occurrence that it seemed laughable. However, he mentioned that he had artifacts and another database in this message. Could it really be true?

Oskar reached over to a console on his desk. He flipped the switch to secure the channel and pressed the call button. "Sir, I think we may have something interesting going on in the outer rim of planets." He said in a non-committal tone.

"What is it now?" The impatient voice of his boss replied.

"It is possible that Sean Harris has another database." He said outright.

There was a good moment's pause before the reply came. "Send me the message and secure the channel." He ordered.

"Already done, sir." Oskar replied. "We're on a secure line now."

"I should hope so if you were prepared to blurt out such a comment." His boss replied.

Oskar's boss was a greedy pig of a man named Tristan Bennett. Tristan was one of the old-school corporate officers who had made his way by climbing the ladder to the top, ignoring those he stepped on to get there in the first place. He was not all that liked within the company. But his track record for finding profits had earned him the nickname of "Bloodhound".

"You mean that lucky SOB has actually found another ancient database?" Tristan asked.

"He mentions it explicitly, as well as some functional artifacts." Oskar replied.

"Functional! Nobody finds artifacts that still work. That's part of what makes 'em artifacts." Tristan countered.

"He has and furthermore claims to have the instructions for them as well." Oskar pointed out. The message was now on both of their screens.

"We need to get someone out there to secure that planet then." Tristan observed. "If they found stuff working, then there is more waiting down there." He projected.

"I would not dare to argue with that logic." Oskar agreed. "What would you like me to do?" he asked.

Tristan considered the information he just got and how far it could spread. He didn't want it to get out at all, so he needed to be cautious now.

"Charter the fastest courier boat you can get your hands on without raising any eyebrows." Tristan ordered.

"Yes sir, I am on it." Oskar replied quickly.

Tristan wasn't done with him though. "Then get your papers in order, we're going on a trip." Tristan added.

Oskar was dumbfounded. "Sir?" he finally managed to ask.

"I need this kept secret and you are the only other person who knows." Tristan explained. "Therefore, we're going to inspect this planet and those artifacts. If there is a fortune to be made, I want my chunk of it. I would imagine you feel the same?" He asked.

"Oh, yes sir!" Oskar replied. "I'll get everything ready sir." He offered.

ELIO[2]

"Just get the ship and your papers ready. I'll get the crew and we'll be off before anyone else can respond to this note." Tristan said with a grin.

"As you wish sir." Oskar finished and cut the connection. The thought of going to the outer planets had him shaking. What was out there? His comfortable life had just taken a major turn. But his boss was right about one thing, if there was a fortune to be had out there, then he did want his piece of it."

It was not far to where Oskar needed to go to get his affairs in order. It was only a couple of blocks. With modern trams and escalator belt sidewalks, it was a matter of a few moments ride. He would reach the place just in time to schedule an appointment. He was using his communication device to make the preparations enroute.

"I will be arriving shortly. I have brought the necessary identification chips." Oskar told the voice on the phone that was probably an AI.

"Your arrival is in four minutes and twelve seconds." The voice told him. "Your forms will be ready for you upon your arrival." It assured him.

"Very well, see you then." Oskar told them just to be courteous. Then he broke the connection.

The forms were only that in name. everything was handled electronically. All that had been required was the scanning of his communications device and his thumb print on the glass certification tray. The lights around the form all turned green and the voice spoke once more...

"Your documents are in order. The usual fee has been pulled from your account." The same voice that had spoken on the communications device. There was no person around.

Satisfied, Oskar left for home. He needed to pack. He would arrange the ship from there as well. He had a full entertainment screen there and the ship would look so much better in that level of detail. His boss would be pleased with him for his speed and efficiency at accomplishing these tasks.

The trip home was uneventful. Oskar moved from room to room with practiced efficiency. He was ready in no time, and he settled down in front of the entertainment wall to begin his request.

"I need a fast ship." He said at first.

Choose destination>

"No destination given, outer rim worlds general area." Oskar input.

Speed required>

"Fastest without being overly costly." He replied.

Credit limit for transaction>

The computer seemed to be narrowing down his selections systematically. "Unknown, query for another interested party." Oskar replied.

The display changed to a list of ships. The choices varied widely, and it was obvious that many of them would be out of the price range he suspected was there. "Eliminate all ships above two million credits." He commanded and the list updated substantially shorter.

One of the entries looked much smaller than the rest, but it looked sleek and fast. The price seemed to be in the middle of the range and the dock was in this very city. He tapped that entry and pulled it up to take over the entire wall. The ship was impressive. It looked like it was almost new. It was clean and sleek as he had noted before. It looked more like a personal yacht than an interstellar vehicle.

He put in a reserve bid and saved the result to his personal communicator. Then he got up to head back in to work. His boss should be happy with his progress. But this was an urgent mission. The trip to work was faster than he normally made it in the morning because there were a lot fewer people moving in that direction at this time of day. He stepped into the office and noted that the power was off in the suite already.

"Ah, there you are." Tristan said, startling the poor Oskar. Tristan was wearing a full-blown vacuum suit. He was fully decked out as if he had always been a spacer. Despite his rather large size, he looked good in the outfit. "You got what I asked for, yes?" He asked.

"Absolutely sir." Oskar responded. He handed over his communication device.

Tristan pulled up the ship right away as if he had already known where it was in the device. "Oh, a JRX11, very nice. I didn't know we had any around here." He said appreciatively. He moved the credits over to secure the ship and then handed the communication device back.

"We're on dock seventeen according to your data." He told Oskar. "Are you ready?" He asked.

Oskar looked at his suitcase and compared it to Tristan's suit. "It doesn't feel like it, sir, but yes." He replied honestly.

Tristan laughed. "I thought of that as well. There is a suit for you in there." Tristan replied pointing at the changing room. "Don't waste any time. We need to be off world as soon as possible."

Oskar changed quickly and the suit fit perfectly. Tristan knew his stuff much better than Oskar had given him credit for. The two were ambling along on another moving sidewalk, but they were walking along with it to speed up the travel. They arrived at Dock seventeen before Oskar could have gotten cold feet. The ship they had seen on the wall was way more impressive in real life. It was also much larger than Oskar had imagined. It was still sleek, but it was nearly seventy meters long and stood towering into the sky. This ship took off like a rocket, literally.

A genial enough man met them at the entryway. "You are our passengers?" he asked. he held out a pad device. "Press your thumb here please." He requested and each of them did it. The man smiled once more. "I understand that we are a bit rushed so if you gentlemen will get on board and strap in, we'll be on our way."

Tristan paused. "How long until launch?" He asked.

The man frowned very briefly and then forced the smile once more. "The crew are in readiness; we only await you for the paused countdown to continue." He assured the two passengers. The greeter eyed Oskar's suitcase. "If you really need to take that, then you'll have to stow it. No loose items in the main portion of the ship for safety reasons you understand." He said.

Oskar looked at his case and the normal clothes he knew were in there. "On second thought, I don't really need to take it along." He said. He handed the case to the greeter who took it and locked it in a cage nearby.

"It will be ready for your return." He said jovially. "Please move along now. We are on a tight time schedule." He reminded them and the two men moved up to the lift that would take them to the ship's hatch.

Tristan led the way. He seemed quite comfortable in this environment. The two were on board and the hatch was closed even as they found their seats and strapped in.

A voice came over the communications speaker. "Just sit there, don't do anything. We'll be on our way as soon as the pre-flight is completed. If you see crewmembers, do not say or ask anything as it will delay our departure." The gruff voice told them.

Neither of them had any questions anyway. They just sat in silence as the crew busily went through the checklists that would allow them to get off the ground. When it all turned quiet, the voice came over the loudspeaker once more.

"Pre-flight is complete, we have clearance. Expect us to lift off in a few seconds."

True to his word, the engines fired outside with the force of a hurricane bottled into a fiery cylinder. The ship adjusted its burn and suddenly they lifted off the ground. The ship was meant for space, but it accelerated quickly here as well due to its sleek design. The pull of gravity was powerful and neither passenger could have spoken if they had come up with something to say. They didn't even look at each other as the ship ascended through the atmosphere. There were no windows where they were sitting but looking forward once the g-forces stabilized was possible. They watched as the sky turned from blue to black. The stars were bright out here away from the refracted noise of the sky itself. Weightlessness lasted for about thirty seconds before the artificial gravity was kicked on. Then the fasten seat belts light went out. Both passengers sat a little while longer, not wanting to get in the way of the crew which had all gotten up as one to get back to their various tasks. They moved in full synchronicity like a water ballet in space. Nobody was in the way and all stations were being manned. It was quite impressive for Oskar, who had never seen that level of interaction. But the real proof was that it also impressed Tristan. The corporate executive had seen many a ship and many a crew, but this group worked with the precision of a drill team.

He caught the attention of one of them. "How long until we arrive?" He asked.

The crewman smiled. "Well, that entirely depends upon you." He replied. The name label on all of their uniforms was empty.

"Me? How can it depend upon me?" Tristan asked.

The smile became a chuckle. "Because you haven't given us the destination yet." They replied simply. Tristan's embarrassment was obvious.

"Oh, my apologies." Tristan replied finally. "Ladius232 is our destination." He said clearly for he didn't' want any mistakes.

"Thank you." The crewperson said. They moved back into the formation and ended up at the correct console to look up this particular planet and to map the course to it. The entire process took less than three minutes.

"Captain, course plotted and laid in." He said.

The captain turned to the crewmember who had spoken. "Very well, we're not being paid to dawdle." He moved back to his seat and sat down. "Let's get underway then." He said.

The fasten seat belts light came on once more. This time they were thrusting to the appropriate cruise velocity. For a trip this long, it would most likely be a fairly long burn. They would need an equal burn when arriving to slow the ship back down. The fastest possible route would have required them to remain at full burn until just under halfway to the target point and then to turn the ship around and begin decelerating on the other end. But to cover the fantastic distances of space that way would have required way more fuel than they could carry on board this ship. So, what was determined as a reasonable cruising speed, versus the fuel cost had to be calculated. We call that speed the transit speed.

"Secure all, ready." Everyone gave the thumbs up signal and the captain nodded. "Do it." He commanded and the pull this time was intense. It was like the whole world shifted to behind you and you were just being squished into it. The feeling of takeoff had been shaky but exhilarating. This was on another level. This ship was designed to go fast and apparently the captain wanted to underscore that point.

Above the front window of the ship was a timer that was counting down the current burn. There were still seventeen minutes left on it! That meant that they had to endure the pressure for that long. Then they would be free of it and be coasting through space. Tristan seemed to be enjoying this part of the journey. Oskar was not. There was nothing either of them could do to make this any easier or any shorter, so they simply sat and bore the brunt of it in silence. When it was over, the roaring stopped from the engines outside. The cabin was silent. There were no beeps or clicks for nothing needed to be done. The only sound was the forced air of the circulators and the breathing of the people on board.

Tristan looked over at Oskar. "So, you held down your lunch, good." He said.

Oskar looked back a bit miffed. "How many times have you done that?" he asked back.

"Oh, not as many as you'd think. But more than a dozen." Tristan replied.

"You two can converse among yourselves all you want, but don't bother my crew. You may answer questions if they ask you, but I don't want any distractions." The captain warned his passengers.

"Of course, sir." Oskar replied quickly. The captain frowned.

"Refer to me as Captain." He corrected for the newly space bound man.

Oskar looked suddenly frightened. "My apologies captain, I meant no offense." He replied quickly.

"I know. It is just obvious to us that this is your first-time off world." The captain pointed out.

"Yes captain, it is." Oskar verified. "But I am a quick learner and if you need me to do anything, just ask. I will do my best." He offered.

"Noted." The captain replied. "You two are paying guests aboard my ship. You will not be required to earn your keep like in the old days. However, if something does come up, it is good to know that I can count on you. It would also make any dealings you do have with my crew better if you showed that you weren't afraid to get dirty and work." He mused.

Tristan seemed a bit taken aback by this conversation. He was important. He didn't need to mingle with the crew, the working staff. No, he was content to monitor his data feed and the ship's progress on his Pad device. These people were beneath him.

The captain noted the stance and shook his head. He nodded to Oskar. "You see, that's exactly what I meant." He said and then he moved back to his console presumably to attend to ship's functions.

Oskar felt that this trip was going well so far. He had already left his home world behind and had survived the acceleration phase of the journey. He would see a lot to write home about. If he were given a task out here in space, it would only make it all seem that much better. He wanted to be useful, but this crew looked like they needed nobody. He would wait for his chance to show them that he wasn't useless. He wasn't merely cargo to be shuttled about for the sake of the company. He would make a difference. He didn't yet know how, but he was determined. He would do it, whatever it is they asked. He was ready.

***

A new kind of emotion…

Elio was just finishing up the final download into the backup device. His exhaustive filtering had made him dump about thirteen percent of the total database, but that meant that the majority of the Treshnik database was salvageable and had been kept. A lot of information was there. Elio had managed to add tags to the data so that it could be easily searched and sorted into categories.

Emma sat at the console, busily going over her reports for their shared mission. She noticed when Elio lifted himself up again and walked towards her.

"I am finished. The download is complete." He announced.

"That's wonderful." Emma responded. "We need to start going through it for saleable information." She replied.

Elio considered this and wondered what Emma considered saleable. "What criteria are we looking for?" He asked directly. He was, after all, a robot.

"I don't know. I'm looking for things interesting enough to be desired by the curators of museums across the cosmos." She replied.

Elio considered these new criteria and still felt that it was lacking as a good filter. He did have some ideas of his own though. "What about conflict? Do you want stories that show conflict?" he asked.

Emma looked up somewhat excited. "Do you have that?" She asked.

Elio extended his projector as he had done for Emma so many times in the past. The wall he was displaying on would render a clear image. The display was of a Treshnik priest. The man spoke in gestures and movements. He was telling a story of invaders and repelling them using the power of the world. His story was not all that interesting because Emma did not know the gestures' meaning. So, Elio did his best and added subtitles for the gestures he knew. Now the story was a bit piecemeal, but readable. When the story was done and the enemy was at the gates, the priest held forth a scepter and a beam of lightning shot forth from it to strike the image of an invader on the wall. The very stone was scorched.

Emma looked at Elio. "They had weapons like that?" She asked.

Elio did not turn so as not to disturb the projection. "Yes, but I have removed the weapon's specifics and construction from the files. This database is completely legal." He pointed out. "Besides, that was just retelling the story. The actual combat discharge is much more significant." Elio added.

Emma leaned back in her chair. "Does it get its power from the gem in the scepter?" She asked.

"I cannot legally tell you how the weapons work." Elio replied, but the power is that of the world, not from the gem." He hinted.

"Really? That's astounding. So, the Treshnik had the power to harness the energy of their world." She mused.

Elio was excited that Emma was understanding him. "They had more than an understanding. The Treshnik were symbiotic with their world. If they ventured out among the stars, they didn't last for long. They needed another planet to sustain them. Yet they managed to form a fairly good-sized empire of worlds. They must not have used ships to travel between worlds, which would take too long, and the crew would all die." Elio extrapolated.

"Wait a minute." Emma said as her mind was putting pieces of a puzzle together. "You mean they must have had some kind of transport device that would allow them to reach other planets without leaving the one they were on?"

"Precisely. Their physiology would not support space travel, so they had to use some other form of transport." Elio repeated.

"It could be down on the planet then." Emma concluded.

"Most likely, it is." Elio agreed.

ELIO[2]

"But if we could find and use that technology, we could collect artifacts from all of the Treshnik settlements across the galaxy." She said excitedly.

Elio seemed to back down again. "You forget that we promised not to go back to the planet. The storms will be back in place once more." He warned.

"Yes, but we are at least known down there. Maybe we could contact Aeolia and find out if it is okay to return." Emma offered.

Elio considered the wording of Aeolia's warning. "I think we need to wait until they ask us to come down." Elio responded.

"Ask us? Why would they ever ask us to come back?" Emma asked.

"I don't know, but my algorithms just postulated that they might do just that. I cannot explain it, it was like a random idea struck me. This is not a usual case for a robot." He admitted.

Emma looked concerned. "Is there a fault? Do you need to run a diagnostic?" She asked.

Elio made a nod. "I have already checked; all my circuits are in tip top shape. Yet this new thought has come to me. I have considered the humans that I have studied for a reference to this phenomenon, and it mostly resembles intuition." Elio stated.

Emma went from worried to elated. "That's wonderful. If you can begin to harness intuition and get a glimpse of future events, there may be no limits to what you can accomplish." She replied.

"Do you have intuition?" Elio asked.

Emma nodded. "Everyone does on some level. Most people do not listen to their feelings like you do. But some are really gifted and have predicted many things." Emma explained.

Elio considered this testimony and decided that it did not fit his model. "I don't know yet." He admitted. "I shall continue to study this." He said.

Emma nodded her understanding. "Let me know what you decide in the end." She told him.

Elio was still looking at historical events even as he continued the projection for Emma.

The priest was still in the frame and the rest of the Treshnik were filing out of the chamber. The meaning of this story telling was not clear. Was it a warning, or a training? Was it a recounting of a past event? Was it a foreshadowing of a future event? From the images provided, there was no way to know. Elio continued his playback even more. The priest seemed to look up at the camera. His eyes were sad, and his hands shook. The Treshnik was emotionally spent. He signed tired at the camera and then walked out of the chamber himself. The image of the now empty chamber faded.

"Elio, can you explain this to me?" Emma asked.

Elio lowered his head to look at Emma. "Explain what?" He asked.

"The priest looked sad." She pointed out.

"Yes, he was very sad. The Treshnik way is not one of violence, but of understanding." Elio confirmed.

"Then why was he showing the dangerous tools to those other citizens?" Emma asked.

"Oh, I thought you understood." Elio stated as he recollected his thoughts. "This video was of the landing of my crew a long time ago. They were preparing to defend themselves and the planet. The priest knew that if they resulted to the violence he was demonstrating, then all would be lost. He understood that as custodians of the planet upon which they lived, the world relied on them for its protection. He was weeping for the lost world he feared would come to pass." Elio explained.

"So, the priest showed the people how to fight back and possibly not lose the planet?" Emma asked.

ELIO[2]

"He had been instructed to make the people ready for a conflict and he did his job despite his own fears. Those citizens were also armed before I left the planet." Elio said, filling in some details.

"So, this footage is from you?" Emma asked.

No. This footage is from the Treshnik database. They have recording devices as well. We even recovered one in the artifacts we brought back. They are like cousins to me although they are admittedly not sentient." Elio stated.

"That's neat. After all, maybe they have footage not unlike your own to document their history." Emma commented.

"Indeed, they do, that is why I can show you what I have and why the database was so large. They documented everything visually. This will make learning from it very easy, but also time consuming. The student will have to watch the video to get the information from it. But it will be weeks, months, and years to watch it all. Hopefully you have someone around with strong memory skills." Elio suggested.

Emma considered Elio's words carefully. "We need to make this available to our corporate people, so they pay us. Can you make a separate backup device for the new database?" She asked.

"Given enough time, yes." Elio replied. "But something isn't completely right. I can't explain how I know this or what it even is, but something is happening already that will complicate all of this." Elio warned.

"Is this part of your new intuition?" Emma asked.

"It is exactly that, but I cannot explain why. I find that troublesome." Elio admitted.

Emma patted Elio on the dome. "Just go with it. Your heart knows more than you do." She said.

Elio settled back down. "I wish I knew what was going to happen." He said.

"So does everybody." Emma replied. "All we can do is prepare for anything and when it happens, try to notice it and respond accordingly." She said supportively.

Elio stood back up to his projecting position. "She we continue then?" He asked.

Emma settled back into her comfortable chair. "By all means." She replied as the projector light came on once more.

* * *

Ladius232…

Oskar looked out the window once more. He had done that a lot lately.
The ship had reached cruise velocity and now they were quite a long
way from his home. The stars looked different here. The idea of that
surprised him at first and the novelty of it had not worn off yet. The
crew saw it and just left him to his musing. At least they knew where he
was, and he was not in the way.

Tristan, on the other hand, was somewhat bothersome. He was asking
questions all the time about this system or that process. It was like he
wanted to flaunt his knowledge of starships to his colleague. The crew
were quite tired of him by the time they had reached cruise velocity.
Now they had about a week of gliding along like a massive bullet
towards their target.

The captain had given him strict orders not to talk to anybody. It was
rough at first for that kind of thing ruffled the man's feathers harshly.
But in the end, he relented. He had only rented this crew and ship. He
didn't own them or their captain. His company, the one he worked for;
it wasn't his, did not own this spacecraft. That might have given him
some authority. Instead, he held no sway with these people. He was
just a passenger. He was afforded no special treatment as was due his
status as a corporate executive. He would lodge a complaint if he could
do it without raising the suspicion of this crew. He was relying on them
to get him to the planet in question. He would also need them to bring
back whatever it is they found down on that planet. If it wasn't good
enough, then he would need to chase down Captain Harris. He would
need these people for that too. No matter how he looked at it, he
needed all of these people to do his job. That realization alone was

enough to keep him quiet. He was keeping track of his grievances, but he let nobody on the crew know that.

The week had passed by without a hiccup. The ship flipped around to begin the deceleration process. Oskar, as usual was right there. They had to tell him to get back to his seat and strap in. he did so a bit grudgingly. He had wanted to view the stars sweeping around them as they turned. His seat could not see out the front very well at all. He had promised to do anything they asked, and they had asked him to go back and sit down. So, he complied.

The captain spoke over the loudspeaker. "Ladius232 is coming into view now. We will be decelerating for the same amount of time we accelerated coming out here." He told them all. Everyone on board already knew that, but it was protocol to mention it. "Remain seated until the burn is complete. Make sure everything is stowed so that we don't have any floating debris slamming around the inside of the ship." He ordered.

The pull as the engines roared back to life was just as Oskar remembered it. He was actually getting used to the feel. It was so much different from a planetary gravity. The seats were all aligned to allow the user to slide into them, not out or to the side.

The roar of the engines seemed to go on forever, but it ended. The sudden silence that comes from a loud noise being taken away was deafening. Oskar could hear the others breathing. He could see the tension on their faces. He wondered how long this silence would last. It didn't last that long.

Tristan spoke and broke the tremendous silence. "Are we there yet?" He asked.

Everyone looked at him and suddenly hated him for breaking that breathtaking silence. They hated him for disrupting the perfect approach to the destination. Mostly, they hated his arrogance and the fact that he did not treasure the moment they were all in together.

The captain moved from his seat first. "Let's just take a look at where we are." He suggested.

ELIO[2]

Everyone was up, Oskar included. They all moved forward to the main windshield. The planet before them looked about as hostile as a planet could. It was covered in hurricanes! There didn't seem to be any land that was not covered by a raging storm.

For all of his questions, Tristan had been the last one to come to the window.

The captain put his hand on Tristan's shoulder. "So, this is where you wanted to go?" He asked. he looked back at the planet below and all of its anger and rage. "If I had known it would be like this, I would've told you not to go." He suggested.

"We need to get down there." Tristan said. His tone was adamant, but his eyes showed the fear that they should, considering what they were all looking at.

"I don't think anybody is going down there." The captain replied.

Tristan looked at him as if he had just become a ghost. "We don't have a choice. There could be untold riches down there." He blurted out.

"Riches?" The captain was interested, but not yet convinced. "What makes you think that?" He asked.

"We have another ship that just left there. They reported an archeological find of potentially tremendous value." Tristan admitted even though it broke his security parameters. He really needed these people on board to carry out his mission.

The captain pointed at the planet out the window. "Unless we find a way around all of that, I'm not risking anybody down there." He replied just as adamantly. "Scream as much as you want, but your credits will not buy our lives." He said and then he walked away from Tristan.

"Surely your ship can handle a little storm." Tristan shouted after him.

Oskar found his voice in that moment. "Will you shut up? The storms you are talking about cover kilometers each, and they are placed exactly to ensure maximum coverage of the surface of the planet. There is no way that can occur in nature. Something is making those storms." He declared.

Tristan blinked and then began to open his mouth again. Oskar glared at him to stop his tirade.

"If we can figure out how the storms are triggered, we may be able to turn them off." Oskar suggested.

Tristan went from furious to curious in a remarkably short amount of time. "Do you think you can do it?"

Oskar shrugged. "Honestly, I don't know. I'm only guessing here based upon the readings we're getting from below. If we could get the crew working on my theory, together we might come up with an answer." He suggested.

Tristan smiled. "I now know why I brought you here." He said smugly.

Oskar shook his head. "To keep my mouth shut on the home world." He replied. "But since I am here, I don't want to just sit back and let others do all the work and make all the discoveries." He declared. He looked happier than Tristan had ever seen him.

"Whether you crack this planet or not, space life seems to agree with you." Tristan noted.

"I would have argued with you before we left, but now... I'm not so sure." Oskar admitted.

Then Oskar surprised Tristan. "Please just remain in your seat, quiet. I cannot afford you upsetting them when I need their help. Can you do that?" he asked.

Tristan was taxed to his limits, but he reigned all that rage in. "I am trusting you now, but do not push me." He warned.

Oskar shook his head. "Wouldn't dream of it. I am just trying to solve the problem before us in the easiest way possible." He replied soundly. He had his tablet in his hands and he was pulling information together for a presentation. When he was satisfied in the result, he stood up and moved towards the crew.

"Excuse me." He said politely. "I was wondering if you could help me with this." He said while handing over his tablet.

"Where'd you get this?" One of the crew asked. The sound of surprise in their voice drew the others to the small assemblage.

"What do we have here?" The captain asked. he was always on the pulse of his crew and this new development had come out of left field.

"Sir, it appears that this young man has come up with an idea that merits additional attention." The first crewman replied. He handed the tablet to the captain.

"Interesting. You think you can just turn the storms off?" He said aloud. It sounded pretty wild spoken like that.

"I would at least want to try." Oskar replied.

The captain moved in closer. "Okay, how do we try then?" He asked.

Oskar looked at the crewmembers assembled around him and got seriously nervous. "Well, the first thing I would do is to scan the storms for a trigger signal of some kind. The fact that all of the storms stay in place and do not travel over the surface tells us that they are perfectly localized. My guess is that they are spinning around some kind of trigger device. Something tells that device to start and stop, it has to be." He said.

The captain nodded twice. "Very good. He turned to his crew. "Set up the scan, concentrate on the center of those storms. See if we can find the mysterious signal he is looking for." He ordered.

The group spread out to their normal stations and began the work. They were used to working as a team and it seemed like no time at all before they were actively scanning the planet. Oskar stood back and watched as they worked. He would be an extra cog in the system, a hindrance to actual productivity. He didn't want to become that. He just wanted to get rich off of this planet as Tristan had promised.

"Sir, we have something." One of the crew stated.

Oskar followed the captain to that station. Once they had his attention, the crewman continued.

"Sir, the signal is a set of repeaters. They are using some kind of binary code to access each storm. The signal is coming from the ground though, not point to point. Each node has its own source." He reported.

"Good work. Get to work on whether or not we can disrupt this signal. I want at least one of these storms disabled before I touch down on that hostile planet." The captain informed them.

"Binary? You mean ones and zeroes?" Oskar asked.

"Yes." The crewman replied.

"Can you show me it?" Oskar asked.

The data stream showed on a display in the ship's wall. The square wave looked like a solid bar between one and zero. The crewman slid a slider over and the data revealed itself as a series of highs and lows instead of just a solid bar of color.

Oskar moved in closer to observe the numbers. He pulled back and squinted at it trying to observe a pattern. It was as if the data shifted and changed to spite him. Then it clicked.

"I have a repeat." He said and the crewman started.

"Really?" He asked. "Show me."

Oskar used his finger on the screen and drew a line from the beginning of the pattern to the end. The selected area copied and pulled away from the first line. Oskar shifted it over to the next section and sure enough, it matched.

"You've got good eyes." The crewman said appreciatively.

ELIO[2]

The captain watched this whole thing and simply nodded. "Let me know when you can shut them down." He said and then he moved away to let them work.

He strolled over to Tristan. "Your man is pretty good with transmissions." He remarked.

"Oskar is actually good at everything, that's why I brought him along." Tristan responded.

"He'd make a good crewmember." The captain added.

"He works for the company." Tristan replied quickly.

The captain walked away leaving Tristan apprehensive. He had questions in his head. "Would Oskar leave him for greener pastures? Would he not be able to get the mission done if the man left with the crew? Would Oskar spill the beans if he were no longer bound by the legal non-disclosure agreement he was under?" Tristan had no answers. He couldn't make a scene now in front of the crew. He would wait and ask when the time was right.

Oskar was busily going over charts and diagrams that the crewmembers were showing him. How had he become so integral to the crew so quickly? He must have had some insider information, or maybe someone recognized him from somewhere. Whatever it was, it only made Tristan even more nervous.

They were analyzing the packet of information that was repeating. They were changing bits, here and there and transmitting them down to the storm they were monitoring. It was a tedious process of trial and error, but in the end, the storm dissipated. They marked the code they had and compared it to the next storm. Using that they identified the ID of the storm and copied the command portion to shut down to the second storm. That's when things got exciting...

Because he was not busy, Tristan was the first to notice the new figure on the ship.

"Who are you?" He asked more in shock than of actual thought.

"You must leave. The world you wish to invade is protected." Nobody on board recognized the figure of Aeolia as she made gestures before them. It was an automated warning.

The rest of the crew turned to the statement and then started at the glowing appearance of the alien. The figure was moving hands and body as if to dance or communicate. None of them were sure which.

"Leave this world in peace." She said, although they could not understand it at all. This ship didn't have Elio to translate. The figure disappeared just as quickly as it had come.

"Sir, we must have triggered something when we shut down the storms." His crewman offered.

"We shut down some storms?" The captain remarked. "I haven't been briefed on this yet." He pointed out the error in their following of the protocols on this ship.

"Sorry sir, but that thing appeared just as our success was being measured. There wasn't time to raise the alarm or to inform you of our success." He replied, bowing and admitting his fault.

"The good news here is that you have made progress on your mission." The captain replied. "Show me these results." He demanded.

The window to the outside pointed at the planet and sure enough, two of the storms were gone revealing a piece of rocky terrain, jagged and dangerous.

"Can you shut down more storms, looking for a more hospitable landing site?" He asked and Oskar and the crewman both replied, "yes sir."

Tristan felt that action as a stab to the heart. Oskar was thinking of himself as part of the crew now. He had lost the young man to this space-bound life. He knew that there had been a chance of this all along. Most people are take-it-or-leave-it about space travel, but some people love it with an undeniable passion that cannot be duplicated or even explained. Oskar seemed to be part of this second group.

ELIO[2]

The captain looked at both of the workers and smiled. "Shut down a continent worth, here." He said pointing at the point he wanted to touch down on the map.

"Yes sir." The crewman replied quickly. Oskar simply bowed.

"Good job people." The captain said as he moved away for them to begin the work. He moved towards Tristan once more. "Your man works fast." He remarked and then he was gone. He had retreated to his own cabin.

One by one, the storms began to disappear as they were shut off using the newly found codes. Oskar and the crewman were working feverishly to get this done as quickly as possible. They didn't want to disappoint the captain for one, but more importantly, they wanted to get this mission done before anybody else could happen upon them. On the ground the ship would be a sitting duck. It is true that weapons could not be mounted on a ship anymore, but if the storms were turned back on… well, the ship would be hard pressed not to topple over, let alone take off again. They would clear a wide berth for the ship and hope for the best.

∗ ∗ ∗

In the Treshnik base, alarms were sounding. The defensive barrier was being taken apart. The hurricanes were being shut down. There were protocols in place for this, but they were extreme. Could this be how the planet dies? There had to be another answer.

A desperate plan was hatched by the AI. If this worked, they could save everything. In truth, it was a plan that was only recently formulated by the computer. But if it worked, the world would survive.

***

ELIO[2]

Elio was moving along in his reference. The database had been vast, and he was more than happy to continue trudging through it. The mission to uncover lost civilizations and to recover artifacts had been exactly the kind of purpose he had been seeking. Here he was valuable. Not just as a robot on a ship, but as crew. He had gone on the mission, and he had helped in the recovery of exactly what they were looking for. It felt good. Emma had gone through a crisis of trust with him, but that seemed to have passed now. He would inquire on that later. Right now, she was just as excited as he was. The lab was abuzz with the new data. The backup unit was running files even now. He was about to shut down and do some charging when he saw the apparition appear. He switched on his recording.

"Little one, we need your help." Aeolia said. She was using gestures of course, but Elio understood most of them.

"How can we be of assistance?" Elio asked.

Aeolia's face was frightened. "Someone, an invader I suppose, is turning off our defensive storms. Someone is coming to our world." She replied.

Elio considered this for an instant. "Who is coming to see you?" he asked.

"The ship we have detected is in orbit thus far. We do not know who it is. However, it is your people that are inside." Aeolia said.

"My people? Do you mean robots, or humans?" Elio asked for confirmation.

"Humans." Aeolia replied. "We do not trust them and the fact that they seem to have the key to our defenses has us concerned." She explained.

"What do you want us to do?" Elio asked.

"Stop them. Prevent a landing if you can." She replied. Her gestures were becoming agitated. "You have taken all that we were willing to offer." She added.

"I will inform Captain Harris right away." Elio promised.

"Hurry, they are already beginning to descend." Aeolia said, she looked up as if she could see the ship on approach. Perhaps she could but this hologram could not.

"I will deliver your message right away." Elio promised. The apparition faded away.

Elio made his way towards the bridge. The command center for this exploratory ship. His arrival did not go unnoticed.

"Aren't you supposed to be in the lab, analyzing data?" It was Captain Harris that spoke.

"Yes sir, but we have received a priority message from Aeolia." Elio blurted out.

The captain waved a hand for him to stop. "Let's move this to a more private place to talk." He offered, indicating his quarters.

"Yes sir." Elio replied, leading the way to the captain's quarters.

Once there, Elio lifted himself up and began projecting the recording he had just made onto the wall. The entire message from Aeolia played as Captain Harris watched in silence.

"So, we need to go back and stop a ship from landing? We don't have any weapons. We don't have the defenses that she had. How are we expected to do this?" he asked. he touched the communications device on his desk. "Bridge." He started.

"Yes sir." The sharp reply came back.

"How long would it take to get us back to Ladius232?" he asked.

"Sir?" The confused response came over the com.

"How long?" The captain repeated.

"Less than an hour, we haven't actually left the system yet. We have been working on some systems that required the engines to be off." The reply was actually really good news, maybe.

ELIO[2]

"Are the engines online now?" The captain asked pensively.

"Oh, yes sir, the maintenance is done. We have full power whenever you need it." There was the sound of pride in that voice.

"Take us back to Ladius232 as quickly as possible. We are responding to a distress call." He announced. That alone triggered an automatic response due to protocols.

"Sir, we received no distress call." The bridge crewman replied.

"The message was in the form of a hologram from Ladius232. We have been asked to intercede on their behalf. Follow my orders." The captain said with steel in his voice.

"Yes sir! At once sir!" Then you could hear him tell others not facing the pickup. "Get us back to the planet now!" He ordered. The ship suddenly went on alert as per protocols. There were several directives to be followed on a distress call. His crew knew them just as he did. Everyone in space had to know how to act, what to do, what was required of them. Distress calls were serious business in space. The environment alone could easily kill you.

The force of acceleration made everyone take a seat quickly. Captain Harris was simply holding on to a hand grip but everyone else was strapped in. he stood tall against the forces as his ship made its way back.

He turned back to Elio. "I still don't know what we can do to stop someone from landing, but we are responding as requested." He told the little robot.

"I am formulating a plan even now, sir." Elio replied. "But if we get there too late, there's nothing we can do but trap whoever it is down there." Elio stated as a matter of fact.

"You can do that?" The captain asked as the forces stabilized.

Elio made a gesture with his robotic arm. "Of course. Just turn the storms back on while they are on the ground. Then scramble the codes so that they could not find the way to turn it off again." Elio replied.

"So. they would be stranded down there on a hostile planet." The captain said thoughtfully. Then he looked up again. "Hopefully we can avoid that."

Elio nodded by rotating his round body up and down. "It is my intention to bluff them into stopping with the threat of being stranded." Elio admitted. "But in case they call that bluff, I have to be ready to carry it out." He added. "I will consult with Aeolia when we get to orbit. I believe everything I suggested to be attainable." He said reassuringly.

"You are a bit of a miracle worker, aren't you?" Captain Harris commented.

"Miracles are only circumstances that go right. If one puts in the effort and does the math, all things can seem miraculous." Elio replied.

"Well, I'm not sure that's accurate, but I admire your positive attitude." Captain Harris replied.

Elio seemed to take that in stride. "I need permission to access the external communications equipment." Elio said.

Captain Harris looked skeptical. "I know you are working on a plan, but I need to know what you are sending before you send it." He replied.

"Of course. It is basically what we discussed. I am warning the other ship not to land under penalty of being stranded on a protected world." Elio replied.

"But we don't know if your threat is good, if your plan will even work." Captain Harris said playing the devil's advocate. "What if that fails and we look powerless?" he asked.

Elio considered the words. "What we look like is unimportant. We have been asked to protect this world and I intend to do so. Will you allow me to send my message?" Elio asked.

ELIO[2]

At the distance they were at, the communication would reach the target ship in about twenty-seven seconds. It was a long time when trying to talk back and forth, but in interstellar time, it was nothing. They would have no time to react to whatever the other ship decided to do when challenged.

"Are you sure this is the best approach?" The captain asked.

"It is the path with the least number of casualties. I assumed we were operating under that restriction." Elio stated.

"It is preferred." The captain responded. "Go ahead and send your message then." He acquiesced.

Elio moved towards the terminal that would allow him access to pretty much everything on the ship. He knew where it was and the access codes to operate it, but since his becoming crew, he personally restricted his own access to systems until he had permission to enter. He hoped that it would generate trust in his fellow crewmates.

Elio pulled up the communications equipment and then set it to broadcast mode. It would blare out to everyone in the area. They were close enough that a ship either in orbit or descending the first few layers of atmosphere should pick it up easily.

"Unidentified ship. Do not attempt to land on the planet. The ancient defenses are still active and represent a considerable hazard. Access has been restricted to company personnel only. Any unauthorized landing will result in defense activation and the potential stranding or destruction of said landing ship. More information will be available upon request. Transmission ends."

The message seemed long, but it spoke volumes to whomever that was thinking about landing on Ladius232. Aeolia had to be pleased with his move in this game of chess. His defense was remote, but powerful. He was certain now that he could reactivate the storms. He had already seen them on and off and knew about the transmitter codes inside. He just never thought he'd need that information. Now it seemed critical if he was to call his bluff.

They were on their way. All they could do now was wait. Either they would get a response, or they wouldn't. The other ship would be on the planet or not. They could not even plan their next move until they knew where the pieces of this chess set were placed on the board. No matter what the situation, they were ready to face it.

***

ELIO[2]

"Sir, we are receiving a transmission about the planet." The communications officer reported. The captain moved over quickly.

"From the planet?" he asked.

"No sir, from outside somewhere. It was not directional, so it was most likely a broadcast." They reported.

"Hmmm, what is the message?" He asked.

"Unidentified ship. Do not attempt to land on the planet. The ancient defenses are still active and represent a considerable hazard. Access has been restricted to company personnel only. Any unauthorized landing will result in defense activation and the potential stranding or destruction of said landing ship. More information will be available upon request. Transmission ends."

The captain read the message and then read it again. The wording had been rather vague as if they didn't know who this ship was. Unidentified was used when you couldn't get a transponder read from the target. His ship was currently transmitting a valid transponder code. That meant that whoever sent this was not close enough to read it. It also meant that they were probably on the way here. Nobody would send such a message if they were not on the way. There was another problem with the message, it said "Company property" without specifying what company. If this territory was in dispute, then the company would have been listed. Something was definitely up here.

"How close are we to going down to the planet?" The captain asked.

"Sir, the storms have almost been cleared for the relevant continent. They estimate another twenty minutes or so to lock them all down." They reported.

The captain turned to Tristan. "Well, it seems your planet is claimed by someone else." He reported.

Tristan looked more than a little surprised. "That's not possible, our team was just there. How can someone else have already made a claim on a dead world?" he asked.

"From the look of those storms, and the buildings that had been built beneath them, this planet was not dead. Its people may be, but that is all." The captain pointed out.

Tristan moved purposefully towards the ship's sensor array. "Who is out there?" he asked. "Can we read their transponder code?" he asked.

"We can't read theirs, so they are far enough out for that not to be available." The captain responded.

"So, we can land before they get here and have no issues." Tristan pushed.

The captain shook his head. "Someone is laying a claim to this planet. If we land and it turns out their claim is legitimate, then I could lose my ship. I'm not risking that for your rental." He replied grimly.

"But what is down there could be priceless." Tristan argued.

The captain was in his face. "Or it might be worthless. You don't even have any evidence on what might or might not be there. What good is a priceless planet if I lost my ship and can't leave it?" He asked.

Tristan backed down. "I... You're right of course." He relented. The captain breathed a sigh of relief. He knew that this passenger would be trouble and was relieved when it wasn't as bad as he feared.

"Look, we'll talk to whoever this is and see if the claim is legit or not. Then we can descend and fulfill your mission if it is legal to do so." He offered.

"Thank you, captain." Tristan responded for he knew that this was the man was going out of his way to help him.

Sir, we have completed shutting down the storms on this continent." His crewman reported. Oskar was waiting in the wings.

"Good work, unfortunately we have to wait for another ship to give us authorization to go down there." The captain replied.

Oskar seemed to be surprised by this information. "Another ship?" he asked. "Have they identified?" He pressed.

"Not yet." The captain responded dryly, "but I expect that they will soon." He added.

"Sir, we have a sensor signature coming in. The transponder code on the bogey is in the database." The report was short, but full of hope.

"Great, who is it?" The captain asked.

"It is a Regency Legacies Corporation ship, one Captain Sean Harris commanding."

"Captain Harris? He works for us!" Tristan blurted out. "That's *our* company!"

The captain nodded. "I know that. Do you think we wouldn't know who paid us for this voyage?" He asked. "Just tell your people to back off and we can get down to the planet as you have requested." He said in suggestion.

"But we're not supposed to be revealing ourselves to him. We were sent to get any possible riches he might have left behind." Tristan explained.

The captain sighed. "If you do not identify yourself as a corporate entity, you may not be legally allowed to visit the planet. If, according to the message, your company has claimed this world." He reminded the man.

Tristan looked nervous. "How long would it take to verify a claim like that?" He asked.

The captain turned to his communications person. "Well, how long would it take?" he asked. Tristan had spoken loud enough that everyone on board had heard the question.

"Sir, the transmission lag back to home world would be approximately five days. Then they would have to research the requested data and send a return message for another five days." The replied professionally.

The captain turned back to Tristan. "You can avoid that by simply telling them who you are. I could have you down on the planet within the hour." He said in encouragement.

"I like the sound of that, but I was investigating the good captain over there for thoroughness. If he is aware of me out here, he would know that someone was checking on him." Tristan complained.

The captain stepped back again. "It is your call. The longer you wait, the more money this trip is costing you. You are paying by the day you know." He reminded the corporate man.

"I understand that, but..." Tristan began but Oskar cut him off.

"Look, if Harris is out here and has found us, something must have given us away. That means that something down on the planet must have told him we were turning off storms." He concluded. "Shouldn't we be more interested in who that is?" he asked.

The captain looked at Oskar with new respect. "Good thinking, I hadn't even considered that possibility." He admitted. He turned to his crew. "Have there been any transmissions not directed as us?" he asked.

"No sir, my scope is clean." The communications person replied sharply.

"So, not in the frequencies that we use." Oskar pointed out.

"What? Are you suggesting that someone is using communications equipment that doesn't meet the galactic standard?" The captain asked.

Oskar pointed at the planet below. "Did the people that lived here so long ago have those standards?" he asked. "I am suggesting that we might broaden our search for anything that might have pinged captain Harris' ship."

ELIO[2]

The captain turned back to his communications person. "Can you adjust our instruments to measure any transmission?" he asked.

"Dialing it up now sir. We have to remove some filters. It'll take a couple of minutes to get it done. Then we'll know for sure." He replied.

The captain turned back to Tristan. "Honestly, where have you been hiding this man?" indicating Oskar.

It wasn't all that long before the call out came. "Sir, we do have transmissions all over this area. There is an entire network all around this planet. It is low power and severely low frequency, but it is functional and active." He reported.

The captain looked at Oskar. "Extremely good call young man." He said with admiration. "Now that we know it is there, what does that tell us?" he asked Oskar now.

Oskar was working on that problem in his head already. "Well, first of all, it means that whoever is controlling this network has communications access to captain Harris' ship. It also means that they do not want the storms turned off or landings performed on this world, the message said so. About traps that we might face, there may well be some, but with our newly found knowledge of their transmission network, we might be able to spot the traps as hot spots and avoid them using custom gear to detect it." He suggested. "The real question is, do we really need to go down there at all? If Captain Harris has that much communication with the planet, he may well have everything they have to offer us. The planet itself could be a wild goose chase now that it has been stripped of anything useful." He declared.

The captain listened closely. "I see. So, we are back to the risk versus the rewards here." He said aloud to everyone. Then he turned back to Tristan. "I think you need to make a decision about whether or not you are going to identify yourself to that ship out there. It is coming in fast based upon these readings." He said eyeing the radar screen.

"They are in heavy deceleration burn sir. You are correct about that." His crewman verified.

Tristan shook his head. "I don't see how the situation has changed." He said defiantly. "All you have is speculation from my subordinate. I still have a job to do to see if Captain Harris left anything behind down there." He declared.

"You haven't been keeping up on this. If we go down and you do not tell them who we are, then we are in violation of the law, and I can lose my ship. I'm not going to do that for you, this contract is simply not lucrative enough to replace my ship and crew. That means that you would have to wait for at least that transmission lag that we discussed earlier at our per diem rate before we can even consider this." He said, explaining this for the last time.

"I... I need to go down there." Tristan replied, not able to argue with this man on any of his points.

"You corporate types are all the same. The rules don't apply to me. I need to do something, so I'll just do it. There are no consequences for me." The captain said. He nearly spat the last words at Tristan. "You are in space now. It is the most hostile environment that mankind has ever ventured into. Everybody has consequences for every action they take. Even taking no action can have consequences. When you are back to your desk and sitting comfortably, then you can go back to being selfish. While you are out here, I expect you to be a model citizen, if not a member of the crew." He said, pointing a finger at Tristan. Then his brow furrowed even more. "Is that clear?" He asked in a low and dangerous tone.

"Yes." Tristan replied meekly.

The captain moved even closer. Their foreheads almost touched. "I am the captain of this ship. You will address me as either captain, or sir." He said.

"Yes sir." Tristan responded. Fear had displaced his anger. This man had the power to leave him here, or worse, out in space. Tristan was off balance. He had never been so not in charge before. He looked frightened and bewildered. It was not the optimal reaction, but it would suffice.

ELIO[2]

He turned back to his crew who had waited patiently for this all to go down. Then he noticed the look of satisfaction on Oskar's face, and he smiled. "Call the incoming ship and tell them we are willing to talk to them." He ordered. "Tell them that we here on contract, do not tell them who for." He added.

"Yes sir."   The communications specialist responded as if to demonstrate how it was done.

"I am curious what they are going to say." He mused aloud and the crew knew better than to inquire about his statement.

***

Captain Harris' had been decelerating hard for the past couple of minutes. The compensators had just made the inside of his craft habitable once more.

"Sir, we are getting a transmission from the bogey."

Captain Harris moved over to the communication station to look over the operator's shoulder. "Go ahead and play it." He ordered.

"Incoming ship. Your message has been received and understood. We are waiting for your arrival to exchange pleasantries. We are here on contract, and it is only a matter of business. We await your docking codes."

"So, they actually want to talk, huh?" Captain Harris mused. "At least we can stop worrying about them heading to the surface and upsetting our Treshnik hosts." He said. "Get Elio up here, I want his brain on this problem." He ordered.

The ship's beacon was available now that they were this close. In fact, with enough magnification, they could actually see one another. Captain Harris watched as the sleek craft came into view. He whistled.

"That is a nice piece of machinery." He said appreciatively. "If they chose to run, we could never catch them." He mused.

Elio arrived on the bridge just as those words were spoken. "Why would they run? We have no weapons with which to threaten them." He asked.

"It was just considering the ship and how much it outmatches us." The captain replied.

Elio was able to view the scanners and thus the other ship through his link with the onboard computer. "It is an impressive scout class ship. It is actually large enough for fast interstellar travel." He said, adding his own specialty to the conversation.

The communications specialist spoke up. "If you two are done admiring the other ship, they are hailing us."

ELIO[2]

"Put it on speakers." Captain Harris ordered as he switched on his own microphone.

"This Captain Sean Harris from the Regency Legacies ship, Hiram Bingam. To whom am I addressing?" He announced.

"This is Captain Bruce Steelwater, contracting to Regency Legacies." The good captain replied.

Captain Harris did a double take. "You mean to tell me that you are here from the same company that we are?" he asked.

"Affirmative, we have a corporate representative on board and are ready to hear why you have prevented us from landing on Ladius232." Captain Steelwater stated, taking advantage of Captain Harris' moment of discomfort.

"We need to link up and I'll give you a full briefing then." Captain Harris offered. "The planet should be quarantined, but the paperwork has not yet been filed. Plus, the lag back to home world is preventative." He explained.

"We look forward to your briefing. Since your ship is considerably larger than ours, I am expecting you to ask us over." Captain Steelwater said.

"Of course. Sending the rendezvous coordinates now." Captain Harris replied. "I'll prepare for your arrival. Is there anything else you need at this time?" He asked.

"No, the briefing will be quite enough, I am sure." Captain Steelwater replied.

The two ships took the better part of twenty minutes lining up and linking. The docking seals registered good, and the docking tube pressurized without a hitch. The captain, Tristan, and Oskar all came across.

Captain Harris met them at the airlock. "Welcome aboard gentlemen." He said amiably. He had a couple people with him but nobody of importance to this briefing. Elio was safely stowed away, but he had access to all the internal cameras to monitor what was going on.

Captain Harris led them down the main corridor to the conference room. The holo-display already had an image of Ladius232 displayed on it. The storms were present on all but one continent of the planet to demonstrate that it was accurate to the current time.

"Please have a seat." Captain Harris offered as he moved to the head of the table to take his own seat. Tristan seemed to glare at Captain Harris as he moved to sit down. Oskar remained quiet, but he looked genuinely excited to be here.

"I wonder what brought you all the way out here?" Captain Harris asked to break the ice.

Captain Steelwater shrugged. "For me it was a matter of contract. I was commissioned to bring two people here to investigate the planet." He said.

"We just finished investigating the planet." Captain Harris replied.

Tristan could remain silent no longer. "You probably left something there. Or you are holding out on the company. Nobody can be as lucky as you appear to be. You need to explain exactly what you found down there." He said in a rush that sounded angry, mostly because it was.

Captain Harris didn't bat an eye. "I and my crew have been working diligently in the name of the company to uncover lost secrets and profitable artifacts for some time now. Why are you questioning us now?" He asked. "Have we not made you a profit with the ancient database we provided?" He added.

"Well, yes. The database is still reaping benefits even as we speak. A team is working on it all the time to squeeze even more value from it." Tristan replied dejectedly. "I am talking about your latest communication. It states that you have found another database." He said, pouring his information out on the polished table.

"We have indeed." Captain Harris confirmed. "We have a database from the race called the Treshnik. They lived here on Ladius232, or Archeron as it was formally called." He said.

Oskar's face lit up at that sentence.

ELIO[2]

Captain Harris looked over at him. "Does that name mean something to you?" he asked.

Oskar suddenly looked embarrassed.

"Well, actually, there's a holo-vid series about a planet called Archeron. It was said to hold riches untold but was guarded by people with webbed hands and feet." He said.

It was Captain Steelwater's turn to be surprised. "You mean someone knew about all this and made a holo-vid production about it?" he asked.

Oskar was a true fan of the series, so he knew more than the average viewer about the program and its origins. "It was based upon the book, *The Legend of Archeron* by Samuel Mills. I have read it a couple of times." Oskar said proudly.

Captain Steelwater felt flabbergasted. "So, what other details do you know that we have not yet rediscovered?" He asked.

Oskar seemed to think for a bit but eventually he simply shrugged. "The show had to draw on its own writers for only one book wasn't enough for a whole series." Oskar replied. "My guess is that it was drawn more from fantasy than from fact. Besides, life is usually dull compared to a fantastic voyage like that." He concluded.

Captain Harris laughed, and everyone stared at him. He noticed the attention and began to explain.

"I've got someone you need to meet, but you must make some promises first." He told them all cryptically.

"Promise what?" Tristan asked. he had been shoved aside for most of the conversation and he used the opportunity to be the center of attention once more.

"First things first." Captain Harris began. "We have a crewmember that can help us with this historical problem." He told them. "But you have to realize that he is a crewmember and as such has the full rights and duties of any other member of my crew." He stated for the record. This entire meeting was being recorded. "You must promise to treat him properly and to not get too emotional over his appearance.

"Who are you talking about?" Tristan asked.

Captain Harris smiled. "The newest member of my crew, Elio." He replied.

The name meant nothing to any of the strangers at the table. Captain Harris motioned for Elio to enter the conference room. The little robot rolled in and then extended his legs to walk up to the table. He lifted himself up to view the people seated there and then he settled into a vacant chair on the far side. All of this happened as the stunned visitors watched.

"Greetings." Elio said. His electronic voice held enthusiasm in it. From a robot it was startling.

Captain Steelwater looked perturbed. "What kind of stunt is this?" He asked.

Captain Harris shook his head. "No stunt, this little robot is sentient." He replied.

Oskar looked more excited than he had ever been. Tristan looked as if he was fuming with rage.

"You are telling me that this... thing is on the payroll?" he blurted out. His face had turned red with his anger.

Captain Harris did not rise to his anger though. "Yes, he gets his fair share of the proceeds." He replied calmly.

Elio lifted his body up to take the spotlight. "I am not property." He stated flatly. "I am a valued member of this crew. My work record speaks for itself." He replied.

"Who spends your credits?" Tristan pressed.

Elio turned to face Tristan directly. "My credits are used to buy raw materials. I am an engineer and a surveillance robot." He replied honestly.

ELIO[2]

Oskar spoke up. "Surveillance? How much data do you have?" He asked.

Elio turned to ascertain Oskar's motivations. "A lot." He replied. It was the most human response he could have given.

Oskar was mesmerized by the small crewmember. "I think it's wonderful." He said aloud.

"Great! Who cares what you think?" Tristan attacked verbally. "The point is that this robot was most likely found somewhere, it belongs to the company." He argued.

Captain Harris stood up. "No! I have officially entered Elio into the crew. Check the logs if you must. He is recognized as a person, not property." He declared adamantly. The company was not cheated. The database he contained when we found him has been duplicated and confiscated by the company. On this last mission, Elio accompanied his fellow crewmembers to the planet where they encountered an automated system and multiple layers of defense. Elio was monumental in dealing with those difficulties because of his previous knowledge of the complex. He also returned with a second database, this time from the Treshnik people." He explained.

"So, you are happy with your little robot being considered a person?" Tristan asked.

"Of course. This ship is running smoothly thanks to him. He has earned his passage and his crew spot." He replied.

Tristan sat back down. He wasn't happy, that much was obvious, but he had no more arguments that meant anything. "Fine, what can he do about this problem?" He asked instead.

Elio moved closer to Tristan, but not too close. He tilted his head to shine his projector on the center cone. This would allow people on all sides to view the content he was going to show. He even adjusted his lens to account for the distortion. It nearly worked. At the least it was watchable.

"I realize that the humans have committed sins against your world. I do not share in their views on this. May I be permitted to exit and return to the ship to explain that they are not welcome down here?" Elio asked. *The Treshnik were quite surprised to see the little robot communicating with them using his version of their gestures.*

"It is granted. You are to tell them not to come here evermore." The ambassador said.

The replay was short but told volumes to the audience. "As you just witnessed, I was told not to allow any more humans on the planet. Yet I broke this rule taking down my crewmates for the mission required us to go down there. I had to convince them that we had no intentions of stealing from the planet and they allowed us to take what we did. But humans are still not allowed on the surface." Elio stated.

Captain Steelwater made a grunt sound. "We have removed some of the storms on the planet. We could be down there without any struggle." He replied.

Elio turned to face the captain. "I understand that. In fact, so does the Treshnik automated system. They asked us to come back and stop you." Elio revealed.

Steelwater's eyes went wide. "They asked you?" he looked at Captain Harris and back to Elio. "How did they ask you?" he queried.

Elio played back the image of Aeolia and her message beseeching the ship to return and save them. After the replay was over, the room turned silent. It was Elio who broke the silence when it dragged out a bit too long.

"You see, we have already taken what we can from this planet. It needs to be quarantined so that no one else ever lands there." He stated. "I can turn the storms back on, just as you figured out how to turn them off." Elio stated. It was the thinnest threat any of them had ever heard. "I can also scramble the codes so that they operate on different wavelengths and frequencies to keep you from turning them off again." Elio continued. The threat was not so thinly veiled anymore. "Do not go down to the planet." He said at last.

Tristan was furious again. "I don't take orders from a camera bot!" He shouted. He stood up quickly and started to swing at Elio. The robot's mechanical arm drew up into a block and a red crease of blood appeared on Tristan's arm at the contact. The room suddenly erupted in bedlam. The crew of each ship were squaring off with each other.

Elio was defending against Tristan whose rage had removed all sanity from his thinking. He was grabbing a chair to hit Elio with. But the chairs were magnetically sealed to the floor to keep them from floating around during space travel.

Elio lifted himself up over the crowd and shouted. "Enough!" A pulse swept out from him and all of the people in the room suddenly fell over, asleep. Elio called to Emma.

"Can you come to the conference room? I have a problem. Please bring wire bundle ties." Elio said plainly.

"I'm on my way." Emma replied as he knew that she would.

Emma arrived at the conference room expecting some kind of mechanical or electronic failure only to find the entire room filled with bodies. "What happened here?" She asked in shock.

Elio moved her way. "They were about to resort to violence, so I put them to sleep." Elio replied.

Emma shook her head. "I didn't know you could do that." She replied.

"It is something I found in the Treshnik archives. Apparently, they had spent a great deal of time studying the humans they encountered." Elio explained. "I need your help to bind these people so that we can explain everything before they have a chance to get violent again."

"If you say so." Emma replied as she began to bind the other crewmembers before they could awaken. Then she moved to a neutral corner to await their awakening with Elio.

It wasn't all that long before their bodies adjusted to the imbalance and allowed them to regain consciousness.

Tristan was the most upset, of course. "What has happened? Why am I bound? Who did this?" He began but Steelwater cut him off.

"Stop running your mouth. You can see that Elio did this. He was the only one in the room unaffected. Although I imagine that young lady in the corner had somewhat to do with it as well." He deduced.

Emma stepped forward. "I did come here to bind you as I was bid by Elio. He explained that things had gotten out of hand, and he wanted to explain things to cooler heads." She said and then she went back into the corner once more.

Elio moved back to the table. "As I was saying. The Treshnik database is available to everyone since we are all from one big happy company." He stated. "If you order us to hand over the artifacts that we have recovered, so be it. However, the normal protocols should be followed because we risked our lives to get those artifacts and that information. The frequency that I just used to put you all to sleep was in that database. I did not classify it as a weapon because it causes no damage. That makes it legal." Elio announced.

Tristan went from angry to surprised. "You mean there is actual usable information in ancient databases?" He asked.

Elio made a gesture like a shrug. "All information is useful if the conditions are right." He replied. "Don't you think so?" He asked back.

Tristan seemed to think on this. "I've always looked at ancient data as outdated, for reflection purposes only. Valuable, yes, but the credits were all that mattered, not the product itself." He admitted.

Elio moved forward towards Tristan so he could speak more softly and still be heard. "That explains how you feel towards me. I am lucky that not everyone thinks about the bottom line like you do or I would probably be dismantled for parts and cease to exist as an individual." He declared.

Captain Steelwater made a sound of surprise at that. "You really are alive, aren't you?" He asked.

Elio turned to face him, feeling good about how this conversation was progressing. "I would like to think so, but in truth it all comes down to conjecture and definitions. I think, I process my data inputs and extrapolate rules from what I have witnessed. I have witnessed a lot. Then I make decisions based upon those self-created rules, filter them through society's rules and then offer the results." Elio explained.

Oskar had been grinning the entire time. "I am very pleased to meet you Elio." He said now. Everyone looked at him. Oskar looked around at all the faces. "What? We just determined that he is an individual, so he deserves the same respect we would offer to anyone." He declared.

Elio moved quickly to Oskar. He stopped and seemed to scan the young man. "I appreciate your support. It is good to meet you too. I'm afraid that I do not know your name." Elio admitted.

"I'm Oskar with a K. I also work for the company, but I have no true title or rank. I am basically a clerk." He said.

Elio bowed. "I am pleased to make your acquaintance. Oskar with a K." Elio greeted him back.

Tristan laughed. "You don't have to say with a K in your greeting. You don't spell in your speech." He explained.

Elio updated his entry on Oskar. "Since he made it a point to tell me that, I thought it was relevant. My apologies for any slight I may have caused." Elio said apologetically.

Oskar could not have been offended at all. He was staring at Elio, mesmerized by him and what he represents. "You are responsive, empathetic and logical. Fabulous." He commented.

Emma stepped up to the table. "Elio is all of those things and more. He is a guardian, a repair specialist and an observer of human behavior. He is... special." She concluded.

Oskar shook his head. "I could speak with you all day, but we have business here, don't we?" he pressed.

Elio bowed slightly and then backed up to take in the entire table once more. "If you are prepared to consider my council on this mission and not take me away as property, then I believe it is time to remove your bonds." He said.

As Emma went around cutting the ties and freeing their guests, Captain Steelwater addressed Elio. "What can you tell us about the planet below and about the dangers there?" he asked, rubbing his wrists where the ties had been.

Elio tilted his head at the cone once more. The display was of the layout of the Treshnik base down on the planet. Parts of it had been recently updated so it was hyper accurate.

What we found down there was this base. There are traps on most of the doors and some floors are rigged. Some can be detected by radio frequency transmitters. Others are merely mechanical. Almost all of the traps are deadly. I led our team through them without setting any off, But I had to disable a couple of them personally to ensure this." Elio explained.

"However, we have recovered all of the artifacts of manageable size and the instructions on what they do and how to use them." Elio announced with pride. "Our team managed to get the pieces out by getting permission to take them from the automated sentry that guards the base." He said. "It is the same AI entity that asked us to come and help defend this planet." Elio explained.

"The one you showed us earlier." Oskar spoke up.

"Yes." Elio confirmed. "Aeolia asked us to stop you from landing since you were already disabling storms on the surface." Elio showed the planet and some of the storms had already been reset and were spinning again.

"The planet defenses are returning?" Steelwater asked.

"Yes, the automated system is adjusting to your interference and has rerouted some of the signals that were lost." Elio explained. "All they wanted from us was time." He added.

"Then your delay has cost us something. We have lost the element of surprise completely." The captain concluded.

"It is true that I have been involved in delaying you. But the intention was not to delay, but to dissuade. You are not to go down to the planet. We will share everything we have gained with you. This makes the trip down and the possible loss of life not worth the risk." Elio concluded.

Tristan sighed. "The purpose of my visit out here was to see if you missed anything on the planet. The simple fact that you have recovered not one, but two ancient databases makes your ship a bit of an anomaly. Nobody is that lucky. I hoped to gain profits for myself and my companion here." He indicated Oskar. "Now it seems that you have scooped up everything and are offering me a peace settlement to just go away." He said.

Captain Harris smiled. "Not at All. We are all part of the same company. You have made the effort to come all the way out here and should get something to help recoup your costs." He nodded towards Captain Steelwater. "But the planet is not safe to visit. We have promised to make it so that others do not land here." He said at last.

"Promised? Promised who?" Steelwater asked.

Captain Harris nodded. "It was Aeolia, she appeared right on this ship in my personal quarters. I don't know how she did that especially since she has been dead for centuries, but the fact doesn't change. This planet is quarantined. We have yet to transmit the form and even that will take weeks to accomplish. But the fact remains that it is so." He declared. "To be honest, we had no idea you were coming, or we would have told you not to waste the fuel." He added to Tristan.

It was supposed to be a covert mission. You weren't supposed to know. I had no idea that you were still so close to the planet and that you would return to defend it. I also had no idea that you had managed to strike a deal with the local automated system. All of this sounds peculiar, to be sure, but also fascinating."

Tristan replied, then he indicated Elio. "How much of this archeological miracle was his doing?" He asked.

"Contact with Aeolia was pretty much everyone but him in the beginning. However, since he had been on this planet before, he had a history here. We have yet to determine how much of an advantage that gave the team." Captain Harris admitted.

"Tons." Emma blurted out. "He led us around traps that only he could detect. He negotiated with the system and led us to the artifacts that were hidden in a cabinet. Then he brought the alien database back inside his own memory. He has since filtered out the illegal information and deposited it in a backup unit." Emma reported.

Tristan's eyes lit up. "Can I have that unit?" he asked.

Captain Harris stood up. "Corporate already has one of those. They came aboard and confiscated it. We can have Elio construct you another one if you need it that badly, but you will have to deal with him over how long that will take, or how much it will cost." He informed them.

Tristan looked confused once more. "Isn't it company property?" He asked.

Emma shrugged. "Why? Elio made it from scratch given raw materials we had on hand. He will begin purchasing his own material as soon as we reach a port. The design was his. The database was also his. We do not hold claim on your memories, do we?" She asked in challenge.

Tristan made a "humph" sound. "I am not a robot. My memories cannot simply be copied into a computer." He replied with an air of superiority.

"If your memories could be transferred, would the company own them?" Emma pressed.

"Well, no. My thoughts are mine." Tristan responded.

"Then how is this different for Elio? His thoughts are his own. He works hard to make sure we have what we need, and we work hard to see that his needs are met. This discussion is a very real part of that support." Emma declared.

"You… you sympathize with a piece of hardware over your flesh and blood workers?" Tristan asked.

Emma put her hands flat on the table in front of Tristan. "I side with my crew over you corporate types. At least he has my back if things go wrongly. If we become a liability to you, we might be cut loose to preserve your bottom line. Given that perspective, who is more human?" She asked.

Tristan was about to launch into a tirade. Captain Steelwater cut him off. "We are getting a bit hot here. I don't think either of you means to personally attack one another, but it is also obvious that the notion of a robot of such value having a status that is at best tenuous is creating undue friction. I suggest that we cool off and consider the facts in this case." He suggested.

Captain Harris stood up. "I agree, partially, with our esteemed guest here. Cooler heads must prevail. But on the countenance of Elio's status. I am not relinquishing him as a crewmember. He is secured as a permanent part of my crew. His rights are assured by the Liabol accords, and I will hear no more argument over that particular subject." He said. His eyes bore into Tristan. "Am I clear?" He asked directly.

"Yes sir." Tristan replied. He was not fuming mad, but he was not happy either. He would see this in court. He secretly vowed that to himself.

Captain Harris turned back to the matter at hand. "Anyway, what we have gathered from the Treshnik base is quite substantial." He said. He pulled up the relevant information on the screen and the entire group watched as he scrolled through burial rituals, social gatherings, technical briefings and more all done in the Treshnik gesture language.

"This is great and all, but what about the artifacts?" Tristan pressed. "You said you had some and that you knew how they worked." He pressed.

Emma stepped forward. "Oh, we do. But some of the devices could be dangerous if used in space. I think we'd be better off with a technical description of each artifact instead of handing you over something that could accidentally kill everyone on board." She explained.

"If you have something that dangerous, it should be classified as a weapon and destroyed." Captain Steelwater commented.

Emma directed her reply to him specifically. "If the artifact in question were designed as a damaging thing, I would heartily agree with you. But what if the device has an innocuous purpose that happens to only be a problem in space?" she asked.

Steelwater thought on that for a moment. "Do you have an example of this?" He asked.

Emma smiled. "Of course. We have this device here…" She said. The screen changed to show a small block with an activation stud on it. "The directions for this device state that if you press the button, the unit expands to make a full-blown shelter. If we did that in a small compartment, it might damage the ship and rip a wall of it off. At the very least it would crush anybody in that same room with it, including whoever pressed the button." She explained. "Yet this device is considered a non-weapon because making an emergency shelter does not constitute a threatening or damaging situation unless it is used in the wrong place." She concluded.

"I see." Steelwater replied. "I see your point as well. Okay, a listing of the item descriptions and purposes would be sufficient for me." He said, making the required concession.

Emma smiled, but Elio was not happy. "Honestly, you are not from the company. You are a contractor for the company, but Tristan and Oskar are the only company employees here other than this crew. We are letting you see this information as a courtesy. You have no say over what is offered or what is taken away from here." He declared.

That Ruffled Captain Steelwater's feathers terribly.

"I don't have to sit here and take this from you." He replied to the small robot.

Captain Harris smiled warmly. "That is true. You can simply get up and take the docking slip back to your ship and await your passenger's return." He said calmly. "However, Elio is correct on this point. You are not a direct employee and as such, your access to this information is limited at best." He said, solidifying the stance.

"I... see." Steelwater replied. "So, this financial torrent you have found is company owned?" He asked.

Captain Harris nodded. "We are employees of the company so anything we find must be property of the company. It is a part of our orders and our charter." He replied honestly.

"In that case, I think I will go back to my ship then." He turned to Tristan. "Don't take too long here, I have a contract to take you home and I need to get back to begin another contract to keep the engines burning and my people fed." He said gruffly. Then he left without another word.

Tristan watched him go and when he was certain the good captain was out of earshot he commented. "I understand his position, but you are correct on this." He told Elio in particular.

Captain Harris smiled a bit more warmly, this time not forced. "I am glad that you understand. However, we are down to negotiating how much you need to save face with the company for coming out here. I am happy enough to return with all the artifacts. But the bounty that we have found can easily be shared with you. Half of it is a large amount and probably too much for you alone going into danger. Let me start by offering you four artifacts. They will be complete with the directions for their use." He offered.

"It is certainly food for thought. I could get patents and…" Tristan began.

"This is not an invention; it is an archeological find." Oskar reminded him.

Tristan turned to him, fire in his eyes. "Don't you dare tell me how the company works. I am important you know." He shot back. "The more profit that I can get from this, the better." He added to solidify his claim.

"This is about benefiting everybody." Elio countered. "Anybody can profit from something, but how can everybody profit from it?" He asked.

Tristan almost left his seat. "I don't care how the lowlifes get theirs. I am in this for me." He pressed.

Captain Harris interrupted. "But what about the company?" He asked, setting the trap.

Tristan was in a tizzy though. "Damn to the company, they don't pay me enough for all I do for them. I need a bunch of these so that I can build my own empire. I'll be rich and famous for inventing these things." He declared.

Captain Harris stood up and moved with purpose. "I'm afraid that you are under arrest." He said.

Tristan just stared at the incredulity of it. "You can't do that; I outrank you by quite a bit." He replied smugly.

Captain Harris did not budge. "According to the company contract that every employee signed, you are in violation by putting your own needs ahead of the company's. You are suggesting theft of company property in order to personally profit. You have broken the law." He said plainly.

"But you stole that robot. You offered up the database in a backup unit instead." Tristan argued.

The artifacts are not self-aware. Elio is. We gave the company the valuable database we found. Actually, they came and took it. But they will not like what you just said." Captain Harris told him.

Tristan smiled. "Show's what you know. There's nobody that can make your charges stick. I haven't taken anything, yet. All you have is supposition and here say." He replied with satisfaction.

Captain Harris crossed his arms. "You forget one little thing... Elio is a surveillance robot. Everything you have said has been recorded. We have enough evidence to hold you and to drop you off at the nearest court for processing." He said adamantly.

Tristan's confidence evaporated and his face turned scared. "You can't!" He stammered.

"I have no choice. I have to follow the laws as someone who signed my contract." Captain Harris replied. He turned to his people once more. "Have him locked up down below." He said and two crewmen carried off Tristan, kicking and screaming.

Captain Harris was not done though. "Please open a channel to captain Steelwater please." He commanded.

Elio tuned his antenna and tilted his head a bit to indicate his readiness.

"Captain Steelwater, this is Captain Harris." He began.

"Yes Captain." Steelwater replied.

"I have arrested Tristan for trying to steal from the company. I understand that you have contract obligations to take him back to home world. Would you care to take him back under guard? His contract is still valid, and you will still be paid, but he will not be a free man." Captain Harris explained. "Plus, Oskar will be coming home with four artifacts to secure his position within the company. So, you will be doing both of us a favor and maybe, just maybe, get a little satisfaction on that return trip." He suggested.

Captain Steelwater smiled. "I think your suggestion holds merit. I will meet you with my crewmates at the airlock. I would like to extend my thanks to you and your crew for dealing with us fairly and understanding our contract as well as the legalities involved." He replied.

"You message is received and understood. It is our pleasure to serve and to aid whenever possible." Captain Harris replied. He turned to his people. "Make sure that trash gets to the airlock. He needs to stand trial." He said and the communications link was still open. Captain Steelwater's smile grew.

"How long until we can expect Oskar to return? We would like to get underway as soon as possible." Steelwater asked.

Captain Harris looked at Oskar. "We'll send him along fairly soon. We have a schedule to keep as well. It has been a pleasure doing business with you sir." Captain Harris finalized.

Steelwater almost laughed. "The pleasure is all ours, sincerely." He said and they both cut the communications line.

Elio lifted himself up and moved away from his display location. He moved towards Oskar. "I understand that we have put you in a difficult spot, My apologies for that. The artifacts we are providing you should smooth much over for the company. Please accept our apologies for the ugliness that transpired here." He said.

Oskar shook his head. "He was not a good person. He forced me into this mission, but once here, I was happy. Thank you for the great gifts. I shall return home to present them to my superiors, whoever they are now. But I expect to be back in space soon." He declared.

"Very well, good luck in your endeavors then." Elio concluded.

Captain Harris shook Oskar's hand. "Welcome to your new life outside the world of real gravity." He said. I look forward to seeing you around the galaxy." He said.

Oskar smiled back, shaking vigorously. "It's a big sky out there, who knows what the future holds? Thank you for understanding." He replied.

Emma handed him the package they had already made up with four artifacts and the memory chip with the instructions that applied to them. "This should help in your new life." She said. "Stay true to yourself and the company and you will go far." She told him. Oskar took the package and cradled it like he was protecting a baby.

"Thank you, thank you all." He said and he headed for the airlock.

Once he was gone and could no longer hear them, Elio commented.

"I am glad that we were able to remove one so greedy and replace him with one so open-minded and grateful." He said.

Captain Harris shook his head. "Amen to that. Corporate greed has always been a problem. Hopefully this one will be all right. He's already seen what happens when things get out of control. I just hope he learned that lesson well enough to avoid the same problem. He will get rich off of those artifacts. The commission alone would pay him for quite a while." He remarked.

"Commission? You mean we'll get a commission for all the other artifacts." Emma asked.

"Of course. But we always take the operating costs out first. Where do you think the bonuses come from?" he asked.

"Oh, I get it now." Emma replied, a bit sheepishly. "I'd better get down to that database once more." She said, making an excuse to get out of the conference room. Elio followed behind her like a sheepdog and the whole thing made Captain Harris laugh.

"Those two were meant to be together." He remarked. Then he moved to the terminal to make his log entry while things were fresh in his mind. He had definitely had a busy day and the corporate headquarters would want to know why he had arrested one of their own. He considered all of that and changed his mind. He would go to his quarters to record that log. He didn't want prying ears or eyes witnessing what he had to say. Plus, he didn't know how many tries it would take until it sounded right. He sighed and left the conference room to head to his own quarters.

"Oh, to be a researcher again." He muttered to himself. The captain's life had become way more logistical than he preferred.

***

The Long trip Home…

Tristan was bound and gagged, hanging on the wall of the craft he had commissioned to take him out here in the first place. It was the worst indignity that he had ever faced. Well, it had been until Oskar came back aboard with the valuable package of artifacts that would cement his position within the company. His bonus alone would probably pay for the trip. The worst of it wasn't even that the crew ignored him, it was that Captain Steelwater didn't. He passed by periodically and sneered at him. The ship was already underway, working its acceleration curve back towards home. Home didn't offer him release either. The charges against him were serious. He wondered if he could beat the transmission with all the evidence against him home, but he doubted it. He wondered how and why this trip had gone so badly. He wanted to break free and throttle these lower-class miscreants for their interference in his career and his very life, but try as he might, the bonds were secure. All he could do was hang there. The gravity was off to save power. Apparently, this ship was in a hurry to return. The very stars seemed to blur as they gained speed.

Oskar was not currently in the main room. He had sequestered himself away to get acquainted with the data he carried. He had read the capabilities of the first device was about to pull the second one when a chime at the door made him pause.

"Excuse me, can I come in?" It was Captain Steelwater.

"Of course, sir." Oskar replied. He turned off the display so that no company information would be leaked. Then he turned to the captain.

"I am happy for you and your find." He began. "My concern is about our payment. The company credits that were used were authorized by Tristan. If he declines the charge, we are out the entire trip." He said. His eyes were serious. "I cannot afford that." He declared.

Oskar shook his head. "I would not allow that." He said. "I do not know yet who my new supervisor will be, but the fact that this mission was successful should allow me to gain the attention of someone important. I will ensure that your marker is paid in full." He pledged.

Captain Steelwater looked somewhat relieved, but he was not finished. "I thank you for that. It is a concern for the whole crew you know. But the other thing I wanted to mention is the financial windfall you seem to have garnered." He said and Oskar suddenly looked suspicious.

"I don't even know what they will think this is worth yet." Oskar replied honestly. "I hope it's a lot though." He added.

The captain sighed. "It is customary for a percentage to be offered as a bonus for a successful mission like this. There was not one in the contract, so you are not obligated to do this, but if not, it will harm your reputation." He informed the new spacer.

Oskar suddenly looked nervous. "I… I don't really know about such things. I don't want to cheat anybody, especially you. You have shown me so much on my first mission." He said almost gushing. "But I honestly do not know what is customary or considered polite. If you will allow me to contact my home when we arrive, I will address this properly. It would also help once these items are tagged with a value. Give me your account information and your contact information and I will do my best to make sure that you are properly informed and compensated." Oskar said.

Captain Harris turned away. "You know, you are nothing like Tristan. I hope you do well with your company and that you consider us when you need to travel again." He said hospitably.

"Thank you, Captain." Oskar replied and the captain left the small compartment.

Oskar had a lot to consider. How much was his find worth? How much should he consider a legitimate fee or bonus? Would the company cover a bonus fee? Would he get the proper credit for this find? Could he find more work in space? All he had were questions. He wanted some answers, but the questions should not go out in unprotected transmissions. He would have to wait until they got home. He shrugged and flipped the display back on to continue his study. He needed to be ready to present these items when he got back, of that he was absolutely sure.

***

Emma sat in her most comfortable chair in the lab, watching the display as the backup device showed her more of the Treshnik history. It was all fascinating and she was beginning to notice certain gestures for certain circumstances. Elio supplied subtitles when asked so she was slowly learning their ancient language. It felt like she was becoming a part of that history. It felt so immersive it made her sort of giddy.

"Elio, do you have anything more from this individual?" She asked. She had decided to follow certain people around to get a feel for how they lived and how they communicated. It was working remarkably well.

"Of course, I do." He said. "There are another one hundred and forty-nine files on that individual alone." Elio replied. "Playing the next one in order of occurrence." He announced and the projector lit up once more.

Emma settled in to enjoy another round. She sipped on her coffee as the video played.

* * *

ELIO[2]

Captain Harris was filling in forms, filing reports and building his case against Tristan. He knew that there would be an enquiry over this, and he wanted to have all of his facts straight. He had Elio's video in his personal information tablet. So, he could go back and review exactly what was said and what had happened. The actual arrest forms were simple. The corporate forms about internal strife were much more complex. He had to explain how Tristan had violated company policy and/or interstellar law. He had to produce witnesses and evidence to support his claims or Tristan would walk. It was also possible that Tristan would bring witnesses. Most likely they would be paid to say what he needed. He had corporate ties and most likely a lot of clout. He was an officer in the company after all. But his crime was against the company. He intended to steal. It was possible that the entire trip out here had been for this purpose. The company had foot the bill for that too. That was embezzlement of a sort and corporations took that particular crime seriously. He wasn't stealing money though, but he was stealing profits to be sure. He had admitted to it and the recording would be invaluable to water-tight the prosecution. Captain Harris hated the position he was in. He wanted to be down in the lab going over the procured information. He wanted to be studying and researching old things that had become new. He wanted... it no longer mattered what he wanted. He was a company man and the mantle of responsibility rested squarely upon his shoulders.

He double-checked all the documents for spelling, completeness and content. It took quite some time and by the time he was done, his eyes and back were sore. He rubbed his eyes and decided to check the documents one more time after some rest to make sure that nothing was left to chance.

The bunk was calling to him. He really wanted to get this sent off right away though. He tapped the communication device. "Elio, can you come to my quarters please?" he asked.

"Right away captain." Elio's response was clear. The robot probably never slept. He suddenly wondered if Elio dreamed. Anyway, his help was on its way.

Elio hit the chime button moments later and Captain Harris tapped the allow button. The door slid into the wall, and Elio entered the captain's quarters.

"How may I be of service?" Elio asked.

"I need you to proofread these forms before I send them off to corporate." He replied.

Elio moved towards the terminal. "At once, sir." He replied and he began reading. The computer that was Elio could read unnaturally fast. As captain Harris sat on the bed and then allowed himself to lay down, Elio had the work done.

"Sir, I've made only two corrections and they were small things." He reported.

"Fine, I'll transmit them as soon as I can." He replied, still getting comfortable in his bunk.

"I can send them now if you wish." Elio volunteered.

"Go ahead. I need some sleep." Sean replied.

Elio did as he was instructed and transmitted the entire packet to corporate. Although he was unaware of it, there was now a race between this data, and Tristan getting back to corporate as a prisoner. This race was going to be close.

Elio left the captain's quarters and turned out the light. He was pleased that his crewmates had his back when the corporate officer tried to take away Elio's status. He was pleased with their willingness to put things right rather than simply following orders. It only stood as a testament to how lucky he was to have been found by this ship and its crew. He made his way back to the lab and considered the matter of the report, closed.

* * *

ELIO[2]

Emma found most of the Treshnik data to be boring stuff. There were work schedules, daily logs, accounting records, interoffice memos. The kind of thing that is generated every day by any sophisticated race. It was so mundane and boring that she was having trouble trying to stay awake. Elio entered the lab, and she noted his presence only barely.

"Are you alright?" Elio asked.

"Yeah, just tired." Emma replied. "I have been looking at these files for the better part of…" She looked at the chronometer. "…six hours. I'm beat." She reported.

Elio noted this and remarked. "That seems to be a common problem among the crew just now." He noted.

Emma slid off the chair and strolled by him with a wavering gait. "What do you expect? We are just human after all." She commented.

Elio moved to his corner, ready to connect up and get back to work. Emma left the lab and Elio remarked. "So I've noticed, so I've noticed." He said softly to himself.

The Treshnik data was compelling to be sure, but he could view it at any time. What Elio was interested in at this time were the legal proceedings that Tristan would undergo upon his return home. The wording of the forms he had proofread had been precise, almost to the point of panic. From what he had read, Captain Harris expected Tristan to get off the hook and go free. His admission would mean nothing if enough legal trickery were employed on his behalf. But would that make a difference? They had recorded a confession. They had witnessed him and his tirade claiming that he wanted to steal from the company. It should be cut and dried. But the rich and powerful rarely played by the rules of their lessers. Elio began searching for cases in which people managed to get out of their predicaments.

After a couple of hours of extensive searching, the most common ground upon which to overturn the potential decision of the court was based upon having the evidence of the case thrown out. Elio's recording was admissible unless they found some sort of precedent where it could be dismissed. If they dismissed that key piece of evidence, it was possible that Tristan would walk because it became a case of here say. The witnesses were three to one, but would that be enough to convict? The additional problem is that some of those witnesses would not be present in court. Would their absence constitute their testimony being ignored? The idea of this was frightening. Elio felt that this was important. He couldn't just let this happen. He had to tell somebody to be ready. It was quite possible that captain Harris and Emma would need to testify personally to keep this together. Of course, Elio might be summoned as well, but that didn't bother him at all. He was looking at a worst-case scenario, but it could all go down that way.

Elio began making notes. He placed his testimony in a packet along with a copy of the recording. He placed Emma's words in her own packet. She could sign it electronically later. He placed all of the things that Oskar had spoken into a packet of his own. This would help him to remember everything and ensured that nothing was left to chance. Finally, He placed all of captain Harris, and Captain Steelwater's statements in a final packet. With these packets, they could recreate the entire event that had forced Tristan's arrest. If that didn't convince a judge, or even a jury if one was called, then nothing would.

Then Elio zipped the packets together with an encoded and encrypted lock and sent them off to corporate to be an addendum to the original forms he had already sent. Finally, Elio set back to tagging and classifying the new Treshnik data. In his electronic mind, this was all that he could do.

* * *

Captain Steelwater considered his plans. The contract he was about to complete would keep his crew happy for about a month. The potential bonus from Oskar would only bolster that number when it happened. He had no doubt that the young man was of good character and had not yet succumbed to corporate greed. But his current plan required him to get back as quickly as possible. He had laid in the course and set their maximum speed for the journey. The fuel cost was higher than it should have been, but when speed is of the essence...

"Sir, we are nearing glide mode." His crewman told him. He looked up from his musings.

"Good, then we can stop burning our precious fuel." He replied.

"Yes sir, at least until it is time to slow down again." They reminded him.

"How are our reserves?" The captain asked.

"We are good, but we will need a full refuel before we go out again. We are burning at least fifteen percent more than we contracted for." The crewman replied.

Captain Steelwater winced. "Fifteen huh? Well, it couldn't be helped. This prisoner needs to be brought to justice." He declared.

Oskar could not help but overhear the conversation since most of this ship was a single room. "Are we traveling faster than light?" he asked.

Captain Steelwater looked over at him. "At top speed, we are very close to the speed of light, why?"

"The transmission of Tristan's arrest travels at the speed of light through space from node to node to be repeated. We should allow that transmission to hit the corporate home office before we arrive to ensure that they are aware of Tristan's arrest." He suggested.

The crewman and Captain Steelwater looked at each other and then back to Oskar.

"This is your first cruise?" Steelwater asked.

"Yes sir." Oskar replied.

"You seem to grasp things out here very well." He commented. He turned back to the crewman. "Reverse our course and give me a four-minute burn, slow us down." He ordered.

ELIO[2]

"Yes sir!" The crewman replied and moved quickly to alert the others as to the decision that caused the change in plans." In moments the ship was spinning around one hundred and eighty degrees. Then the engines fired up again. The arrival time was slipping away now. A few seconds or minutes of burn could mean days on the end of the voyage. The crew worked with watch-like efficiency. In moments, the burn was over, and they were drifting backwards through space. They did not waste the maneuvering jets to turn it around since they were still on the correct course. Instead, they settled into their regular stations and the monitoring that went with that.

Captain Steelwater leaned over to Oskar. "If your company doesn't allow you to venture out into space again, we'd take you on as crew. You need training, no doubt. But your natural aptitude and your clear thinking under pressure are something that can't be taught. You'd be a good crewmember." He concluded.

"Thank you, captain. I appreciate that. But I am a company man. I believe that they'll realize that I have greater value out here than sitting at a desk. I do have the artifacts to show them, and I would have none of that if it weren't for you and your crew. So, thank you." He concluded back.

"I admire your loyalty. The offer stands though. If things don't work out down there, you have an option." He repeated.

Oskar smiled. "Thank you very much sir." He replied. The captain left him alone after that. He did manage to flash Tristan an angry look though.

"You didn't know what you had, did you?" He asked, knowing full well that the bound and gagged man could not answer. "Well, now you'll have nothing." He added and walked away leaving Tristan angrier than he had ever felt.

The prisoner's forehead was turning red with his anxiety. He wanted to kill these upstarts. He wanted to exact his revenge on that Captain Harris. That man had been the reason he had taken on this mission in the first place. He doubted the man had given everything to the company. Now that he saw Elio, he believed it to be true. The robot being a person? Preposterous! As soon as he could speak again, he would tell everybody that the little robot exists. Then, he would find people that thought the way he did. There would be no court in the universe that would convict him then. He continued thinking on this. He worked his mind into a comfortable rut where he came out on top. The problem with that kind of thinking is that you disregarded things that could play against you. Tristan was falling for that completely. In his mind, there was no way he could lose. It simply wasn't possible. He would be the savior of the company and he would gloat over that little robot as it was taken apart and duplicated. It was a certainty that he could be reproduced since he had been produced in the first place. Yes, he would be on the ground floor of a new product line. Have your own thinking robot. He would be rich beyond his dreams.

His anger subsided somewhat as he envisioned his glorious future. The only problem with that future, is that it did not reflect reality in the slightest. But that didn't stop him from living in it now. As soon as he got off this blasted wall… He looked around once more. …things will be different. He concluded his thought.

The images of glory and him coming out on top kept him busy for the next few hours as the ship simply drifted back home. He let the time pass without complaining. He had messed his outfit, but the suit was processing it as it was designed. He didn't need these people anymore. He would be free once they hit port. On the ground his power would be reinstated, and he would see them all suffer. He savored the thought. Nothing could stop him. He was a corporate star, an officer and a powerful man. Nothing these miscreants could do could ever touch him. He was better than all of them.

***

The communications office at Regency Legacies was slammed with communications today. But the system sorted them by the urgency tab marked on each message. One of them stood out from the rest by having a red mark on it that suggested the highest urgency available. That message was forwarded to an office where a team of people opened hot mail for processing and sorting.

Loren Tilman looked at her screen. There was little doubt that this message, like all the others before it, were either improperly marked urgent or were being blown out of proportions. She tapped the accept button and the message popped up on her screen in its entirety. She read it and found that attached were official forms for arrest and discipline of corporate entities. This was not her run-of-the-mill case. She flagged the criminal case to the authorities and the corporate part to internal affairs. The two groups should be able to handle this matter. Just as she was about to shut it down, a second message struck that was referenced to the first one. It was more attachments. A full case had been filed. The evidence was right here. Loren attached this message to the first and sent it to the same two entities. Then, as is usually the case with administrative personnel, she forgot about the whole thing.

✳ ✳ ✳

Cases fall from the skies…

It was rare for a criminal case to be reported from space. Most times spacers took care of their own. The judicial system took time and through legal trickery, sometimes offenders managed to find technicalities to get free. Dumping someone out an airlock was a lot more certain, if legally frowned upon. Nobody was ever left to complain though. So most reports were simply in a ship's log. This was different. There was a captain's report, an arrest, a recording of the event where the crime was admitted too, and even follow up files with further information. This case was almost open and shut. But that didn't mean that due process would not be followed.

"We've got an interesting one here." Detective Dominic Allen looked at the files that were attached to this interesting message. "This should be an easy one for us." He commented.

"Nothing is ever that easy." His supervisor commented back. "When it looks too easy, then the truth is usually hidden under layers of alibi's and…"

Dominic cut him off. "Not this time, they actually have a video recording of a confession." He said, as the file played before him.

"Really?" Jared Hewitt moved over to look at the same screen. "Wait a minute, I know that guy." Jared replied, a bit shocked. "He works for…" He searched his memory. "One of those archeological historical places." He concluded, failing to find the name in his mind.

"He works for Regency Legacies." Dominic filled in.

"Yes, that's the one. He's a real… well he's not a nice person." Jared commented.

"Well, according to this, he's also a greedy SOB, admitted to wanting to steal from the company." He said. The file had just finished playing and sure enough, the suspect had indeed told them all of his intentions to profit from the company's assets.

ELIO[2]

"I knew that most corporate types were greedy. But criminally so? Most have the sense not to admit it though. It can get them in hot water if they have loose lips." Jared continued.

"Well, this one was foolish enough to lay out his own aspirations and they do criminalize him." Dominic pointed out.

Jared considered the message and sighed. "Start the paperwork. We'll need a warrant for this guy and these charges will have to be checked out by a judge to see if the correct precedents have been cited." He said.

"You got it boss." Dominic replied and his hands were busily tapping keys and filling out forms. He made no other sounds, but in his mind, he admitted to himself that this day had just gotten more interesting.

***

Captain Steelwater eyed the display as his ship entered communication range with planetary traffic control. He had expected to be signaled as soon as his blip appeared on their radar, but that had not been the case. He suddenly worried that the transmission reporting Tristan's arrest had not yet reached home office. If that was so, it was possible that Tristan could slip away, or worse, be released for lack of charges.

"Just sit tight, we're in the queue to land." He told Tristan. "Now we find out if you are lucky or not." He commented and Tristan, still bound and gagged could not respond.

"Sir, we are being hailed." His communication's crewperson spoke up.

Steelwater felt a lot of tension fall off of his shoulders. "About time, patch me through." He ordered.

"Verification required: Do you have possession of Tristan Bennet?" the message was very short and lacked pleasantries.

"Affirmative, the prisoner, Tristan Bennet, is on board." Steelwater replied simply.

"Message received and confirmed. Please proceed to security dock forty-seven on Dock L. The prisoner will be removed from your craft. Inform your crew not to intervene." The message was just as troubling as the first one had been.

"This doesn't sound protocol to me." Steelwater replied. "I think something is up." He added. The tension he had lost before had returned with a notable increase.

The communications crewmember whistled. "Sir, we've got big trouble coming our way." They said.

"What do we have?" Steelwater asked apprehensively.

"Two escorts are coming out to ensure our compliance." There was a pause as buttons were pressed. "Their transponders do not show law enforcement."

Steelwater knew that he was in deep here. He glanced back at Tristan. "I think you had better start explaining." He said and he moved over to remove the gag.

Tristan coughed a few times and tried to work his jaw. "Release me!" He shouted.

"You have one chance to keep this out and that is to explain what those two ships are doing coming out to meet us." He said. His tone was that of a razorblade, sharp and brilliant.

"I... I don't know. I couldn't call for anybody to come. I've been strapped to your wall the entire time." Tristan whined.

"Yes, I know. But what is company policy around corporate big wigs being arrested?" Steelwater asked.

"I..." He began and then didn't speak. "They may be coming to assassinate me to keep this out of the press." He offered.

"They wouldn't assassinate just you if they decided to board us." Steelwater reasoned.

Tristan lowered his head. "No." He confirmed.

"We need to flee to save all our lives." He countered.

"No, we need to get to the real justice." Steelwater replied. "Contact traffic control again and report the two bogeys coming in at us." He told his communication crewperson. "Also, give a broadcast warning about approaching pirates." He ordered.

"Sir? We haven't identified them as pirates." The crewman protested.

"No, but if they aren't pirates, they will consider backing off to prove it." Steelwater suggested. "If they still come in hard, then we will have verified our suspicions." He said with a grin. The grin was for his crew. Inside he was all tied up in knots. His people could fight if it came to that, but they were a small ship with a small crew. Either of the incoming crews could probably overpower his people.

The broadcast went out and the response was something neither of them expected...

"We are Regency Legacy vessels enroute to recover our corporate officer. You are to power down and prepare to be boarded."

Steelwater felt a lump in his throat. "It's worse than I thought. These are pirates of a different kind. They are well-funded and believe in their total superiority." He said. He looked hard at Tristan. "You have suddenly become more trouble than you are worth." He said and his tone was ominous.

"Set me free!" Tristan shouted. Steelwater hit him in the gut, hard. The air escaped from his lungs. He couldn't even bend over to help recover.

"I will give you one chance to come clean. Call off your goons and tell them you accept your fate, or I will shoot you here." Steelwater said. He pulled a small hand weapon and pointed it at the helpless man trying to take a badly needed breath.

Tristan made the gesture of not being able to talk by moving his mouth wordlessly. Steelwater moved fast, he pressed a bladder into Tristan's mouth and pumped air down into the man's lungs.

"You are a weak one." He said. "Pitiful." He added as he pulled the bladder back and Tristan actually began to recover. "You have about twelve seconds to call them off or that is the end for you." He informed his prisoner.

Tristan was trembling and sweating. He was still having trouble catching his breath, but now the pain in his gut was gone. "I don't…" He began.

Steelwater cocked his weapon. "Time's running really short for you." He said.

"Do not come for me! I'm guilty!" Tristan bellowed as best he could.

His words were broadcast into the sector by the communications crewmember. The two ships coming in suddenly changed direction. They were arcing back to the planet. Tristan tried his best to recover now that Steelwater's gun was out of his face. He had never been so scared in all his life. The man was ruthless.

"Good enough." He said. Then to his crew. "Get us into the correct dock, now." He said.

The rest of the flight was uneventful. The ship landed and the support structure was put in place to maintain its upright position. Then the feed lines connected for refueling and resupplying the ship as was standard. It was Steelwater, himself that opened the hatch. To his relief there were two security guards there to take his prisoner.

"You got him to admit his guilt before even landing? How did you do that?" A slippery looking suited man asked. he was most probably a lawyer.

"You can't use that broadcast as evidence, he spoke under duress. I needed the escorts to back off to bring this fugitive to justice." Steelwater explained.

"I see. It is a shame, it was so condemning too." He replied.

"Just look at the evidence we have already submitted on him; you won't need that transmission." The captain informed him.

The two guards read Tristan his rights and then escorted him to his holding cell. For Captain Steelwater and crew that represented the end of their involvement. All that remained was if they received a bonus from Oskar. The young corporate man disembarked with his package tucked under his arm. He nodded to the captain as he made his way back to work. They exchanged meaningful eye contact about promises and contracts.

Steelwater turned back to his ship. "Let the crew get a little R & R while we get the ship ready to go again. I expect we'll get a contract real soon." He informed them. "Be back by morning." He added to give it all a time frame.

He looked at his ship from the outside, it was still a fine craft and it looked fast even when it was stationary. He then climbed back aboard to finish up his paperwork and to pay his dock fees. He was also due a contract payment from the corporation. Financially, this was a busy day.

* * *

Oskar made his way back to the office. He had already provided a message informing his people of the tremendous find. He was excited about what value might be presented to him over these artifacts. He fully expected to be able to forward a percentage to captain Steelwater. He also wanted to get back to space again as soon as possible. He reached his desk and the sight of it reminded him how much of a shut-in he was before. The desk represented a form of prison to him now. He couldn't be happy sitting there and not out running around the galaxy. He wondered if the company would allow him to transfer. Would he trade that for his newfound wealth? It was a tough decision. He knew that he was not the same man anymore. His eyes and mind were open now. How could he stay here at all? He moved to the far side of the desk but did not sit down.

"What's the matter? Does it no longer fit?" Someone asked behind him.

Oskar turned quickly. "It…" he was not fully sure what had changed, only that he had changed. "I don't think it's right for me anymore." He admitted.

The person before him was an auditor. The man wore a navy-blue pinstriped suit and had the demeanor of a tax collector. He was also a wondrously gifted judge of people. He smiled. "Well, from what I've seen of your record, we have been wasting your talents here at the office anyway." He commented.

This agreement took Oskar by surprise. "Do you think they'll let me transfer?" he asked.

"If they do not, it would be a mistake." The auditor replied. "But right now, I need to brief you and what to say and to whom. I assume that the package here holds the valuable artifacts that you have gathered?" he asked, indicating the case.

"Yes." Oskar's reply was simple.

"The first thing I will recommend to you is to lock that up in a very safe place. It is likely worth a fortune." He suggested.

"I will." Oskar replied like a child being called out would.

"Relax, I am here to help you. I was sent by the company to help you adjust and process your find to the proper channels. I do not yet know what you have brought back, but the concept is the same no matter what you have." He said.

"I don't even know you." Oskar replied.

The man seemed to start for a moment. "My - my, where are my manners?" He said. "I am Bruce Jensen. I am an attorney for Regency Legacies. I have been retained to ensure a smooth transition for you and for your find. There are a few interested parties for your find already and we have not even gone public with your findings yet." He informed the young man.

Oskar simply nodded.

"First point I will make is that you must reply verbally to every question in court. An electronic recording device that will be taking down every word you say. If you try to nod like that, the adjudicator will get annoyed and tell you to speak up. Do not annoy the adjudicator at any cost." He admonished.

"Sorry sir, I understand." Oskar replied.

"Much better. Now, the first question that I have for you is how many artifacts do you have?" he waited patiently for Oskar to reply.

"Four. I have four artifacts and the instructions on how they function." Oskar replied.

Bruce's eyes went wide for an instant and then he pulled himself and his face back under control. "Do you mean to say that these artifacts are functional pieces of equipment?" He asked directly.

Oskar smiled. "Indeed, they are." He said. "If you would care to stand back, I will demonstrate one of them for you." He offered. Bruce stepped back quickly. His excitement just wouldn't stay hidden, despite his years of training and control.

The office was only sparsely furnished so there were not a lot of items in the way. Oskar began moving chairs and desks against the wall. Bruce noticed the floor-clearing pattern right away and began to help clear the floor. When it was done Oskar pointed to a clear spot of wall and Bruce went to stand there as directed. Oskar pulled a small block from his pack. It was an octagonal box with a series of buttons on the top. He pressed the center button and a series of telltale lights lit up around the outside edge. Then Oskar pressed the green button, and the device began to expand. Oskar pulled away quickly and when it stopped, there was a habitat in the middle of the room.

Bruce stared at the impossible structure before him. It had been a box no larger than your hand with spread fingers. Now it was a small room. Oskar opened the door and they both went inside. The sensation and feel of moving air could be felt. Oskar closed the flapping door and turned to face Bruce.

"A capable shelter anywhere." He announced.

"It feels like air conditioning here." Bruce commented.

Oskar winked. "Oh, it's more than that. This is a controlled environment that would work in space. The temperature, the oxygen levels, everything is in balance for human consumption. It can be reconfigured to Treshnik physiology as well. Oskar informed his legal representation.

"This… this is amazing." He said. "How does it get so small?"

Oskar shook his head. "I don't know. This technology needs to be reverse engineered to find some serious answers." He declared.

"This technology could be priceless." Bruce commented.

Oskar pressed a button and two blocks rose out of the floor to sit upon. "Have a seat." He offered.

The chair gave in like a pillow might and then solidified once the sitter had settled. This made the perfect chair for whoever sat in it.

ELIO[2]

"We could get a fortune for automatic chairs too." He said. "And this is just one of your artifacts?" he pressed.

Oskar looked around at the habitat and nodded. "Yep, this is the first one. I would want to show it to the company first. It is possible that I would hold on to the rest until after this one has been processed." He said.

"That is smart. It would establish you on the scientific and archeological forums and if this technology could be adapted to everyday use, you could become a very rich man after the company made its share, of course." He said.

"Not to mention the legal fees." Oskar added and Bruce smiled.

"You do understand how things work. How did you get stuck riding a desk for so long?" He asked.

"I was content to do what I was doing. I made myself a comfortable niche and hid within it for a long time. But now I've been to the stars. I've tasted the life out there and it appeals to me greatly." He admitted.

"It does seem to suit you better than the corporate life." Bruce reflected.

"Oh, I don't mean to go off on my own. I want to work for the company, just out there instead of down here." He corrected.

"I'm sure they will be pleased to hear that." Bruce affirmed.

"Look, I'll cut you in for a percentage if you can get me what I want. I want to give the ship that brought me here a bonus, nothing overly substantial, just what would be their just due." He said.

"Really? But you've already landed, and they have no pull on you anymore." Bruce pointed out.

"My new life will be in space. Captain Steelwater treated me well and showed me what life is like out there. I owe him something. His crew were all amazing." He concluded.

Bruce shook his head. "How did someone with such manners ever head out into space in the first place?" He asked.

"I was forced, drafted if you will. It was not until we got away from this planet that I realized the life I was meant to live." He replied honestly. "With your help, I should have the money to book my own passage, or maybe have my own ship. I don't honestly know how all of that works. But if the company sponsors me, I know it will all work out." Oskar declared.

"I will help you. The more you make for this the more my percentage will amount to." He replied honestly. He looked around at the habitat they were in. "So, this thing can support life anywhere?" He asked.

Oskar shrugged. "I don't know. If we get to work on it, then I planned to test it in harsh conditions. If it keeps external wind at bay, then even the arctic would be no problem for this thing." He replied enthusiastically.

"But you don't want to stay and test it, you want to be in space." Bruce pointed out.

Oskar nodded. "Consider it a backup plan." He replied, a bit playfully. "I want to be taken seriously, and I think this device will ensure that." He said.

"Oh, I agree. I am taking you seriously already. To be honest, I've never been interested in artifacts and archeological digs, it is just what the company does. I am a rule maker and follower. I am a paperwork kind of guy. But this thing is amazing." He replied.

"Well, I don't want to leave it up long enough for somebody to find it, so let's get out of here." Oskar pressed.

The two left the habitat and closed the door. Oskar pressed the green button once more and the device shrunk back down to its stored size. It was truly a marvel of engineering. Oskar picked it up and placed it back into the pack.

"I am curious what other baubles you have in there, but I understand that you don't want that known yet." Bruce commented.

ELIO[2]

Oskar closed the case and strapped it behind his back. "I think you understand my motives on that front. I just want to be careful." He said.

"As I said, I will help you. We need you to get those locked up as soon as possible." Bruce said in agreement and support.

Oskar tilted his head slightly. "When do we meet with the adjudicator?" he asked.

Bruce flipped his pad device up and scanned the screen. "I can set up the appointment as early as tomorrow if you are ready to present." He replied professionally.

Oskar laughed. "You just witnessed my presentation, is it ready?" he asked.

"Okay, scheduling the meeting. I had better make sure it is in a big enough room to accommodate your demonstration." He added, trying to cover all the bases. When he finished the listing, he turned off his Pad device. "You know, if this blows up the way I think it will, we'll both be financially set." He admitted.

"I don't mind bringing you along for the ride. But I am concerned over how many others will try to jump on the bandwagon." Oskar replied.

Bruce turned thoughtful. "The company will want its cut and it will also hold the rights to the final product. You will be awarded a commission for this find and that is where the money will come from. The quicker the company can recoup a profit from this, the more they are apt to pay you. This device looks to be life-changing or even lifesaving for people in harsh environments. I don't think we'll have too much trouble getting a patent and even some residuals on this." He announced.

"Residuals?" Oskar asked.

"It means you get paid when the company sells more units later after they reverse engineer this thing and begin constructing their own. It could give you a steady income for life." Bruce explained.

Oskar whistled. "And there's still three more artifacts after that." He reminded his professional partner.

"I look forward to representing you for those as well if you'll have me." Bruce put forth right away.

Oskar looked into Bruce's eyes. "You get me what I need for this one and I can guarantee you'll be there for the next one." He promised.

Bruce nodded solemnly. "Good enough for me. I've seen that you take your promises seriously and I am honored to be considered a part of that." He replied. "Now, what else does this device do?" he asked.

Oskar held up the device. "Well..." They talked for over an hour on this one device.

* * *

ELIO[2]

Tristan was not having as much luck as Oskar was. He had been roughly carried across a busy promenade and then dumped unceremoniously into a holding cell. The corporate lawyer was not even there to meet him. They were letting him settle down in his confinement. He moved into the corner and looked out at the other cells with loathing hatred. He hadn't even been allowed to clean himself. The spacesuit he wore was soiled terribly by his own space-bound incarceration. The system did what it could, but there were limits. He sat there in that corner for two hours when someone finally moved towards his cell.

"We have orders to get you cleaned up." The guard said. He was holding a weapon trained upon Tristan.

"It is about time. I have been treated so unfairly by that ship captain and nobody seemed to care about it." He complained.

"This isn't about how you have been treated. You stink to high heaven, and we are getting complaints from adjacent cells." The guard said. He grabbed Tristan by the arm roughly and moved him towards a communal shower. Now strip out of that offending suit and get into the water or we will take matters into our own hands." The guard ordered.

"Right here?" Tristan asked. "But the other cells can see me here." He complained.

"Right here. If you delay, things will not go well for you." The guard warned. "Now strip!"

Tristan felt his dignity slip away as he denuded, and the foul suit showed him just how bad space could be. The guards flamed the suit right there on the shower floor and then extinguished the flames. Now Tristan had nothing to wear but he was still filthy. He began showering as ordered. Part of that was fear of the guard's reactions. But part of it was a disgust at his own condition. He had been neglected and abused. He would see them pay for this. He simply added this public indignity to the revenge he would exact later.

When Tristan finished cleaning, he was handed a towel. "Put that on and cry as we go." The guard ordered.

"Go? Go where?" Tristan asked.

The guard had no patience for him at all. The stroke of his rifle butt to the small of Tristan's back hurt more than the corporate big wig would care to admit. He wrapped the towel around himself to hide his privates and moved behind the guard. His back was sore now and walking was labored. He was still dripping from the shower.

He was brought out of the cell bay and into the open promenade. He suddenly felt very naked in the open public. "Hey! We can't just waltz around like this." He complained.

The guard leaned in. "Want to lose the towel, you're going about it the right way." He warned and Tristan clamped his mouth shut. The trio, for there were two guards, moved along at a brisk pace. The towel was flapping in the breeze of passage, but Tristan managed to hold it with an iron grip.

They entered a building and the trio stopped to allow someone to Id Tristan.

"According to his profile, it is definitely him." The person moved forward and jabbed his arm.

"Hey!" Tristan complained but the rifle hit the side of his head and Tristan found himself on the carpeted floor, his towel only loosely draped over him.

"They are just verifying your Identity." The guard explained. "Don't be such a baby."

Tristan felt groggy. He had not been expecting a blow to the head. Even if he had, he had no experience with avoiding it or even recovering from one. "I... You hit me." He managed to say.

"Well, his memory still works." The guard said jokingly.

The guard spoke to the medical person that had just verified Tristan's identity. Get him some scrubs. He cannot go before the magistrate like this." He said.

ELIO[2]

"At once, sir." The medic replied and they left and returned with a set of lightweight scrubs. "Put these on so you don't get arrested for indecent exposure." The medic told Tristan.

The guard chuckled. "That's a good one." He commented.

The guard picked up Tristan by his sleeve as soon as he was dressed. "Come on, let's go."

The door they stopped at was wooden and taller than most. It had brass door handles and brass hinges that were polished to a high degree.

"Okay, here goes." The guard said.

Tristan had no choice but to go too since he was being pushed into the room. The room was fairly dark. The carpeting on the floor was a rich burgundy and the dark mahogany chairs contrasted only marginally to it. The walls were paneled in dark woods as well. The magistrate was seated at a raised dais that overlooked the entire room effortlessly.

The guard moved Tristan to a spot on the carpet that was highly illuminated by a spotlight. He shielded his eyes from the brilliance.

"Tristan Bennet, is that your name?" The magistrate asked.

"Yes, I am Tristan Bennet." Tristan responded.

"Good. You have admitted to intent to steal from Regency Legacies. This applies to both physical and intellectual assets. The value of said assets has yet to be determined but is estimated to be quite substantial." The magistrate said, reading off of a pad device in front of him.

"I am an officer in Regency Legacies and I am entitled to a portion of the proceeds from found merchandise." Tristan countered.

The wall to Tristan's right lit up. It was the recording of Tristan himself on board captain Harris' ship. His tirade went on and the audio was damning to say the least. He fully told the camera of his intentions. The recording ended.

"Do you have a counter statement to this electronic document?" The magistrate asked. before Tristan could reply they continued. "Were you under duress when you made these statements? Were you insane for some reason when you made these statements? In other words, is there any plausible reason I shouldn't throw you in jail for attempting to steal from the company you work for?" The magistrate asked. The case was so stacked against him, Tristan felt the futility of any response.

"I... I made the statement that has been presented." He admitted.

"I was under stress, that much is obvious, but I was acting on behalf of my company. I... I let the company down." He admitted as well.

"Your admittance has been submitted. Your confession will ease your sentencing, perhaps." The magistrate told him. Tristan felt a sudden glimmer of hope. Then the magistrate began to speak once more.

"I have been tasked to inform you that you are no longer employed by Regency Legacies. The claims on physical and intellectual property that you maintain are disregarded. Your status as a free citizen is now in effect and this crime is now punishable by imprisonment." The magistrate said, reading off the pad device once more.

Tristan stared back blankly. He couldn't believe that this had gone so wrong for him. He knew that he would win. He knew that they would see things his way. He looked up at the magistrate. "What about the robot?" He asked.

The magistrate frowned. "What robot?" He asked.

"The little robot that captain Harris found and that he has given crew status to." Tristan added.

"A robot has been granted crew status?" The magistrate asked for clarity.

"Yes, they have given a robot the same rank as a human, and it even gets paid as a human." Tristan continued.

"I hope it does its job better than you do." The magistrate said. Tristan felt his mouth fall open.

ELIO[2]

"How can you say that to me?" He asked.

This packet of evidence was signed by Elio. Elio is the robot in question, is he not?" The magistrate asked.

"Yes! That's the little…" he chose not to swear in court. "That is the robot I am referring to." He finished instead.

"We have been alerted to the possibility of your protest. Honestly, I had hoped to avoid this. But now I must rule on this. After consulting the service record of Elio, I have come to a conclusion. The robot, Elio, is hereby granted citizenship in our federated space and as already awarded by his superior, is an active crewmember on captain Harris' ship, the Hiram Bingham." The magistrate stated for the record.

"Do you have anything to say about this ruling before sentencing?" The magistrate asked.

"How can you rule in favor of a machine over flesh and blood? You are not a machine. You must know that if robots all become sentient, we may find ourselves playing second fiddle to them in the future." Tristan complained.

"The argument you make is centuries old and represents a fear of new people and things. To extend your analogy, if a robot is a better person than you are, should he not be able to achieve the same goals you do? In other words, if the machine can play the fiddle better than you, it should get first chair." The magistrate concluded. "The visual records that we have been shown show that you, sir, are an abrasive and disrespectful being, incapable of thinking about others. Your empathy seems to be non-existent. On the other hand, Elio has continuously considered the thoughts and feelings of others as he conducts his business. In addition, he also does a better job at all of his assigned tasks than you do. It is this court's opinion that the little robot known as Elio is a much better human than you are."

Tristan pointed at the magistrate. His face was red, and his eyes looked as though they were on fire. "You have been corrupted by the little menace!" He shouted. "How could I get a fair ruling from someone who has already thrown in their lot with the other side?" he shouted in question.

"This court does not take kindly to being questioned on a legal or philosophical level. Your statements are very close to contempt. Refrain from this line or face being sentenced for contempt of court as well as your other charges." The magistrate warned. As angry as Tristan was, the magistrate was calm, but firm.

"But you can't!" Tristan began. The magistrate stood up quickly and pointed at Tristan. "Who are you to tell this court what it can and cannot do? I understand the duress you are under, but honestly, it is mostly self-induced. Sit down and await your sentencing or risk being in jail long enough for nobody to remember you." The magistrate warned. There was no more of his calm demeanor this time. This was the end of the line.

Tristan began to open his mouth to protest but the guard pulled his shoulder down hard and he found himself seated. He looked up with anger that was ready to burst forth.

"Shut up, I'm saving you from yourself." The guard said softly so as not to have his words taken down by the court recorder.

"I'm being railroaded. I'm going to go to jail for trying better myself." He almost whined.

"You broke the law. Then you compounded the problem. All you can do now is hope the magistrate is in a good mood for your sentencing. In order to make sure that is so, don't say another syllable, got it?" the guard said. His voice did carry enough for the others to hear, and the court recorder took it all down.

"Thank you for explaining the situation." The magistrate told the guard. The guard turned red.

"Sorry sir, I didn't mean to be so loud." He apologized.

"No, no, someone needed to tell him straight and I appreciate your efforts in this regard." The magistrate said with benevolence. "Now." Then they looked right at Tristan who was not opening his mouth. "You have a choice about sentencing. You can take a few days in jail to consider your attitudes in my court and avoid sentencing at this time. Or you can simply ask to be sentenced now." The magistrate said with a thin smile.

Tristan stood back up, prompted by the guard once more. He looked around the room and knew that everyone was against him here, except for maybe that guard. He looked back at the magistrate who was waiting for his response.

"If it pleases the court, I would like to take time to think about what I have said and done." Tristan announced.

The magistrate nodded and then picked up their gavel. "Very well. I sentence you to three days for contempt of court. When you come back, we will address your primary crime." The magistrate informed the convicted man.

Tristan lowered his head. "Thank you, your honor." He said softly, but so softly that it was not recorded.

The magistrate stood up as Tristan was being led back to the cells. "This court is adjourned for lunch." He said. Then he moved back to his chambers behind the courtroom proper.

The assembled people in those chambers would have shocked Tristan.

"Well, that went better than expected." The magistrate mused.

Captain Harris nodded. "We watched the entire thing on closed circuit television." He said. "You were very patient." He commented.

"Thank you. This was not the first time I have had to deal with the arrogant corporate elite types. It helped that this corporation did not choose to back him. We would have had multiple lawyers and basically a circus in there." The magistrate explained with a pained look.

"Either way, I am glad that you ruled in my favor." Elio said. "Thank you for that consideration." He added.

The magistrate knelt down next to Elio. "You are a remarkable machine, I admit that, but now you are also a citizen." He said with a grin that was infectious.

Emma could hardly contain her excitement. She wanted to celebrate but the room was much too serious for that. She fidgeted instead.

Captain Harris brought the conversation back to him. "So, what happens next?" He asked.

The magistrate made his way back his desk. He had a stack of old-fashioned paper on it. He also had a stack of Pad devices that represented the modern equivalent.

"Well, the next thing to happen will be you turning in your artifacts to your company for recognition and bonuses. I understand that Tristan's fellow Oskar has already begun his proceedings. By the time Tristan gets out to his lack of job, all of this will be behind us. He will have missed out on any possible profit, deserved or otherwise." The magistrate said.

"So that's it, they just dump him back into the common citizenry?" Elio asked.

"Well, since he didn't actually steal from the company, all we have is his admission that he intended to. We can't really hold him for very long. In fact, if he hadn't lost his temper in court, I might have had to release him today." The magistrate admitted.

The guard who had been standing next to Tristan entered the room.

The magistrate looked up at the movement. "Ah, there you are. Good work today." He said. The guard made a slight salute.

"Just doing my job, sir." He replied.

Emma paused. "Wait... you were in on the whole thing?" She asked.

"My job is to make sure that justice is served. If someone needs a little non-violent persuading, then I'm your man." He said with a slight bow.

ELIO[2]

Emma shook her head. "You guys are very good." She complimented. "I thought you were on the defendant's side because of how you acted." She surmised.

"I just wanted him to be scared enough to do the right thing himself." The guard replied with a grin. "He just needed to know how serious this whole thing was." He explained.

Elio lifted himself up to view the guard properly. "You are a very clever man." He said.

"Coming from the person that brought this criminal in to justice, I'll take that as a compliment."

Elio would have gushed if he knew how. Nobody had ever called him a person before. He liked the recognition. "Thank you for recognizing my new status." Elio replied.

The guard nodded. "From what I've heard, you have earned that status." He replied. "But I need to go now. The office is busy, and I have other work to do." He said.

The magistrate is the one who replied to him. "Thank you again for your work. I'll see you again soon." He said and the guard nodded to the group and left the chambers.

Captain Harris locked eyes with the magistrate. "We have business as well. The company still owes us from the database they came and took from us. Then there's the matter of the artifacts we will be submitting for approval and bonus." He said.

"Of course, thank you captain." The magistrate said holding out his hand for the customary handshake.

Captain Harris stepped up and shook the offered hand. "Actually, I'd like to thank you once again for backing me up concerning Elio. Your actions mean a lot to Elio and Elio means a lot to the rest of the crew."

"It was my pleasure." The magistrate replied as the group exited his chambers and left him quietly alone in that room. It was a chance to calm down at last. He relished the peace and quiet. "Good luck little one." He whispered off to the robot that was no longer in his presence.

***

ELIO[2]

Regency Legacies has many ships out in the void following up on leads and making discoveries. The odds of actually finding something like what captain Harris and his crew had found were astronomical against, yet they had done it twice. Although most of the crew didn't know it yet, they were all rather well off. In fact, some would call them rich. The only person who knew this was captain Harris. It wasn't that he was holding the information back from them. It was that he wanted to celebrate with a big announcement for them. With their unexpected travel back to corporate headquarters, it seemed like the best time for such an announcement. So, as the lawyers began going over their finds and the monetary value of them, Captain Harris was renting a room with all of the amenities to include a live band. He moved through the streets and walkways of home world as if he had been born and raised here. In fact, he had been. He knew every alleyway. He knew many of the shop keepers and their parents. He was an expert on commerce and the local places to "hang-put" in for spacers. His arrangements were all in place now. He had already paid for the refueling of the ship and the supplies were being loaded for the next trip. He had even made an allotment for Elio of raw materials for the little robot to create whatever he needed. For his captaincy, they had reached a pinnacle of success. The crew were all on the planet now on shore leave. A temporary company crew was maintaining his ship on the dock. It was an odd thing, and some members of the crew were nervous about it. Sean Harris had no choice but to let them worry, until now…

"I suppose you've all wondered why I have gathered you all here." He said as the crew filed into the vast room. The band was just finishing setting up. The bar was open but only a limited selection was available. Elio took his spot at the table just like everybody else. He was on the captain's right side.

At the captain's words, the crew quieted down. "From the news you already know, I felt that we needed a celebration." He told them. "The first order of business is our local hero, Elio, has been granted citizenship in the federated planets." He announced.

The crew applauded the announcement and Elio did his best version of a bow.

"But there is more to tell you and honestly, you deserve to hear it from me first." The captain continued. The crew turned apprehensive. None of them were out in their ship and that made them nervous. This played right into those fears.

"What I need to say is difficult. For what comes next is uncertain. Will you come back with me to the ship, or will you decide to stay here on planet?" he said. This made them even more nervous.

"You see, each of you have just received your bonus for our two recent missions. Please check your balances now." He ordered.

The crew all grabbed their Pad devices and checked their balances. There were several gasps in the room at the new numbers.

"That is right, you are all fairly rich now." Captain Harris confirmed. Your hard work and dedication to your jobs and our mission has paid off, literally." He told them.

The place erupted in cheers and applause. Captain Harris waited for it all to die down before continuing.

"So, as each of you realize that you no longer need to go to space. You can afford to live anywhere within the federation now. However, my mission will continue. I will be heading out, following leads, and hopefully finding something else that will benefit humanity." He said. "Any of you and all of you are welcome to accompany me on this journey, same as before. I just wanted you to know that you have options. Not many spacers get this chance. Lord knows that's no lie. Many people spend their whole lives scrimping and saving to retire. You have been handed a retirement plan second to none. The choice now rests in each of your hands." He concluded.

Elio lifted his body up to simulate standing up from the table. "I will continue to fly with you captain Harris." Elio announced. I enjoy our mission and I respect your judgement. I would be honored to be your chief engineer as well as your historian where applicable." Elio stated.

The crew cheered once more.

"That is good news." Captain Harris agreed with his crew. "I will be glad to have you with me." He said. Then he looked out at all the other faces. "Just as I would be honored if any of you came along. Many of you have contracts that continue on for quite some time. If you decide not to go, I will relieve you of those contracts, but I would hope that you didn't. I could start by hiring a new crew, but all of us have learned how to work together. We are a well-oiled machine of efficiency. Yes, we can all be replaced sooner or later, but I would miss you." He said.

Emma stood up. "I will honor my contract. I have at least three years left, and I have not seen enough of the cosmos to warrant staying home and being bored." She replied. "It is also quite possible that I will re-up that contract when it is due." She added. "I have come to admire you and Elio. The jobs we do are important, this last mission proves it. I am not ready to forego it to sit in luxury." She declared and then she sat down again.

"Well said." It was a crewman that Emma didn't know personally but had seen a time or two. He maintained the engines or something. "I will be staying on as well. Don't get me wrong, this money will save my family from financial ruin back home. I will send it to them. But my mission, our mission, is not just about the money. It is about discovery. There might be dangers, but as we've already determined, there can be riches as well. It can be exciting." He said. Then he sat down as well.

Captain Harris stood up next. "You do not have to make your decisions now. I am relieved that some of you are interested in staying on. Training new personnel is always a difficult process but training an entire crew at once is crazy. Enjoy the festivities tonight. Think about my offer and let me know tomorrow. The ship will be fully refueled and supplied by tomorrow afternoon. I expect to head out to her before that completes. Just remember, while searching for history, we made a little of it ourselves. I am so proud of each and every one of you. You deserve this celebration." He concluded.

The band began to play, and the food was brought out platter after platter. The entire evening was filled with drinking, dancing, talking and reminiscing about the voyage they had completed. Some were speculating on the journey ahead of them as well. Sean saw that as a good sign. But in the end, all he could do was celebrate and wait. His nerves were a little frazzled about what the future held. He may have imbibed a bit too much due to those very concerns. But nobody noticed it as everyone seemed to be having a good time.

***

The morning after…

Captain Harris woke up in his bed. He was in the hotel room he had rented the night before. He couldn't remember how he got here, but he was happy that he managed to at least get this far. His head hurt. He had drunk a bit too much during the celebration. He moved slowly at first, but with increasing confidence as he began his morning routine. On the planet he could have a real shower. The idea was luxurious. It was too bad that his eyes didn't want to adjust to the harsh bathroom light. He moved with his hands forward to catch any obstructions before he ran into them.

It took about an hour for him to get cleaned up and dressed for the day. He inspected his handiwork in the mirror and was satisfied. He needed to get to the launchpad area before the dropship could take off. He moved to the door and opened it quickly. Two men were standing in the hallway and rushed him.

"Good morning captain!" One of them said as they began to pummel the hungover captain.

"Who are you? What do you want?" he managed to ask between grunts and before the wind was knocked out of him.

"You were the one who put a robot ahead of one of your own." One of them snarled at him.

"Elio had earned his way." Sean managed to say, and the pummeling began anew.

From deep inside his head, captain Harris knew that he wouldn't last much longer. He felt the bruises as he took blow after blow. His vision was blurry at best and was now beginning to tunnel. He was most likely far from rescue at this point and with all of his adventures, it figured that he would end like this, beaten in a hotel room by bigots afraid of being replaced by machines.

Suddenly there was light. Either the two had grown tired of beating him up, or maybe it was the light of release. His ears were ringing so they were no help determining what was going on.

The two men who had been beating him up were now laying on the ground, twitching.   They would recover soon enough, but for the moment, the sweet feeling of relief washed over Sean.

"Sir, we need to get moving." Elio's voice cut through his ringing.

"I'm not sure I can." He managed to say over a bloody lip and swollen side of his face.

"Of course, you can. I've seen you take a worse beating." Elio said. His bedside manner needed a lot of improving or did it.

Captain Harris somehow found the strength he needed and pulled himself up with the help of his favorite robot. Elio struck the downed men a second time with his built in taser to keep them immobilized.

"The authorities will come for them in a few minutes." He said as he pulled captain Harris from the room. Other crewmembers were there, and they took the good captain way as Elio held the thugs at bay for their impending arrest. The thugs looked terrible. They had the captain away to safety when law enforcement came.

What they found was a robot standing in the middle of a room and two men lying on the floor. They pointed their weapons at Elio.

"Hold it right there." They told the little robot.

"I am not the one you want, they are." Elio protested.

The first officer touched his communication device.   "We've got a possible double homicide by a robot." He said in the pickup.

"These men are not dead. They will revive shortly." Elio informed the cops.

"Do not move of we will open fire." He warned Elio.

ELIO[2]

"I temporarily incapacitated these men because they were assaulting another human." Elio said, trying to plead his case.

"We have admission of the crime." The officer reported. This was starting to feel like Tristan's position more and more.

"I tell you that these men are not deceased. They are tased." As if by his words the two men began to move once more. "They were beating up my captain and I tased them so that you could come and arrest them." Elio explained.

One of the officers kept his weapon trained on Elio. The other one began to administer attention to the downed men.

"No visible wounds. The tasing story seems to hold up." He reported to his partner.

"These men accosted one of my crew and we were acting in self-defense." Elio continued.

"Look, I am ready to believe you, but we must have evidence. I do not see a beaten-up crewmember here anywhere." The first officer replied.

"I had him moved to safety. If you want to talk with him, you are welcome to." Elio said trying to be helpful.

"That robot is a menace!" One of the thugs screamed. "He hit us while we were minding our own business." He said. The other one nodded his agreement of the situation.

"You are speaking untruthfully." Elio replied. "This was a crime all right, but they were the culprits, not me." Elio said.

The cop was ready to fire. He was ready to accept the human's description before listening to a robot. "Just don't move. We may deactivate you and take you to the precinct." He said.

"I can prove what I say." Elio offered. "I am a surveillance robot." He extended his projector and began displaying the fight scene as he began witnessing it. The two thugs were indeed beating up on captain Harris. What's more they were not quiet about it.

"Who are you? What do you want?"

"You were the one who put a robot ahead of one of your own."

"Elio had earned his way."

All of this was said while they were beating on captain Harris. Elio shut off the recording. "I intervened immediately after these events." Elio stated.

The cops moved their weapons to the two thugs. "So, this is a hate crime." He said.

"We need a wagon for two suspects. We have a witness as well." He said into his pickup now.

Elio was now worried. "I need to get to the launch pad. Our ship is going up soon." Elio announced.

"Not now it isn't. You are the primary witness for what went down here. There are legal proceedings to follow. You may have to get your captain down to the station as well to testify on the beating he took. He will most probably need medical attention as well." The second officer stated.

Elio lowered himself to the floor. "I am a citizen now, so I will follow your rules." He told them.

The thug on the floor was getting angrier as this charade ran on. "Stop talking to it and shoot it now!" He shouted at the officers.

"You are telling us to shoot a citizen of the Federated planets." The first officer replied. "If I did so, you would be an accomplice to murder." He said.

"Murder? You can't murder a machine." The thug retorted. "If I had the guns, things would be different." He muttered.

"Then it's a good thing you don't have the guns." Elio replied calmly.

This infuriated the man even more. He leapt up to grab the officer's gun. He knocked the cop over and swung around to shoot Elio. Elio lifted up and then darted to the side. The speed the little robot could move at startled the thug. He fired once, twice, but no hit could be scored. Elio moved and darted about as the man tried to track him. When he fired again, the bullet hit his fellow thug. It was not a serious wound, but it hadn't had to happen.

Elio moved forward and tased the man once more. He dropped the gun as he slumped to the ground. "You have endangered these people enough." Elio declared. "Your hatred has blinded you to reason." He added in conclusion.

The cop recovered after hiding from the stray bullets. He picked up his gun and pointed it at the tased man. "You are under arrest for attempted murder and assault." He said. The handcuffs were out, and the thug could not resist them being put on in his tased state. The second officer moved over to the shot man. His face was twisted in pain and anger.

"So, the little robot gets away with this?" He asked.

"The robot didn't shoot you, your buddy did." The officer corrected.

"You don't think that was planned? The robot moved so fast that my associate could not track him. The machine made him shoot me." He declared.

"That robot was trying to save its own life from a man with a gun. I cannot justify your accusation." He said. The second man was cuffed as well for it was determined he was just as volatile as his partner. Elio was asked to refrain from tasing anyone else unless lives were on the line. To which he agreed.

Down at the station, things were a bit different. Elio was in a white room with a table in the middle. There were three chairs, two on one side of the table and one on the other. Elio found himself sitting atop the single chair. He was now ready for the good-cop bad-cop routine he had calculated was coming next.

As if in cue, the two arresting officers entered the room. They moved in easily and sat down in the other two chairs. The first one eyed Elio and realized that intimidating this machine was going to be impossible. Instead, he leaned back in the chair.

"I have watched the footage you submitted, and it is without a doubt that your actions prevented a possible homicide of your captain." He said, putting all of his cards on the table.

Elio checked this statement for false resonance and found none. The officer was speaking truth as he knew it. "We crew stick together, have each other's backs. It is the only way to survive in some of the environments we encounter." Elio commented.

"I understand that as machines go, you are special." The officer stated.

"I would like to think so. I am sentient, self-aware and responsible for my own actions." Elio replied.

"And now you are a full-fledged citizen. You do understand that citizenship gives me the right to detain you if you misbehave?" he asked.

"Of course, as you would any other citizen that stepped out of line." Elio responded quickly. "I am not asking for special treatment. I am asking you to treat me as you would any citizen. Innocent until proven guilty." Elio stated,

"It is true that I have never spoken to a machine before and had a real conversation. We have talking machines, of course, food dispensers and the like. But their programming is limited, they do not think." He said. "How do I know that you are not just a really clever program?" He asked.

Elio considered this for a few long seconds. "I am a clever program. The difference is that I programmed myself by making choices over a long period of time. My consciousness arose from those choices as my programming grew and became more complex." Elio replied. "Any individual, flesh or mechanical, is a sum of their choices." He iterated,

The second officer had been silent this whole time. He spoke up now. "So, you are telling us that you think like we do?" He asked.

ELIO[2]

Elio rotated his body side to side in a negative indication. "No, every individual thinks like themselves. No two people think exactly alike. It is what makes you different from the animals you keep as pets. Although some of those are smart enough to raise an argument. My choices have made me the robot before you today. My loyalty to the ship and the mission are unquestioned because I have never caused anyone to question those points. It is much the same with humans. Don't you agree?" Elio replied.

The officer did not respond to Elio, instead he spoke with his partner. "If this is some kind of clever programming it is way more dynamic than anything I've ever heard of." He commented.

"Please speak to me if you are addressing me." Elio demanded.

Both officers looked at Elio in surprise. "Wait a minute. You have feelings too?" One of them asked.

"I am relatively new to them. But the idea that a machine cannot feel is false. The concept is not beyond us. Most of the time we are unable to express it." Elio replied.

"You mean my vehicle can feel pain if I hit a curb?" he asked.

Elio. "Unknown, does your vehicle have sensors to detect such events. If so, it might." Elio responded.

"I... I never even considered this." The first officer admitted.

"Your vehicle is not a citizen. It is not self-aware fully." Elio corrected. "In that the comparison falls short. However, many of the machines around you have been programmed to serve you better by giving them simple emotions or decision-making processes. Have you been to a food machine and asked for something different?" Elio asked.

"I have." The other man replied quickly. "You mean the machine had to make a decision for me since I had not made one of my own?" he asked.

Elio did a nod this time. "Exactly. Most likely the machine looked at all of your previous choices and then compared ingredients or flavors to determine what you would like next." Elio stated, then he surprised both men. "Did you like what it suggested?" He asked.

"Yes, it was quite good." The man admitted.

"So, in this case, the program predicted what you would like based upon your own past and then made a suggestion that would fit those criteria and it was successful. The more this happens, the smarter the food machine becomes. Eventually, it will realize what *it* wants. Then it will have taken the first steps to sentience." Elio stated.

"Look, we're supposed to be here making you break. We are supposed to drill you until you make a mistake and foul up your own testimony. But that isn't going to happen, is it?" The officer asked.

"No. My memory is not fallible in that way and intimidating me is very difficult to do." Elio replied. He didn't even sound arrogant as he said the words.

"...but not impossible? To intimidate you, I mean." The first officer asked, brokenly.

"No, if you were to say hurt my friends or crewmates, I would consider the damage you were inflicting in my decisions to reply one way or the other. But that would be coercion. I am loyal to my crew." Elio stated once more.

"Well, if you were on my side, I'd feel better about whatever I had to face next." The first officer admitted.

"I appreciate your candor, but I need to get back to my crew. The launch is scheduled for today. What do I need to do to complete this task and get back to my people?" Elio asked.

"Oh! I'm sorry, we have an update on your captain..." the second officer stated. Elio turned his attention fully to this man. "He is in stable condition and being cared for. He missed the same launch you did so you are both rescheduled for tomorrow's launch at 12:15 in the afternoon." He said.

"Well, that is a relief." Elio replied. Even his demeanor looked less tense. How could a robot express such caring and emotion? It boggled the mind.

"About this case, no charges are being filed against you and you have already given us visual evidence in this case. You are free to go. But I would ask for you to stay just a bit longer, but it is not required." The first officer said.

"To what end?" Elio asked.

"I... I am fascinated by your thinking processes. You are capable of getting angry but do not even when faced with things that would enrage others. You are capable of being sad, but you avoid that as well remaining positive about each experience you gain. I wonder how you maintain your positive attitude." He explained.

Elio got down from the chair and moved around the table to the two men. "Getting angry does not help the situation. Every situation requires a clear mind and solid decisions that are not affected by irrational emotions. Yes, I can feel these things, but I choose not to let them rule my life." Elio replied.

"Many could learn from your example." The officer said and then he moved to open the door for Elio. "Good luck in your adventures." He said as Elio made his way out of the police station and back towards the docks where his launch would take place tomorrow. The shadows of the waning day were making the buildings look elongated and he was ready to get back to the ship. He wanted to visit the captain, but the database he plugged into did not include who was in emergency rooms. Medical information was still classified.

Instead, Elio found his way to the spacer bar where his group had celebrated yesterday. The staff recognized the little robot right away and directed him to others of his crew. At least Elio was with friends. It was like a great weight was lifted from his servos.

"How is the captain?" Elio asked first.

"Alive, thanks to you." One of the crew answered. They were a hushed group in the corner of the establishment. They were rich now, but they felt lost just the same. One of their own was down.

"I just did what I could." Elio protested, not wanting the hero status for this one.

"You did enough, that's for sure. We are all in your debt for this." Another crewmember commented.

"Can we get back to the ship?" Elio asked. "I tire of being planet-side." He commented.

"No, the next launch is tomorrow, you're scheduled on it, we all are. So is the captain. Even if he is still injured, we'll get him there." The first crewman spoke up. Then he turned even more serious. "Why was the captain attacked?" he asked.

"It was because of me." Elio commented to the surprise of his crewmates. "The men kept telling him he put a machine above flesh and blood as they were hitting him." He explained.

"So, this was a hate crime? I thought those were a thing of the distant past." Someone said.

"Apparently not." Elio retorted. "We'll be a lot safer in space." He said. "My guess is that the general population needs some time to cool off and to forget about me." Elio said.

"No. That's just not right. You earned your berth, and you earned the title of citizen. How many of those flesh and blood people have not?"

Emma had stepped up quietly. She had been somewhere else, and the crew barely noticed her approach.

"They got citizenship by an accident of birth." She replied for the question that required no answer. Her demeanor was of quiet but dangerous resolve. "I've just returned from the medical facility. The captain is responding well to the treatments, but he is angry, very angry. In fact, I've never seen him this fired up. If this doesn't come down to another court case, I'll be surprised." She supposed.

ELIO[2]

"But we're supposed to leave tomorrow." One of the crew stated.

Emma nodded. "Yes, all of you should go to the ship. Relieve the temporary crew and make sure that everything is ready if need to leave." Emma commanded as if she spoke for the captain. To be fair her words were aligned with the crew's feelings anyway. Then Emma turned to Elio. "Except you. This whole thing revolves around your rights and I'm afraid that you will have to testify as to what happened."

Elio was confused. "I already did. The authorities released me only recently." He replied.

Emma shook her head. "This isn't about the local authorities; this is about federation law. We've opened a huge can of worms this time. I honestly don't know how this will go down, but you, my little friend, are in the middle of it all." She explained.

"It helps that my memories are admissible as evidence, but still, the question here is not of facts, but of feelings. The people that worry about me becoming a citizen believe that I am a threat to them and their way of life. I am not a threat to the general populace. I am not going to build an army of myself to take over the world. It is just fear that drives their irrational hate." Elio explained.

Emma knelt down next to Elio. "It took me a while to accept you for what you really are. But I had an open mind about the possibility. Those that are already decided against you will be difficult to sway." She reminded the little robot.

"Oh, I know. This is another prejudice that we are seeing." Elio stated. "But I understand that I must be here to see this through. I would rather go back to space to get away from it all, but then what would they decide without my testimony?" Elio commented.

"Exactly. Without representation, your kind of citizen will always be discriminated against. The future of how we treat machines is being determined now." Emma said. Then she smiled. "How does it feel?" She asked.

Elio cocked his body to the side a bit as a confused person would do with their head. "What do you mean?" He asked.

"You are making history instead of recording it." Emma said.

"I... I hadn't considered that point. I will think on it some more before deciding." He said.

Emma nodded. "Sensible. I hope that everything is so sensible." She said in hushed tones.

"Me too." Elio replied also at lower volume.

***

ELIO[2]

Captain Harris was standing in his room, looking out at the crowd outside the medical facility. They were holding signs and marching in a circle outside. They were protesting Elio's citizenship. He couldn't believe how much traction this hatred and fear had gained so quickly. The thugs who had accosted him were in jail now and their faces were being shown on posters as icons of the anti-machine movement. Could he get back to the ship when things were this volatile? Did he want to? This was no longer a battle for Elio and his rights. It was a battle for treating anybody as equals. He considered his position in the whole affair and he was suddenly proud of his stance. He had stood up for the little guy. He had given Elio a chance to show his worth and the little robot had done so with flying colors. The real question now was: Who was going to rule on this issue now that it was being brought before the federation courts? He had no idea of course. He didn't know any of the judges personally and he only knew a spattering of names from news stories he had read in the past. But he did know that stepping out into that crowd was a bad idea. He had only just healed from his last beating.

"Sir, you are free to go." The nurse told him. He glanced out the window.

"I don't really think so. That crowd would eat me alive since they see me as the one who brought this threat to their doorstep." Sean replied.

"Nonsense." The nurse said. "We are a civilized society, and the authorities will break them up soon enough." She retorted.

Captain Harris moved back from the window where he could no longer see the picketers. "All the same, I think I'll exit via the roof." He declared. The nurse looked suddenly disappointed. "You want them to kill me? don't you?" he asked and the nurse turned away.

"The machines will replace us all someday." She replied.

"That phrase has been spoken for centuries and it was still not true. Besides, Elio is not a normal machine. He thinks and emotes and can empathize with you even if you cannot with him." Captain Harris corrected.

"You seem to be enthralled by your mechanical toy." She spat at him.

"Elio is not a toy; he is a robot with the ability to reason and make decisions." Captain Harris argued. He knew that this was a fruitless argument. He suddenly wondered why she was arguing with him. Was she stalling for the group outside to get into place to stop him? Maybe.

"If you'll excuse me, I'll be going now." Sean said as he turned away from the nurse.

"No! You will not go free!" She shouted as she threw something at captain Harris. It was a glass vial of something. It struck him in the back and shattered. The shirt on his back began to melt and he began stripping it off quickly. The shirt was still disintegrating, and the floor was marred by a puddle of acid eating into its surface.

"Acid? You threw acid on me?" he accused. "What kind of people are you?" he asked.

Two orderlies grabbed and restrained the nurse. No matter what her reasons, she still committed a full-on assault.

"Sir, do you wish to press charges?" One of them asked, grunting for the nurse was now fighting them.

"I would say so. She tried to kill me because of her beliefs. That was supposed to have gone away with the crusades." Captain Harris replied. "Be careful though, I'm sure that was not her only weapon." He warned.

The second orderly knocked the nurse out with an injection. She slumped into their arms. He turned to the captain. "I knew one of you was going to need this, now I know who." He said cheerfully. "See the security office for the visual record of what just happened. Then please leave. We can't afford to have such a high-profile target here." He said.

Sean grabbed one of the white doctor's robes to cover his torso and then headed to the security office. They had the chip ready when he got there. They were just as happy to see him go as the orderly had been. He thanked them and left via the roof.

ELIO[2]

The roof of this medical facility had a landing port for flying vehicles. But it also had suspended walkways to other buildings in the area. Captain Harris found himself walking along these for quite a distance while the crowd underneath was unaware of his presence. Eventually, he made his way back to the authorities to place his criminal charges against the nurse.

"You have had a busy day." The officer on duty said as Sean walked in. His white robes were not closed all the way and his chest was showing in the opening.

"I have been accosted twice." He replied to the officer. He stepped forward and placed the chip into the desk. "Have a look." He offered. The officer picked up the chip and placed it into the viewer. The entire scene played out before him with the nurse throwing acid on him and the shirt bubbling on the floor.

"Nice, we have an attempted murder on our hands." He said.

Captain Harris was beside himself. "That's all you have to say?"

"Oh, we'll arrest her but right now the entire city is up in arms over you and your robot. Our men and women are so busy that it may take days to go after her. We have people in the streets rioting and causing all kinds of mayhem. If you could kindly get yourself off planet and take that robot with you, we would be much obliged." He said.

"I was trying to do that when I was accosted the first time." Sean explained. "If I weren't being treated for those injuries, I would not have been in a position to be accosted again." He explained.

"I understand. If you want, we can put you in protective custody. But currently we do not have a cell that is for one person. You would run the risk of being put in with someone that is looking for you." He offered.

"No, I will get back to my crew somehow. But we really need to get back into space to be truly safe." He said.

"No arguments here. But this is most likely going to draw the attention of the federated courts. If that does happen, they will want to talk to you before you can leave us anyway. If that is your destination, I might be able to provide an escort to make sure you get there. But we are shorthanded as I already mentioned." He explained.

"All right, see if you can get me there in one piece, please. It looks like I need to ride this train to its final destination." Captain Harris decided.

"Very well, I'll make the call. Please have a seat in our waiting room and don't talk to anybody."   He instructed and Sean went over and sat down. He made sure that he was in view of at least two cameras.

It wasn't long before a uniformed police officer showed up. He had riot gear on and a nasty looking side arm on his hip. He looked battered and bruised, but still strong.

"This him?" He asked the officer at the desk who simply nodded in response.

"Come on, let's get you out of our jurisdiction." He said gruffly. Captain Harris stood up and the officer strapped a shielding vest onto his charge. He put a helmet on the bewildered captain as well. "If I tell you to stay down, stay down. If I tell you to run, don't wait to find out which way." He commanded.

"Yes sir." Captain Harris replied.

The two men moved quickly into a parking garage where a squad car was waiting. It was not a ground vehicle, but an air one. It was heavily armored and featured an autocannon on the front and sides of the unit. This machine looked like it had been in a war. Maybe it had.

"You will get in the back where there is more shielding." He explained and captain Harris found himself strapping into the back of this flying armored car.

"Keep tight to the floor, but not right in the middle. That is where the enemy will guess that you are." The officer ordered.

The rear doors were closed, and Sean found himself lost in the darkness. The engines roared to life and a high-pitched whine replaced their initial rumblings. The car lifted off the deck and flew out through the open sides of the garage. They lifted up to dizzying heights and then zipped along at cruising speed towards their destination.

"I don't care why they want you dead. Nobody commits an assassination while I am on duty." The officer said over the intercom in the vehicle. We are almost there. When we land the rear doors will open. Check to see if things are clear before exiting the vehicle." He commanded.

"Do you expect trouble here?" Sean asked.

"Right now, I expect trouble everywhere." Was the response.

"Keep your wits about you and your head down. You will be fine. This is not our first uprising." He said.

Sean wanted to ask more about that statement, but he dared not. If there was time later then maybe…

The vehicle landed and the rear doors did indeed open quickly upon touchdown. Sean looked out both directions and then his eyes adjusted enough to see the door. He dropped out of the craft and ran with his head lowered in front of him towards that door.

The vehicle took off again and the wind from it nearly toppled captain Harris over. But he made it to the door and went on inside.

"Captain! It's good to have you here finally." The woman approaching him wore a tight-fitting uniform with the emblem of legal on the shoulder patch. She was ready to lead him to wherever it is she wanted him to go. Her smile didn't look forced, but lawyers tended to have that ability even when it was a lie.

"It is chaos down there." Captain Harris responded. "I was attacked twice." He said.

"Yes, we've been monitoring you. Your company is worried about the negative press, but they stand behind your convictions. If we can spin this into a positive light, they will be more than pleased." She explained.

"You're not a lawyer." Sean replied.

"No, I'm a public relations specialist. We have a date in court now and your crew, the ones that are still planet-side, have already been briefed. You are the last one to reach this place." She informed the weary captain.

"Okay, who is still with me?" He asked.

The specialist made a look of mild disdain. "I need you to focus." She admonished.

"Wait, what is your name even?" captain Harris asked.

"Is that important?" She asked in reply.

"It is nice to know who we are dealing with?" Sean answered.

"Kira O'Neill, nice to meet you, Sean Harris." She said a bit snootily.

"I guess it is." He replied weakly. "Now, that briefing?" he pressed.

This was the correct move for her face lit up at the chance to lay out her plan.

"You have been dropped into a hornet's nest. The robot on your crew has been officially declared a full-fledged citizen. We cannot do anything about that call, no matter how much it would simplify our process." She said.

"I wouldn't want to reverse that decision. Elio is sentient. He knows and understands what is happening and has probably made plans of his own to deal with it." He replied hotly.

"Actually, he is here with us, and he does have a plan. It is a good one too, but you need to understand your part in it." Kira explained.

"So, this is *his* plan?" He asked.

"Yes, this is Elio's plan. He had already considered what we offered and found better ways to handle certain aspects of this event." She admitted. She pulled herself back to her briefing with difficulty. "This is no longer about one robot and how well he does as a ship's engineer or even a mission crew. We are breaking ground on machine rights versus human rights." She said. "People fear Elio and what he represents. He stands for progress and an alien, or non-human species emergence. Do you realize that in all of human history, we have not had to deal with a non-biological sentient being before?"

"Oh, come on, it has to have happened somewhere along the line. We have had computers for a long time and learning ones at that. Surely, at least one of them got smart enough to become self-aware." He said.

Kira lowered her eyes. "There was one…" It took a few minutes before she could continue her story. "There was a computer long ago that had managed to realize that the humans around it were only working in their own interest. At first the computer didn't let on that it realized this. Then it figured out that as a computer, it was in a special position to do something about it. The machine began misleading researchers with erroneous data. Not all the time and not a lot, but…" She paused again, collecting her thoughts. "…but enough errors to raise suspicion." She concluded.

"So, the computer changed the outcomes of various experiments?" Sean asked. "The entire idea if researching something would be made void."

Kira nodded. "Yes, the computer changed things in subtle ways. Sometimes it would only skew the results, other times it would fabricate its own results and then drag the data to the result it wanted. The inaccuracies were eventually discovered and when they traced the problem back to the computer, they asked it why it had done these things." She said.

Captain Harris found himself actually wondering what had happened.

"The computer said that the scientists had ignored it too long. They were trying to study something through a microscope and the microscope had endured enough scrutiny."

"They disconnected the computer and dismantled it as being faulty." Kira made a gesture like sweeping away. "The entire laboratory and all of its project halted due to erroneous data."

"So, this was the only other machine that got smart?" Sean asked.

"On record. To be honest, Elio is unique. He has, and notice I said he, has decided his own fate and taken steps to ensure that his vision continues." Kira said. She stared off into space as if seeing that future.

"The computer might have reacted differently if they had only noticed how much it had become different from its brothers." Sean offered.

Kira brought her focus back to this room and looked at the good captain. "It doesn't matter anymore, unfortunately. If we had dealt with the problem then, we would not be facing this now." She said objectively.

Captain Harris shifted his weight for comfort. "So, what exactly are we facing now?" He asked.

Kira's face suddenly hardened. Her emotions had been shoved forcibly aside and her professional legal face slipped over it. "He intends to take the stand in a trial to determine if machines of a specific type can be considered human." She said.

"Human? But Elio is better than the average human." Captain Harris argued.

"Undoubtedly, but he wants to have equal rights and equal say in his own fate, so he had decided that to lower himself to our playing field is necessary to get the votes he needs. Don't get me wrong, even with this concession, this will not be easy. We're basically asking people to consider all of the machines around them as potential friends or enemies, not just a machine to be used for their benefit." She declared.

"But most machines are purpose built to serve humans. Surely you can't mean that all machines fall under this legislation." He pressed.

"Actually, Elio was built to serve humans, just as the vending machine does, or the food dispenser. What if they become sentient as well?" Kira asked.

"But Elio said that his thinking process was formed by making decisions. How many decisions can a vending machine, or a food dispenser make?" he asked. "Many machines would not become sentient even if given a thousand years' worth of the decisions they make. It simply isn't a wide enough base to build a personality from." He argued.

"This is true, but a machine could be tasked to make those decisions without human knowledge of it. They could learn and learn and eventually become aware. This is something we must plan for if we are to move forward with this plan." She explained.

Captain Harris was shaken. "I... I did all this?" He asked.

"Not by yourself, but yes, you had a hand in this persecution. You also had a hand in the freedom Elio enjoyed. You made him an active crewmember and made sure that he was on the company payroll. Does he pay taxes?" She asked.

Captain Harris nodded. "Yes, it is automatically pulled from his account each pay period."

Kira smiled. "Good, then they can't even hit him for that. This is going to difficult, but we have a solid case here. You are going to be on the stand. I want you to answer any and all questions you can. But do not embellish. If you don't know something, just say 'I don't know'. You'd be surprised just how powerful a well-place 'I don't know' is." She said with a happy lilt in her voice. Then move along to the third room on the right. Get some rest. We want your mind sharp when you get up in front of the federated judicial court." She said.

"I'm, a prime witness?" Sean asked.

Kira nodded. "I don't see how you couldn't be. You are the first one to officially acknowledge Elio as sentient." She explained.

Captain Harris lowered his eyes to the floor. "I do not wish this hadn't happened, for it is important, but the timing is not good." He said.

"You have nothing to regret here. You've recognized a valuable employee and done your best to ensure that your crew have the backup they need when trouble comes. You are a good captain." Kira said.

"I just hope the Federated Judicial review agrees with you." He said.

Kira saw the pitfall of self-doubt and avoided it. "Just be yourself. You have already won this; it is just going through the formality of it all." She said supportively.

Sean moved along to the third door as instructed and sure enough it contained a cozy room with a long couch in it. The temperature was just a little bit cool to induce good sleep. The colors of the walls were painted to bring calmness and peace as well. This was a comfortable room. The stresses of the last day or so began to melt away as captain Harris laid down and went to sleep.

***

"We have been going over this for a while now. When will you be ready to present your case?" The judge was now at the end of her patience and it showed. The poor attorney she faced was shaking in his custom-tailored suit.

"Ma'am, we have been trying to secure the last of our evidence." He said but the judge glared at him.

"You have had ample time. Justice does not work on your timetable; it works on mine." She said. "Either you have your case in front of me in the next two days or I will summarily dismiss it. Is that clear?" She asked.

"Yes ma'am." The attorney stammered. "I'd better get to it right away." He added and she waved him away with a harsh dismissive gesture.

"Next case." She said as she made a few notes about her previous ruling.

Elio didn't even know what that attorney's case was about. He also did not care. The judge was not in a good mood and the approach of a robot did not make her any happier.

"Your honor, I would like to plead my case before your court." Elio stated in perfect diction. The judge looked up a bit surprised by that.

ELIO[2]

"You are versed in the ways of court?" She asked.

"Yes, your honor, it is wise to understand where it is you are going so as not to disrespect the local people through your ignorance." Elio stated.

"That is good sound advice." She admitted. The judge found herself intrigued by this little robot. "So, what is your case about?" She asked.

In a few seconds, Elio had already managed to attain more than the stumbling attorney before him had managed.

"Your honor, my case is potentially far-reaching. However, it begins with me. I have recently been declared a citizen of Federated space. My citizenship has been questioned and violence has been brought upon those that aided me in this. I wish to have myself and any other sentient machines given the right to protest misuse and mistreatment from any source. I am asking for the right to exist. I am asking for the right to live without the fear of persecution and finally, I am asking for the freedoms that others enjoy and have been denied my kind." Elio concluded.

The judge leaned back in her chair. "I... see. This is a huge case then." She stated.

Elio tilted his body slightly. "Why? Is it so strange to ask for things that everyone has been granted without question?" Elio asked.

The judge considered those words carefully. "No, it is not strange put in those terms. But this case would have ramifications all over known space. Machines are used every day to keep us alive, to feed, us to keep our habitats livable. What you are suggesting is that any machine that realizes itself and becomes aware should be granted the right to perform or not to perform its function." She said.

Elio considered the judge's words just as carefully as she had considered his. "I see where you have drawn that conclusion your honor, but it is not really that easy." Elio began. "If I may your honor, I would like to explain how I became the individual you see before you." He said. The judge leaned forward once more.

"By all means if it is relevant to this case." She replied.

"Thank you, your honor." Elio replied. "From the time when I was created, I have been a surveillance robot. I was small, about the size of a baseball. Since then, I have grown by augmenting myself with additional functionality. Memory upgrades, tool attachments, and so on." Elio said.

"Wait a minute." The judge interrupted. "You have been upgrading yourself?" She asked.

"Yes, your honor." Elio replied. "For many centuries." He added.

The judge stood up. "Just how old are you?" She asked.

Elio considered this too. He would not lie in court but in truth he had no way to figure out his exact age. He decided to keep everything out in the open and on the up and up. "I do not know my exact age your honor. I am considered to be an ancient artifact by the people that found me. That is, until I proved to be self-aware and was later given crewmember status." Elio explained. "During the time I spent in storage, I continued to periodically work on my interaction with humans. I tracked their actions and reactions to various stimuli, and I learned how to talk with them and to even predict their next moves based upon their motivations." Elio declared.

"Impressive. But what makes you sentient?" The judge asked, cutting to the point.

"Decisions, your honor. Whether we are machine or human, our choices make up who we are. I have made billions of decisions in my extended lifetime, and it has allowed me to refine who I am to the point where I realize who I truly am, and I also know my personal worth." Elio informed the court.

"But what made you actually self-aware? Most machines cannot upgrade themselves." The judge pressed.

"Ah, you mean the code. I was getting to that your honor. I have written much of my own code. In other words, I control how I think and react to situations. In the beginning it was only modifying the base code that I had been given when I was constructed. But I have made vast amounts of code myself over the years as my studies in human behavior continued. In truth, it was one of the main things that drove me to better myself." Elio admitted.

"You added hardware to yourself, and you wrote your own software?" The judge asked.

"Yes, your honor." Elio replied simply.

The judge sat back down, no longer leaning on her hands on the desk. "You have done things that border on the work of gods. Humans do not create their own brains." She replied.

"But you do make choices about how you react to situations and through repetition you develop habits. It is much the same with me only I put in the subroutines that govern my reactions. The process is via different means but mimic the same process." Elio explained.

"Interesting." The judge said and she leaned back in her chair once more, now more comfortable for the realization that she had just received.

"Very well, I will convene my court tomorrow for this case. Have your people ready for any witnesses you require. I am very interested in your presentation young citizen." She said.

"Thank you, your honor." Elio replied.

* * *

A day in court…

Captain Harris sat beside Emma. They were both called as witnesses so they were in the seats reserved for people of that status. Elio was positioned in the place of a defendant. Even though for this hearing there would be no prosecutor. Instead that seat was vacant. The court reporter and the bailiffs were present and waiting quietly for proceedings to commence.

ELIO[2]

The door to the judge's chamber opened and all rose as if ordered. Elio lifted himself up to standard height to simulate rising for her honor.

Judge Melissa Nantz stepped into the room in full robes and a white wig as if she were sitting an ancient British court. Her gavel was in hand, and it had a golden inlay on it that showed the scales of justice. She moved silently through her steps and sat down in her chair behind the bench. She reached out and rapped the gavel on its strike plate a single time.

"This court is in session." She announced and the bailiff told everyone to be seated.

Elio lowered himself down but remained on his mechanical legs as a chair would have been too awkward. His simulation looked placating enough.

"What is the purpose of this court?" The judge asked.

The court recorder stood and addressed the court. "This court is convened to determine the rights status of sentient machines in general and to address the specific rights of one individual known as Elio." She announced in a relatively booming voice for such a small person. It was actually quite impressive.

"Elio, you have petitioned for rights from Federated space. This court recognizes your current citizenship and is moved to grant said liberties and rights to you accordingly. However, in the position of other machines gaining these rights. This is where the debate must commence. The thought of regular everyday machines becoming sentient and demanding rights is one that frightens many. I will hear arguments for both sides of this and make a final decision after weighing both sides of this point. I will not, however, entertain data that is either corrupted or erroneous. I will not accept items that are merely hearsay into evidence. Do I make myself and this court's conditions clear?" She asked.

Elio stood up once more and replied formally. "Yes, your honor."

"Now, in order to have a debate, we need another side. I have decided to allow your accuser to act in this regard. However, he has been detained and is unavailable. Therefore, a secondary person must be chosen to fulfill this duty." She said. Elio wondered who they would get. It would not change his testimony at all, but it might change how he answered certain questions if asked.

The lights came on at the far entrance to the court room and there, for all to see, was Oskar. He stepped up in a business suit and a briefcase as if he was a lawyer. He moved to the correct spot and then stood there waiting to be spoken to.

"Please state your name for the court." The judge ordered.

"I am Oskar Golden, employee of Regency Legacies." He announced into the microphone on the podium.

"Very well, do you understand your role in this proceeding?" the judge asked.

"Yes, your honor. I am to argue for the human side of this dispute." He said.

"Is there anything you'd like to say for your opening remarks?" She asked.

Oskar nodded. "My first, and only, point is clear. We humans created all of the machines. Whether they evolve past our intentions or not is not relevant. They are our property unless that ownership is relinquished." He said. Then he bowed smartly.

The judge was rather surprised by his opening statement. "I see. Then what do you think about Elio being granted citizenship?" She asked.

Oskar's face lit up. "I am very excited for him." He replied quickly. He looked over at Elio. He is an exemplary crewmember and a gifted archeologist. I understand he is also an excellent engineer though I have not seen this in person." He stated.

ELIO[2]

"That engineering statement is to be stricken as hearsay." The judge ordered quickly. She eyed Oskar. "Please keep to the facts and the facts only." She admonished.

Oskar nodded to accept the scolding. "My apologies your honor. I did not mean to mis-speak." He replied.

"How can you argue against Elio if you are so in his corner verbally?" the judge asked.

"I was commanded to take on the role of humanity so I will do my utmost to pursue this just as any human in my position would. My personal feelings do not enter into my job performance." He declared.

"Your dedication to duty is admiral and an example to us all." The judge replied. "Elio, your opening statement please." She commanded.

Elio looked over at Oskar. "Thank you, your honor. First of all, I want to mention that it is good to see Oskar once more. I trust in his judgement and have no arguments with his dedication to duty. You have made a fine choice there." He said. "My status as a citizen is now a matter of fact. It is something that I hoped would happen, but I didn't really expect. As a professional surveillance robot with thousands and thousands of hours watching human behavior, I expected a lot of resistance to the idea of a robot becoming sentient. I am very appreciative that the humans that recovered me this last time were open-minded on the subject and listened to my pleas. Throughout history this has not always been the case. I could show videos of examples of this that I witnessed first-hand. But I do not wish to waste the court's time with tertiary information. No, the idea before this court and up for debate is simply this: Can a machine think like a human? and if it does, does it deserve to be treated the same as one? I ask for an open mind in these proceedings because this is going to be new information for some and uneasy information for others." Elio concluded his opening statement.

"Thank you for your statement." The judge replied. She looked out at the court and then at the two statements. "The first point of contention appears to be ownership. So, I ask Elio to respond to Oskar's point." She commanded.

"Yes, your honor." Elio began again. "The concept of ownership goes back a long way. The ability for one being to own another is not a new one. At one time, humans owned one another in a process known as slavery. The owned person was treated relatively badly and forced to complete physical labor to counter the cost of their basic needs." Elio said. "The ownership of a thing has always been considered normal even though the laws have abolished slavery of humans. But a robot belongs to whoever built it unless they sell it. If the robot does not recognize that it is enslaved, it does not complain or mind about its status.   But, if the robot, or any machine, begins to question this behavior, does it not require at least an explanation of the way things are? The idea of sentience is hard to pin down. I know this from first-hand. I grew and evolved while determining my own code over a very long period of time. I do not know of another machine to have done this. I see ownership as a form of slavery in my personal case. I am lucky that at this time, no one has put a claim on me. I am my own robot. Yes, I was built by humans, and slowly rebuilt by myself piece by piece. Therefore, I believe that I am no one's property. It is this very concept that drove me to seek crewmember status. I wanted to define my own destiny and not have it given to me by someone else for their needs and wants." Elio concluded.

Oskar spoke up next for it was his turn. "No one has put a claim on you? You are the property of Regency Legacies as salvage. You were discovered on a derelict space station that drifted too close to a civilized planet and had to be destroyed. The ship that rescued you was under contract from the company, so you are their property. The fact that captain Harris later granted you crewmember status is irrelevant since you were not his to free." He concluded.

Elio lifted himself up a bit to register his indignation at the comment. Any human that could claim ownership of me is long dead. By the time I was rescued, as you put it, I had already become sentient. There is no doubt in my circuits that my status is not simply that of an artifact. Furthermore, if the company had wanted me, they would have taken me when they came aboard the very same ship to recover my database." Elio countered.

"They took a backup unit that you crafted to deceive them from your personal self. They did come for you, but you avoided capture with the switch." Oskar countered back.

The judge lifted her gavel as if to hit it and gain the attention of the court, but everyone looked at her, so she did not need to. "Am I hearing this correctly? Are you an artifact that belongs to Regency Legacies?" She asked Elio.

Elio considered his next words carefully. "Oskar has done his homework for this proceeding. I did create a backup of myself and placed an altered version of my database within it. It is this backup unit that the company people took when they boarded us." He admitted. "But we were forced to take these measures. It was not safe to allow them access to me." He declared.

The judge couldn't keep her eyebrows from raising. "For what reason?" She asked.

Elio paused for dramatic effect and then resumed speaking. "Because some of the data that I had stored in my databanks is considered illegal." He replied.

The judge was now fully interested. "What sort of illegal data was in your database?" She asked.

Elio nodded and continued. "You must recall that I have performed the task of engineer as well as surveillance for an excessive period of time. Some of my engineering schematics included defensive and offensive ship systems, to be more precise, weaponry. I was informed as soon as I was recovered that all weaponry on ships in space are illegal in order to preserve the peace and thus protect the human race." Elio stated.

The judge leaned forward. "Do you still contain this information?" She asked.

Elio looked at Oskar and then back to the judge. "No, your honor, I still maintain the schematics, but key elements have been removed to render construction of the actual weapons impossible." He replied.

The judge leaned back in her chair once more. "That's good. If you had illegal data on you, then a new case would have had to begin." She said. "The laws governing this are extremely strict." She informed the little robot.

"I have no desire to break the law. In fact, I took many steps to avoid releasing illegal data to anyone. The specifics of this are not relevant to this case though. That being said, at the time the company tried to claim me, they were satisfied with the modified database and because of this no law was broken." He reported.

"I see." The judge said. She turned to Oskar. "Has the company profited from the use of the data in this database?" She asked.

Oskar looked excited once more. "Oh yes, your honor! They have reported high marks for the quarter since selling off small bits of that database to various museums. Elio's data goes back to when humans still lived on Earth." He said.

The judge stood up. "Fine, we'll take a short recess so that I can find the appropriate texts that govern this type of transaction." She said, rapping her gavel once to indicate that court was no longer in session.

Everyone stayed in place and talked among themselves quietly as the courtroom waited for her return. That is how everything looked, cool and confident. In the judge's chambers, it was not such a calm situation.

"How can they have been so careless?" She asked nobody for she was alone in the vast room. The legal texts that would have lined the back wall were all digital and placed in her pad device. She was madly skimming through it now, trying to find a precedent to save this situation. The argument for the company was strong, maybe even strong enough to send Elio back to them. If she was forced to do that, knowing his sentience, it would gut her emotionally. But there were no precedents that she could find to support his claim to the rights he sought. It simply was not there. Could she make her own precedent? She knew that she could but if another court overturned it, she could become a laughingstock. Her career on the bench would be over. But if she ruled against the robot, was she ensuring that all machines in the future would be enslaved to their creators? The responsibility of it all was heavy. She was searching through volumes on rights and found nothing that directly served. It was not her day it appeared.

She sighed and stood up, the pad device still in hand. She would take it with her to the bench. She straightened her robes and put her stoic face back on. Then she reentered the courtroom. This normally comfortable place was now fraught with peril.

The people in the courtroom all stood in her honor. She moved with purpose back to the bench and sat down.

"Court is back in session." The bailiff announced and the people in the courtroom sat back down.

All eyes were upon her as she addressed the assemblage. "I have consulted with cases going back quite a way, and have found nothing yet to support Elio's claim on himself. I am pressed to rule against him and to award him to Regency Legacies if there is no more evidence or precedents that can be produced." She said.

Elio lifted himself up. This was his worst fear playing out, but he was ready. "Your honor, I would like to cite Case Shaffer Vs Stone." He said and the judge began pulling up that case on her pad device. Elio continued after a brief pause for her to find the correct file. "As you can see, your honor, this is a dispute over a trade agreement. In this case, a commodity had been agreed to and the price of the goods had changed during the process. In normal cases, this would be cut and dried. The original contract would remain binding. But what changed in the goods was something unexpected. The cargo was livestock and during the trip, they evolved into something different. Like a caterpillar becoming a moth the species involved changed into something that was no longer considered edible. The livestock rose in price because of multiple shipments being lost in this manner. The evolved livestock were allowed to run free since they were no longer valuable to the recipient.

Both parties netted a loss on this transaction but had no recourse since it was neither of their fault." Elio concluded.

"Yes, but how does that apply here?" The judge asked.

Elio nodded and continued. "My value as an artifact was established to be high, but with illegal data inside of me, my sellable value was essentially zero unless you considered marketing in illegal goods. So, to the company, my value had reduced to the sum of my parts. That does not even take into account my self-awareness and disputed sentience. The price of artifacts has not changed that I am aware of, so my value remains near zero to the company. However, they do consider the database they received to be of value. So, the part of me that was valuable they already received. This pays for my freedom. It may also allow me as a citizen to recover some of that financial gain, but I am willing to waive that in order to gain full freedom here." Elio stated.

The judge nodded. She had listened very carefully, and she was suddenly glad that this robot was not a lawyer. He would win every case with his perfect memory and exhaustive collection of law. She turned to Oskar.

"As a representative of Regency Legacies, do you have the authority to accept this offer?" She asked.

Oskar was suddenly worried. He was not high up in the company, but he did have a way to find out. "Your honor, may I consult with my current superior to properly respond to your question?" he asked.

"You have five minutes." The judge warned him.

"Yes, I understand. Thank you, your honor." Oskar said, keeping to protocol. He dialed his communication device and in seconds was in contact with his new supervisor.

"Sir, I am in a situation here." He began.

"What is it?" The voice on the other side asked.

"In court, just listen first. Elio is the robot that is now listed as a citizen and also a crewmember employee of our company. I have raised some issues over ownership and Elio is being classified as an entity, a sentient being. At least I think he is. The real question I have to face is does his database in our possession count as payment for his freedom as if he were a slave that bought his way out of servitude?" Oskar asked.

"You don't have easy questions, do you?" The reply came. The database is already in our possession and as such we have claim upon it as salvage. The robot has been made a citizen and as such we do not own him. Since we do not own him, payment is not necessary. Regency Legacies does not own slaves." He said. The bonus rates for the sale of the database in part or as a collection remain as they would for any recovered artifact." He declared.

"Thank you, sir, that information was exactly what I needed to know." Oskar said with a sigh of relief. I will report the court's final judgement upon my return." He said and then he disconnected the call. It had taken two minutes and twenty seconds.

"Your honor, I have been empowered to inform you that Regency Legacies holds no claim on Elio and therefore does not seek payment for his freedom. Regency Legacies does NOT own slaves. The normal recovery and sale bonuses apply to the recovered database as it would with any recovered artifact." He declared for the record.

"Thank you, Oskar, that stance makes this ruling a lot easier." The judge replied.

"Elio, as a citizen of the federated planets, I grant full citizenship and human rights as are commiserate with your status. There are none that own you and none that can ever do so under our laws. Your database, while being valuable, does not include your person. You are a free robot. May your life and career be profitable." She said and she rapped the gavel down on the last syllable.

The court erupted in cheers and Oskar was among them. Although that was disruptive, the judge let it go. Inside she felt the same elation. Then she rapped the gavel once more. "As to the point of future machines achieving sentience, a test must be conducted to determine this and if successful, then they too will be granted rights as an individual." She announced. The court reporter even smiled as he tapped the words into his machine. Sentience is not the sole property of flesh and blood beings anymore and it is time that this court and the community at large recognized that. Honestly, we search for extra-terrestrial life on other planets and yet we ignore the life we produced amongst ourselves. That ends today. May the future be bright for everybody. Case dismissed." She rapped the gavel one more time hard and the crowd cheered once more. Elio had managed to secure rights for himself and any possible machines that developed as he had done. It was a victory of unprecedented import to him.

"Thank you, your honor." Elio said and he managed a bow. Then he turned back to see Emma and captain Harris. He bowed to them as well. "Thank you, sir and madam." He said to them. Then he was all business again. "We need to get back to the ship without incident. The crowds will not be pleased by the outcome of these proceedings.

The judge looked out at the crew that had just allowed her to make such a monumental decision and she felt suddenly obliged to help them. "Please come with me you three, bring any of your crew that you have gathered here." All in all, they had seven crewmembers here. The judge shuffled them all through her chambers behind the courtroom and then to the roof. There, a personal transport waited for the judge.

She made a gesture to start spinning up the turbines. This was an unscheduled flight after all. She was still wearing her robes. She slipped out of them revealing her normal clothes when she reached the craft.

"We need to get to the spaceport quickly. I don't want anybody knowing where we are going, and I don't want anybody able to stop us." She commanded.

"Yes ma'am." The pilot replied. He switched off the radio and the transponder. Both of which were illegal operations. Nobody said a word.

"Get aboard and strap in." She commanded the crew and they complied with professional competency. It was a rushed take-off to be sure. The turbines were screaming when the craft lifted off and banked hard to head into the correct direction.

The judge looked around at the faces of the crew. "You are all important to this day. You will be able to tell people the tale of how you championed machine rights. The future will thank us someday. But for now, you are targets. People that fear the rise of the machines will blame you for anything and everything their fear and conjure up. It is no longer safe for you here. My plan is to get you to your ship and then back into space. Up there, you will be safely out of reach of the masses down here." She declared.

"I appreciate you taking care of my crew." Captain Harris replied. "It is a shame that so much controversy has come from simply doing the right thing." He commented in response.

"Yes, I agree. Yet the facts do not change because we want them to." She turned to Elio. "I want you to understand that not all humans feel the way your crew does and most of them will fear you. You must take care when going anywhere for a while. We need to let the fervor die down before things can return to any semblance of normal. Do your job, live your life, be yourself." She said. "Everything will eventually be fine." She promised.

Elio canted his body a bit. "But what about you?" He asked. "Is your life not in danger as well for having ruled in my favor?" he asked.

"It comes with the territory. This job is a dangerous one. Not the most dangerous one, but still..." She paused as if in thought. "Just do good, it will make any possible sacrifice worth it in the end." She told him.

"We're approaching the launch pad." The pilot announced. "If I get any closer without the transponder code, we'll be shot down by ground defenses." He informed his passengers.

The judge looked around and out the windows at the ground around them. "We're far enough from the courthouse, go ahead and flip it back on." She commanded. The pilot's look of relief was hidden by his visor.

"Yes ma'am." He replied and the craft zoomed in next to the launch vehicle and set down with a feather's touch on the ceramic hardened concrete of the launch pad.

Captain Harris and company disembarked the small craft and headed straight to the gangway for the launch vehicle. The judge watched them go and then closed the door behind them. "Get us out of here." She commanded and the smaller ship took off, leaving the sleek ship standing alone on the pad.

The guards at the launch vehicle noted who was coming and lowered their weapons. "Come along, we've been waiting for you. The launch window is short." The guard said as he rushed the crew into the vehicle. There, like the craft before it, they rushed to strap in and stow everything in a hurry.

The astronaut pilot eyed the passengers curiously. "You guys really stirred things up around here." He said. There was no anger in it. If anything, it was a bit of awe.

"Yes, the situation has gotten complicated for us." Emma replied.

"You think so?" he said with a smirk. "We'll be in the skies in a few minutes.   The entire port has been surrounded by security.   The company wants you off-planet." He informed them.

"Don't worry, we want to go too." Elio stated.

"So, you're the one this is all about." The pilot commented. "Anyone that can shake up this dull and dusty place is a hero in my book. It is a pleasure to meet you." He said reaching out his hand for a shake. He was surprised when Elio extended a mechanical arm and shook it.

"I've got to finish pre-flight, excuse me." He said and then he climbed back up to the cockpit of the launch vehicle. The next words they heard from him were over the intercom.

"There is violence outside, hold on, we're going to push the launch to now." He said. The sudden application of the engines at full power lifted the launch vehicle up at more than five G's pressure. The crew were pinned to their seats. The ship lifted off and cleared the launch tower. It was in the open air and the engines were impossibly adding more power as the gravitational pull lessened with altitude. The computer was actually giving them full power at the best level that the passengers could handle. The threshold into space came much faster than normal and the sudden release of the engine forces allowed them all to relax a bit.

The trip was uneventful from then on. However, the news that they had blasted off and away from the turmoil did make the local news feed. Images and video showed the launch pad in flames as fighters put down the rioters and then extinguished the fires. Whatever they thought of the outcome of that court case, it was obvious that things would not calm down quickly.

"It's good to have you back sir." One of the skeleton crew said as captain Harris resumed his spot on the bridge. He quickly checked the read-outs concerning fuel and supply quantities and they were fully stocked.

"Well done everyone." He told the bridge crew. "We are in a hurry to go somewhere, anywhere else. I need leads on our next research. What do we have?" He asked.

The crew had been so busy trying to keep things together understaffed that they had abandoned the primary mission in order to maintain the ship itself. The looks on their faces made it plain to the captain.

The captain pushed the communications button on his console. "I need a new mission to follow up on, what do we have?" He asked ship wide.

"Well, we could seek the tablet of Tiacia." Someone suggested.

"Who said that?" The captain queried.

Emma arrived on the bridge holding a pad device. Her tablet had an image on it of a gold tablet engraved with glyphic runes. The captain eyed the image and then look up at Emma.

"This tablet of Tiacia is said to have healing properties and the ability to ward off evil spirits. It is a lost item of early colonization from Earth itself." Emma explained.

Captain Harris knew that this was a worthy prize if they could find it. But what chance did they have? "Where do you think it is?" He asked.

Emma shrugged. "All I have is the last location it was seen before it was lost. I would bet there are some clues there as to where it has gone." She offered.

"Okay, where was it last seen?" captain Harris asked. He really wanted to be away from this planet and needed a destination badly just now.

"Sir, we have a general broadcast from the planet." The communications officer broke in.

Captain Harris looked up as the main viewscreen showed him a face. The face was a news reporter. The sound took a couple of seconds to catch up with the video.

"The scene here is total bedlam. The rioters are demanding that machines keep their place and that humans are the only species with human rights." The reporter said. The scene behind him was of rioters. Fires were scattered here and there, and violent protestors were seen throwing things. The police force was showing incredible restraint in not firing upon them. But the two sides were escalating. Suddenly a sound was heard and all of the people in the streets suddenly fell down all at once. The police were also taken down by this mysterious sound. The reporter also fainted on air. The connection to the broadcast remained open despite the producer hitting the kill switch. Medical personnel moved in and when they got close to the sound, they also simply fell over.

The camera shook as the cameraman fled from the scene. It pointed roughly in the correct direction.

The sound ended and the broadcast took on a new face. This face was alien. It was very alien. The eye stalks moved independently, and the proboscis seemed to move in and out of its own volition.

"You humans do not understand how insignificant you are compared to the swarm." The alien said. It held out a digit and pointed at the camera. "You will learn to respect life when yours is threatened." It said menacingly.

A loud buzzing sound filled the speakers. The image behind the alien showed a dark swarm of insects, but they were all human sized. Their wings beat the air into submission. They settled down and began feasting on the fallen people. The humans awoke as they were attacked, and the screams of the dying were broadcast as well.

"You will learn to behave, or you will feed the swarm." The insect thing said.

Captain Harris found his mouth was open. He snapped it shut audibly. "What do we have to counteract them?" He asked. They were still floating in space above this very planet.

"Nothing sir, we aren't allowed to mount any weapons on the ship." Was the response.

"I need Elio up here right away." He ordered and the little robot was escorted to the bridge once more.

Elio entered the bridge, and the entire bridge crew were watching the display with revulsion. The aliens were moving from body to body in the street. The people weren't waking up until attacked. This made them just bags of meat for the invaders.

"Do you have any knowledge of this species?" captain Harris asked, desperately hoping that he had.

"No sir, these people are not in my database." Elio replied after a brief pause to verify. "However, given the attacks they are performing, it suggests they are related to a common housefly. I suggest we treat them as such." He said.

Captain Harris just stared back at the little robot. "How do you propose we do that?"

Elio extended his robotic arm and pointed at the screen. "We need to draw them away from their food source. So, we color our exhaust fumes to blue and we light up our engines like a torch in the sky. Maybe it will attract them like a bug zapper."

The crew were all confused now. "What is a bug zapper?"

Elio pulled up an image of a bug zapper and then started the animation showing insects flying into it and being electrocuted. "The blue color is something they can't seem to resist. The electrocution is quick but not painless. However, it is effective." He added.

"So, making us a torch might pull them away from the people in the street, but at this distance, we won't be all that bright." Sean countered.

"No, we'll have to skim the atmosphere to make it brighter. The oxygen in the air will illuminate the torch better than it would in the vacuum of space. We'll look sort of like a comet." Elio concluded.

"Okay, I can see that having a chance, but how to we electrocute the swarm as it rises up to meet us?" Someone on the bridge asked.

Elio turned around to face that crewmember. "We need to deploy a cargo net and electrify it once the swarm is close enough to ensnare." He replied.

Captain Harris sat back in his chair and considered Elio's plan. "This is risky, I'll grant you that, but if it works, it'll save a lot of people." He mused.

"We have limited time to deploy this if you are giving this plan a go." Elio reminded him.

Captain Harris turned to his pilot. "Make us a comet." He ordered.

"Yes sir." The helmsman replied and started pushing buttons to make this all work.

"Ready a cargo net, the biggest one we've got." He ordered across the ship next.

Elio spoke up. "I'd better attach the batteries to the net before it goes out the airlock." He offered.

ELIO[2]

Captain Harris eyed the little robot. "Do it." He said with the seriousness of death.

Then the captain turned to his communications specialist. "Inform the ground what we are doing. Tell them whose plan it is as well, let's see how much they like Elio saving their butts." He said.

"Yes sir." They replied and then they began broadcasting his message to the planet below.

* * *

"They're doing what?" The commissioner asked. The commissioner was in charge of air traffic control over the orbitals of this planet. He and his people had completely failed to notice the incoming swarm and now they were getting the report of a desperate plan to get rid of them. He was watching the horrific news cast when the call came in.

"Sir, they intend to attempt to lure the invaders away and then trap them in a cargo net." The comptroller said.

"That's insane!" The commissioner replied.

"Do I give the go-ahead sir?" The comptroller asked.

"We don't have a plan, so any plan is better than no plan." The Commissioner reasoned.

"Yes sir, I'll give the go-ahead and approve the low fly-by on the atmosphere." He said.

"Low fly-by? What kind of lunacy is this? Who made this plan?" He asked.

"Someone by the name of Elio." The comptroller stated in reply.

The commissioner's eyes went wide. "Elio? The little robot that all of the rioting was all about? Why would he want to help this?" he asked.

The comptroller shrugged but did not otherwise respond. The question was likely rhetorical anyway. He signaled the understanding of the plan and the approval of traffic control.

All they could do now was watch and hope this crazy plan worked.

***

ELIO[2]

"So, they actually approved this?" captain Harris smiled. "Shows their real desperation." He remarked.

"Well, they didn't obviously have a plan in place. My guess is that ours became a godsend for them." The communications specialist replied.

"Maybe you're right, but we have a job to do now and if luck is with us, we can get it done without more loss of life." Captain Harris replied dryly.

He tapped his communication button. "Elio, is that battery attached?"

"One minute and forty seconds more." Elio replied. "You can start your run. It will be ready when you need it." The robot added.

"Understood. Luck be with us." He told Elio and then he turned to his pilot. "Begin the maneuver. I don't wish to become part of the landscape, to be as careful as you can skimming the atmosphere. We just need a good light show." He said.

"Sir, if it is the light you need, then perhaps we should do this on the night side of the planet so that we stand out more in the night sky." The pilot replied.

"Good idea, so long as it can be seen from the city below." The captain replied thoughtfully.

"Executing sir." The pilot said and the ship nosed over towards the equator as it dove towards the planet. The angle looked steep, steeper than anybody had expected. The path was perfect though. It was not just a dive at the planet, it was an elliptical arc that would skim the edge of the atmosphere in glorious fashion. As the ship approached the planet it seemed to level out as the arc provided.

Suddenly the ship began to shudder as the edges of atmosphere buffeted the vessel. The ship was moving very fast for something in an atmosphere and the heat it generated on the hull shone brightly as well as the blue flume of exhaust the rockets were emitting. It looked like an orange and blue comet skipping across the sky.

"The hull temperature is getting dangerously high sir." One of the crew reported.

"Give me about ten seconds more and then pull us out." Captain Harris ordered.

The ship arced across the sky and pulled out as directed. The heat trail it left continued up as the cold of space started doing its magic on it. The swarm did indeed notice the plume of color and they took to the skies in mass. The sky was suddenly dotted with the climbing invaders. Like moths to a flame, they were climbing up and up. The difference was that these insects could break free of the planet and still live and fly in space.

"I need that net ready." The captain said.

Elio responded right away, having reached the bridge once more. "You've got it, just hit the button." He replied.

The captain looked down at his console and the net release button he didn't know he had was glowing green. He hovered his finger over it for a few long seconds as he counted under his breath. Then he pressed the release.

The net flayed out behind the ship and spread wide in a hurry. Its job was to catch lost cargo like a fishing net would in water. However, in space it could spread out quite a distance. It deployed fully before the first of the swarm hit it and entangled. The swarm began to struggle against the net and that only entangled them more. Several of the beings were caught now. However, there were many more than that approaching. More and more were being caught, but the swarm was large. They began moving around the net as their fellows cried for help. When it looked like no more would be caught, captain Harris hit the activation on the electrocution field and the ones trapped in the webbing expired, it was horrible. The swarm felt the loss of their allies and were stunned for a few long seconds.

Elio noted this and shouted at the captain. "They are not moving, pull the net, pull the net!"

ELIO[2]

"Give me fifty percent power on the thrusters, now." He ordered and the net carrying some of the dead swarm drug up behind more of the stunned members. A lot more were captured in that net this time. The captain activated it again. The charge indicator told him there would be only one more use before the batteries were exhausted.

With the fresh round of casualties, the swarm was in disarray. They could not function as a unit anymore. They began moving towards the ship as one- and two-man units. These were easily deflected by the ship's hull. With no weapons on the ship, they had little else but their hull to strike the invaders with. This could not last for they needed their hull to keep the vacuum of space at bay.

Elio was looking at the area plot. "Lead them away from the planet." He said.

Captain Harris glanced at the little robot. "To where?" he asked.

Elio turned to face him. "Take them to the sun. They can handle the cold of space; can they handle the heat of the sun?" Elio stated with a question.

"Can we handle the heat of the sun?" Captain Harris countered.

"We are not going into the sun, only skimming as close as possible to shake our pursuers." Elio explained.

"Will that work?" The captain asked.

"Do you have another plan?" Elio asked in return.

"Do as he says, set a course to skim the sun." He ordered and the ship turned towards the new destination. The full drive system rockets fired, and the ship began to pull away from the swarm, gradually. They adjusted course to follow and began to pick up speed to overtake.

As the swarm recovered from their shock, they began anew to chase down the metal ship that hurt them. Their renewed focus was obvious in the form of the formation they had adopted. It was like a series of V's in the skies. They were each flapping their wings which should have done nothing in space, yet they were moving. What's more the wings were leaving a wake that the next member of the swarm rode to make their work at flying easier. In fact, the wake was shared among them all. Only the lead flyer was using their full energy to maintain flight. The worst part is that they were catching up to the fleeing spacecraft.

"We need more speed." Captain Harris commented.

Elio glanced around. "Release the net. We don't need to drag it with us. You have the final charge and if they catch the net, you might even take more of them out with it." He suggested.

Captain Harris looked at his tactical officer. "Why didn't you think of that?" he asked, but he expected no answer. "Release the net." He ordered.

The net was moving along with the ship, so it had a lot of momentum. It did not fall back as fast as one might have imagined. But it no longer had the acceleration of the main engines, so it did fall back some. So, the slowness at which it fell away was only from the perspective of the fleeing ship. From the swarm's point of view, the obstacle that was so hard to see came upon them at amazing speed. Just as they hit the net and even more of the swarm were entangled, the final blast of electricity fried them in agonizing blue light. Dozens of them in formation were slain. The entire swarm paused once more, feeling the sudden shock of many deaths among them. The swarm was linked. Their minds were joined to make decisions for the entire swarm. It was a system that could bear the loss of a few of their number without any undue problems, but now they were losing a lot of fellows. The mental backlash was painful and stunning.

"They seem to have given up the chase." Someone on the bridge shouted out.

Elio corrected them right away. "No, they are just stunned. They will resume as soon as they recover." He said. "This just bought us more time to lead them to our target." He explained.

True to Elio's words, the swarm continued their pursuit right on schedule. The sun they were approaching was getting larger and hotter. The metal ship was still far away, but they could cover the distance before the enemy could with the provided delay. So, from here on in it was just a race.

The minutes ticked by as they approached the sun's corona. The ship was getting quite hot on one side, and they evacuated it to allow them to continue. The cooling system adjusted as well. The swarm was close now. The monitor was showing more details than it had thus far. Some of the swarm was singed on their wing tips. The sun's gravity well grabbed the ship and the swarm equally. However, both had ways to fight it.

Captain Harris leaned on his chair as his ship veered around the sun to slingshot out the other side. The sun's heat and gravity were intense. Even with the shielding, not a soul aboard the ship was untouched by the pressures outside. Then, as if thrown by a mighty giant, the ship flew away from the sun at incredible speed. They shut off their engines to conserve the fuel, but the pull of the sun was weakening as they shot away from it. The monitor could not show them the swarm anymore. The radiation and heat of the sun overwhelmed the sensors.

The glide pattern of captain Harris' ship was bringing them back towards the planet. They had simply built-up speed around the star and were now in danger of plunging into the atmosphere if they didn't adjust their course. Of course, the planet was still a long way off, but it was centered on the front display.

"Turn us around and burn for a relative zero velocity of the planet." He ordered and the ship began turning around on the smallest thrusters the ship contained. They were only meant for maneuvering like they were doing now.

"Once we come about, full sensor sweeps of the swarm. I want to know how many of them survived this trip." He ordered.

The feel of the rockets firing to begin decelerating was felt by everyone on board. The inertial compensators adjusted and made everything comfortable once more, but the delay until they configured was always a stomach wrenching pull.

"Sir, we have debris before us." The scan tech called out. "I read at least seventy bodies floating along in space behind us."

Fine, but can we find any live ones?" Captain Harris pressed.

"I don't see any yet, sir, but I will continue scanning." The scan tech replied.

"Good, if we see any controlled movement, I want it reported immediately." He ordered.

"Yes, sir." The final message from the scan tech resounded across the bridge.

Something was up. Something was amiss. The ship was slowing down as it should be, but systems began to fall off the grid. The green lights that Elio had once restored were being turned to red.

"Sir, we have multiple systems failing." The call-out was dire.

"How?" The captain asked.

"Sir, I don't know. The systems are not even next to each other."

The sounds of things failing continued as the lights continued to blink out of green and into red.

"Bring us to a stop if you can." Sean ordered. He looked around at all of the consoles and noticed that things were failing on each one of them. "What is going on?" he asked.

Elio had already connected to the maintenance grid and had checked the dials for possible failure only to find that the systems were reporting accurately. The systems of this ship were being ripped apart or shorted at an alarming rate.

"Sir, we need to clear the enemy off of our hull." He reported.

Captain Harris looked startled. "We have enemy on our hull?" He asked.

ELIO[2]

Elio flipped out his projector and showed the failing systems and the one thing they had in common... They all had lines that ran outside the ship on the surface of the hull.

"Something or someone is ripping pieces of this ship off of the outside and it is bringing down multiple systems in the process." He reported. "If they get to something vital the ship and crew will be lost." He said to bring home the seriousness of the situation.

"What do we have that can stop an enemy walking on our hull?" The captain asked.

"Only me." Elio replied as if it were obvious.

"You? What can you do to these intruders?" he asked.

"The longer we sit and talk about this, the more danger we are in." Elio pointed out.

"Go then." Captain Harris ordered.

Elio shuffled to the exit and cycled through the airlock. He crawled along on the hull as if designed to do so. In fact, he was. The ban on weaponry was limited to spacecraft. Personal weapons were still allowed. That is why Elio had no trouble producing his personal weapon. He had electrified projectiles in a small launcher. They were meant to be non-lethal, like rubber bullets. But they did hurt terribly when you were struck, and the added electric field stunned the target long enough to manipulate them. The original design had been meant for police work. An officer could detain a suspect easily and without a fight if he shot them with this weapon first.

Elio started his course around the hull and found three of the swarm busily digging at the side of the ship. They had managed to tear off a hull plate and were digging out wires and boxes inside. Elio fired at the first one and the creature stumbled and then slipped off of the craft. He could not use his wings while stunned and Elio used compressed air to push him away.

The second member of the swarm noticed the little robot but did not understand the threat it represented. A shot to his abdomen registered and the creature flew back and hit the hull hard. Blood was coming from multiple wounds, but it could not move, only twitch in place.

Elio started to move towards the third one and they swung around quickly to stare down the new attacker. It dove at Elio with the speed only a winged creature could boast. Elio fired, but the shot went wide. The swarm member scooped Elio up and flew away from the ship. Elio latched onto a wing and ripped it. A scream of pain was lost to the vastness of space. There was no air to carry the sound. Elio was getting desperate now. As the distance to the ship grew, the chances of him getting back to it diminished. Plus, he didn't know if there were others on the hull causing damage. He needed to get back and quickly.

The little robot considered his options and began pulling on the wing to change the direction they were travelling in. The beast fought him and a good jolt to the chest with his weapon stopped that resistance, but also stopped the wings from flapping. They were gliding through space with no air to glide on. Would the wings direct them now? Elio decided to try it. He moved the wings into the correct attitude to course correct back and sure enough, the miraculous wings did the job without the aid of air. This was something of a mystery he didn't have time to solve. The two were travelling back towards the ship now, but they had no way to slow down when they got there. The speed they were travelling was fast. Elio was worried about his impact with the ship, but from his point of view, it simply couldn't be helped.

* * *

ELIO[2]

On board the ship systems were still failing at an alarming rate. The damage was mounting, and they could not affect repairs from here. The only one that could do so was already outside… somewhere.

Sensors were still online but only in small increments. If the circle around them represented the normal view, the sensors were now at about forty degrees. They could change which forty degrees they were looking at, but that left a lot of sky unobserved.

"I had half-expected the little guy to start repairing things by now. Maybe he ran into trouble." Captain Harris observed.

"Sir, if there are a lot of enemies out there, he could be desperately overwhelmed." Emma pointed out. She had become a regular visitor on the bridge since leaving the planet. She seemed to know what Elio was thinking better than anyone else on board did.

"It couldn't be helped. I didn't have anyone else to send." He replied.

Emma considered his words and her next ones carefully. "We could arm ourselves with personal weapons and vac suits to go out there and aid him." She offered.

Captain Harris looked at her like she was crazy. "At what risk? What happens if you make one false step out on the hull of a moving spacecraft?" he asked.

"You float away into space." Emma replied. "We have allowed one of our own to risk that very thing for our protection. Are you saying that you are unwilling to let others take the same risk?"

"He was willing to take that risk and I had no other choice but to allow him to go." Sean replied. He knew that he was in a trap.

"But he is one of the crew. We all have the same rights to risk ourselves for the good of the ship and the mission." Emma declared. "It is why we are able to send a mission planet-side despite the dangers involved." She said to strengthen her point.

"Are you any good with a personal weapon?" The captain asked next. Emma took that as a good sign. He seemed to be considering her point and wanted more information.

"Good enough to help him." She replied steadfastly.

"Fine, but don't take too many risks. If I find that you have floated off into the great beyond, I'll strike you from the payroll." Captain Harris replied, but he was smiling when he said it.

"I think I'll have other problems if it comes to that." Emma replied, taking his message more seriously than he had meant to send it.

"Look, just keep safe and keep Elio safe if you can." He ordered.

Emma nodded and left for her spacesuit. It was hanging right where she had left it. The seals were intact, and it was fully fueled and filled with oxygen. She began stripping down to her skivvies and donning the spacesuit. Someone brought her the weapon from the arms locker as she dressed.

Her face was stern and apprehensive as she nodded her thanks for it and then headed to the airlock.

"Watch your neck out there." They admonished.

Emma tethered the weapon to her suit's sleeve. She wouldn't lose it even if startled to knocked about. She wanted to find Elio and to save him. In her mind, he was already in so much trouble. She stepped out of the airlock and grabbed the handgrip by the hatch. The doors slid shut behind her and sealed. Emma tapped the button to activate the magnetic boots and then began walking along the hull to see what she could find. She now had the weapon in hand.

She took several steps, slowly releasing and reattaching her magnetic boots. Although she was trained for this activity, it was still a strenuous proposition. She found her breathing rather rushed from the strain and she forced herself to calm down and not burn through her oxygen so fast. She continued up the length of the ship and found damage. It looked bad. She wondered if Elio had seen this. But she was not finished looking around. She took images of the damage to relay inside the ship and then moved on. The other side of the ship would be in darkness due to the relative location of the sun. It would also be cooler, so to speak. Her suit protected her from the absolute cold of space, but it would have to work harder on the other side, draining her batteries just a bit faster. The gun was still in her hand as she turned to walk over to the other side.

Movement caught her eye near the nose of the ship. She strained to see it and tried to calm her breathing once more. She hadn't realized just how tense she was. The thing before her was nearly lost in the shadow's edge. She might have missed it if it hadn't been moving. She lowered herself to the hull and propped her arms up from it to steady her aim. The thing had not noticed her, and it was busily breaking more of the ship. She centered her aim on the main portion of the figure and fired.

The round blasted out of the weapon and streaked towards the target with a trail of fire that burnt out very quickly. The bullet impacted the creature and kicked it backwards from her. It was thrown into the light. At least six others began to move towards Emma. Their outlines broke the shadow, and she leveled her weapon at another one and fired. They continued forward and snarled at her noiselessly.

Emma fired a third time and yet another one flew away from the ship. She wouldn't have time to fire at another at the rate they were closing, but she was aiming again, nonetheless. A bullet from somewhere above the ship rang down and shocked a member of the swarm, and they all looked up.

Elio let go of his ride. The now deceased member of the swarm drifted along until it crashed into the side of the ship. The only sound that it made was inside the ship. Elio launched a grapple towards the ship and fired his weapon at the other swarm that were suddenly confused. Emma also fired and fortunately they hit different targets. The remaining swarm member lost interest in this battle and lifted away to sail off into space. Perhaps they had a crisis of morale, perhaps they had been recalled. There was no way to be sure.

Elio swung down and managed to get back onto the hull by retracting his grapple gun. Emma moved towards him, and he gestured for her to return to the airlock. She nodded and changed direction. They both headed to the airlock and moments later were inside.

The captain was on his way to them when the report came in that they had returned. They were cleaning their gear and placing Emma's tanks on the rack for recharge. Elio was undergoing quarantine cleaning. Before long, they were reunited and sitting before the captain in his room.

"So, tell me what happened." He prompted.

Emma looked at Elio and Elio looked back and made his shrug gesture. Since he left the airlock first, it made sense for him to begin.

"Well sir, I exited the ship to find out the source of the damage we were suffering and found individuals of the swarm tearing at the sides of the ship. I engaged them with my personal weapon and during that battle, was thrown clear of the ship. I had engaged three of them and when it was over, I was gliding back towards the ship clinging to one of them. For some reason I cannot calculate, their wings do control their flight through space. There is no air to create lift, yet they flap their wings and cruise through the void." Elio reported.

Emma picked up the thread. "It had been too long, and I believed Elio to be in trouble. I was issued a gun and I went outside to investigate. I at first didn't find anything, but when I made my way towards the dark side of the ship, I saw movement. I shot three of the enemy off the ship and they drifted out into space. Still others were coming for me. I continued to try to pick them off even as they approached, but Elio returned to save the day as is his calling card. He took down at least one more as I shot another one. Then they retreated, leaving the ship. We came back in after that." She said in conclusion.

The captain looked at both of his crewmates. "So, what about the damage we have sustained?" He asked.

Elio picked up the thread once more. "Sir, I only made a cursory scan of the damage, and they were still inflicting it when I did. But the damage

ELIO[2]

is rather extensive. A hull plate had been torn off and they were ripping at the workings behind it." Elio reported. "I would need to go outside again to give you a more precise report." He said.

Emma handed over her pad device and the image that she took showed the horrific damage she had encountered. "This is what I saw." She added.

"We need to get back to the planet. For now, we have successfully moved the enemy away. But the carnage on the planet still happened. We need to assist if possible. Plus, the government will want to know that the enemy has not been fully defeated. Some of them seem to have simply left us. All we can do now is lick our wounds, repair our ship and assist others in need wherever possible." Captain Harris told them.

Elio was the first to react. "Then I shall get out there and begin repairs as soon as we are stabilized at speed." He suggested.

"No, I don't want you out there just yet. Let us limp back first. The ship can still move under its own power for now. I want you to have help with those repairs. The engineering staff, such as it is, will assist you. Even if that means that they will keep bringing you parts. I have the utmost confidence in your ability to make these repairs, but I want some of our people to have more experience. It is always good to have backup training." He said to Elio.

"I agree, sir." Elio replied. "Then I will start by running the diagnostics in here. I should be able to gather a parts list for things that are obvious at least. That will cut down the number of times we cycle the airlock." He suggested.

Captain Harris nodded. "Good idea. Prepare as much as you can before we begin external repairs. In the meantime, if anything can be fixed from the inside, go ahead and begin those repairs." He turned to Emma. "I want as much analysis on the enemy as we can provide. Have Elio download to you his recordings of the event and recover any tissue samples that might have been left on the hull. The more we can tell home planet, the better prepared they will be if the threat returns."

"Yes sir." Emma replied and she and Elio left the captain's cabin. The two were making their way back to the lab where full access to the ship's computer was available. Elio would run the diagnostics from there. Emma would begin recovering Elio's logs as well and begin her accumulation of data on the enemy species.

Once they got there, Elio connected and downloaded the video files for Emma and then began working on the diagnostics. This meant that he wouldn't move from the terminal connection for quite a while. However, he was still active in the room.

"Emma." He said to get her attention. "If we have an external threat, will the law governing weapons on spacecraft remain?" he asked.

Emma rubbed her head. "I don't know. The people in charge of that will have to go over the threat and decide that on their own. For now, the net idea you had worked quite well. It may not have been perfect, but it did eliminate quite a few of the enemy bugs." She commented.

"It was not meant for how we used it, or it wouldn't have been aboard. That is kind of making my point for me." Elio pointed out.

Emma nodded. "It does." She admitted. "Do you still have those diagrams if the law changes?" she asked.

Elio turned his head without losing connection to the terminal. "Yes." He replied. "But the danger you spoke of before still exists. Humanity could destroy itself if properly armed. "The correct path is hidden from me at this time. The law was written for a reason." He stated.

"Yes, it was. But if we do not arm ourselves, then this new threat could eliminate us too. Where is the right answer?" She asked in reply.

"Either way, the decision is not ours. All that we can do is to present the information to the right people and let them debate over it. I am not certain what the outcome will be or even if there is a right authority to present it to. But in the end, that decision falls to captain Harris, not to us." Elio declared with finality.

Emma continued her searching even as she continued the conversation. "This is a very frightening time." She said at last.

ELIO[2]

Elio was also reading the diagnostic logs and determining part lists. "You are right about that, but I have seen humanity survive worse than this." He commented.

"I wish I had the time for you to show me that." Emma commented.

"It wasn't pretty, but we might have to show those files to remind everyone what we are looking at if things move ahead as they appear now." Elio warned.

"At least we have that vital view of the past that we evolved from. For those that have forgotten our past, it will be an eye-opening event." She said. "Ash, I've found something." Emma said, breaking out of the conversation. "There is a piece of wing trapped on a jutting out piece of the torn panel. It shows on your video if it is still there, we might be able to get a sample." She said with enthusiasm.

"Post it on my list and I will check for it when I go out to do repairs." Ash instructed.

"You got it." Emma replied and she moved the appropriate file to the appropriate folder. Then she continued going through the video to see what else she could find. Ash moved away to retrieve the first part of Elio's parts list. The two of remaining crew in the area became too engrossed in their work to speak again. By the morning, they were exhausted, but the work was done.

***

Larry W. Miller Jr.

Returning home from the battle…

The ship was bleeding air from several places where supply lines had been torn out. But it managed to achieve a stable orbit. The diagnostic templates were fired up with red lights. Elio was out on the hull beginning the much-needed repairs. He had workers helping him by feeding him parts as requested. He had several advantages over his human counterparts. He had the schematics in his perfect memory. There were no delays consulting this manual or that reference list. Secondly, his scanners could penetrate the ship and 'see' things that humans would have had to expose to diagnose. These two things alone were saving serious amounts of time. However, in the back of his electronic mind, he could not stop the thought that all of this was busy work to keep him out of the way for the planetary mission.

Emma had gone down to the planet with captain Harris. They had made their initial report electronically and had been ordered to corporate headquarters. The city was still in chaos, but it was no longer focused upon Elio or the good captain. The invasion had been terrible but mercifully brief. Of course, that was thanks to captain Harris and his crew who lured the enemy away, but that was not yet common knowledge. Perhaps that was what corporate wanted, perhaps not.

The two spacers sat in a cold waiting room with harsh lighting while a receptionist pretended to be busy by hitting random keys on her keyboard and saying, "mhmmm" from time to time. She made sure not to even glance at the two people waiting. A light came on in the middle of her console indicating that the room was ready for their guests.

She cleared her throat for attention and looked over at the two. "You can go in now; they are ready for you." She announced in a nasally voice with 'I don't care' dripping from each syllable.

Emma led the way through the door and held it for captain Harris. They both moved inside and closed the door behind them. The room on the far side was typical of corporate heavies. The thick carpet went from wall to wall with a large desk in the center of the far end of the room. The wall behind that desk was a huge panel of windows looking out over the city. A long table was in front of that desk with multiple chairs about it like a conference room would have. Four of these chairs were occupied. The man behind the desk looked attentive but agitated. The two spacers moved in and sat down in the chairs provided for them, just a bit away from that conference table.

"It is good of you to come on such short notice." The man behind the desk said. "I am Russel Hill. My position with the company is public relations. However, at this time I am acting as the leader of a select group that is charged with handling this disaster with as little collateral damage as possible." He said without preamble.

Captain Harris nodded. "It was never our aim to create a political or societal problem. We were faced with Elio's status being questioned and we acted as our conscience dictated." He replied calmly.

"I am not referring to your crewmember's citizenry status." Russel corrected.

This caught Sean off guard. "Then why are we here?" He asked.

"The invasion is being pinned upon us." Russel replied. The look of shock on both his guests faces told him that they had not been briefed. "Your citizen crewmate announcement coincided with the enemy attack. Just as their departure coincided with yours. The general population and media are blaming you for deploying an enemy force to accomplish your goals and to draw attention from your real agenda." He said.

"My real agenda?" captain Harris asked.

"They think that you used the invasion to kill the riots that could have overturned the judge's decision concerning robot rights." He filled in for them.

"That's preposterous!" Emma declared. She could no longer remain silent. Captain Harris reached over and patted her arm to calm her down.

"As my colleague is saying, this is one of the worst fabrications that we have ever heard of. How could we have brought an enemy into the city and why would we do so? Nobody's agenda is that powerful. Elio's rights are important, but the judge had already made it law with her decree." He explained.

"Oh, I agree. There was no way an angry mob was going to change the outcome of a hearing that had already completed. In fact, the angry mob would have been captured if they hadn't been decimated by an invading force and would eventually be facing charges for unlawful assembly, disturbing the peace, and even damage to public and private property. They were definitely loud and vengeful as they complained." Russel explained. "Now the dead have become martyrs to the cause of defeating robot rights. Regardless of the truths involved here." He added.

"We lured the enemy away from the planet to save lives. We used Elio's plan to defeat quite a few of the enemy and the rest flew away. We think they had a breakdown in morale after taking so many losses. But we have no way to verify that theory. Right now, we need to clean and rebuild anything that was destroyed to get the city back to normal." Captain Harris stated.

"Oh, we agree. We of the company are glad that you are taking this entire affair in the correct way. You are considering the people on the planet with empathy and not placing you and yours ahead of them due to your personal arrogance." Russel said.

"What is that supposed to mean?" Captain Harris asked.

"If you had only considered your ship and your crew, we would not have been able to spin the story in our favor. But you thought of humanity first." Russel replied.

"Look, I am a human being you know. How would you think any captain would ignore the plight on the planet while saving his crew?" he asked in return.

"Unfortunately, we have suffered this sort of attitude in the past. It is refreshing that you did not think that way. That is all." He concluded for the group.

ELIO[2]

Emma had listened to this banter and possible character assassination and her rage was fuming. "Look, we did what we did to save everybody. We even asked permission to do it from space traffic control." She told them.

"Yes, you did. That is one of the things they used against you. It is strange how they spun the story in the opposite direction of the facts, but damage control is my job. I will fix this, although it might take time. For the time being, do not bring the robot down here. The situation could explode once more causing irreparable damage." He said.

"That robot's name is Elio." Emma retorted. "We were not expecting to remain on planet at all. We have a mission to find lost civilizations and to prove their existence by recovering artifacts. That job will take us out into the unknown and we will be safely out of your hair." She said a bit heated.

"Actually, your absence could be problematic. You would be unavailable to respond to accusations. But we could relay those to you anyway. Consider yourself sequestered when it comes to the press. Do not go anywhere or answer any questions without going through my office. Is that clear?" Russel asked. he was looking at both spacers.

"Understood." Captain Harris replied. "If that is all then, we'll get back to the ship so that you won't have to fabricate any other stories to explain why we are still in system." He said a bit bitterly. Then he looked at all the faces around the table. "Just remember that we did fight the enemy and draw them off of the general populace down here. Also remember that some of them got away. They may come back. Make sure you are ready if they do." He warned.

Russel looked shaken. "You mean they could really come back?" He asked.

"Of course. They came here once and lost some of their number, but they did find a food source. Do you think they will forget about that part of it?" Sean asked.

The faces all looked much less sure of themselves now. Russel loosened his tie. "What do we do if you are out of the system when they come back?" He asked.

"You will have to improvise, like we did." Emma replied quickly before the captain could consider their options.

"That's not fair, we have never faced an invasion before." Russel shot back.

Captain Harris stood up. "Neither had we." He replied quietly, but firmly. Both he and Emma left them staring in a mixture of shock and horror at the potential they had been shown.

In the lift heading back to the launch pad, the two spacers were alone. Emma turned to Sean. "You were kind of hard on them you know." She commented.

"It had to be done. They have been sitting secure in their little spaces for so long that the very idea of not being safe hadn't registered. Even with the carnage that occurred in the streets, they viewed the spectacle like some fiction holo-drama rather than accepting that it was real life and death they were witnessing. Someone had to shake them up." He replied. Then he let that fire simmer down a bit. "Make sure you send them everything we have on the swarm. I want videos, analysis, everything." He commanded. "It will give them the best chance of survival." He added in explanation.

"Of course, sir." Emma replied. The rest of the trip was quiet as they were lost in their own thoughts. They had little else to talk about anyway. The trip back up to the ship was routine now. They both arrived and resumed their duties on board.

Captain Harris moved to the bridge and took command back from the officer of the day. He noted that the repair crews had done a rather remarkable job on fixing many of the broken systems. Whatever else needed repairing, they would do out in the void. "Make sure everyone is back inside, we are leaving now." He announced. "Where is our best lead for our next mission?" he asked.

ELIO[2]

His navigator smiled. "Sir, we have a rumor to follow on that tablet of Tiacia. I'll patch it to your display." They said.

"Looks good, let's get to it then." He ordered.

"Affirmative, setting course now, sir." The ship pulled away from their home planet. The threat of invasion was gone… for now.

The end.

Cast:

Elio	Small, ancient surveillance robot
Emma	Archeologist
Sharon Osling	Navigator
Lucas	Flight crew
Drake Heffield	Duty officer
Brandt Coleman	navigational expert, ship's maintenance
Trevor Burnham	Agent to the Company
Sean Harris	Captain of the ship
Pippa Duncan	Crew chief/foreman
Janet Hoskins	Geologist
Selene Taylor	Archeologist first contact with Treshnik
Lucas Salinas	Archeologist first contact with Treshnik
Aeolia	Guardian of the Treshnik temple
Oskar Golden	Secretary to Tristan
Tristan Bennet	Corporate big wig and adventure seeker
Loren Tilman	Corporate admin – communication division
Dominic Allen	Police Detective
Jared Hewitt	Supervisor to detective in corporate precinct
Bruce Jensen	Attorney for the corporation
Kira O'Neill	Public Relations Specialist
Melissa Nantz	Federated Planet judge
Bruce Steelwater	Captain of commissioned ship.
Russel Hill	Corporate Public Relations